Praise for *A Novel Summer*

"Rich, satisfying and surprising... A glorious read."
—Adriana Trigiani, bestselling author of *The Good Left Undone*

"Jamie Brenner has outdone herself with her latest
sun-soaked stunner, a fast-paced, feel-good read."
**—Kristy Woodson Harvey, bestselling author
of *The Summer of Songbirds***

"Packed with best friends, betrayals, books,
and the beach, this is the perfect summer novel."
—Nancy Thayer, bestselling author of *All the Days of Summer*

"Pack this book in your beach bag! Jamie Brenner's
A Novel Summer is compulsively readable. An absolute delight!"
—Brooke Lea Foster, author of *On Gin Lane*

"Brenner's latest escape to the Cape is not to be missed!"
—Jane L. Rosen, author of *On Fire Island*

"Rival bookshops, second chance romance, friend drama,
this was the perfect book to curl up and escape to the Cape."
—Pamela Kelley, bestselling author of *Bookshop by the Bay*

"*A Novel Summer* deftly navigates the fine line between
fiction and real life, friendship and success, childhood
and adulthood, and how books connect us."
—Viola Shipman, bestselling author of *The Wishing Bridge*

Also by Jamie Brenner

A Novel Summer

JAMIE BRENNER

PARK
ROW
BOOKS

PARK
ROW
BOOKS™

ISBN-13: 978-0-7783-1084-6

A Novel Summer

Copyright © 2024 by Jamie Brenner

Park Row Books
22 Adelaide St. West, 41st Floor
Toronto, Ontario M5H 4E3, Canada
ParkRowBooks.com

Printed in U.S.A.

For booksellers everywhere.

One

They met on the beach at midnight. Tomorrow, there wouldn't be a time when all three of them could get together to say goodbye. Shelby bent down and carved their names into the wet sand with a mussel shell. She called her friends back from the edge of the ocean to look before the tide washed over it. *Shelby. Hunter. Colleen.*

Behind them, the bookshop was dark. They'd just been inside. Colleen's family owned Land's End Books, so they were able to make a clandestine, middle-of-the night visit. Shelby wanted to see it one last time before she left.

In the beginning, books were the only thing they had in common: studious, vagabond Shelby; carefree, Cape Cod Colleen; and old Boston money Hunter. Shelby and Hunter met freshman year of college and had been inseparable ever since. Their love of books brought them together, and now it was pulling them apart.

"You're more emotional than you were at graduation," Shelby said, putting an arm around Hunter.

Out of the three, she was the most prepared for goodbye. As an army brat, moving away, moving on, was part of life. She was philosophical about it. But Hunter was sniffling.

"Because at graduation we still had all summer. This feels different."

It was different. School was over, summer was ending, and the future was now: Shelby was moving to New York City to become a writer, and Hunter was moving to Boston for a job in book publishing. Only Colleen would remain on that tiny spit of land, the peninsula that curved out into the Atlantic Ocean like a finger beckoning, *Come here. See what you'll find.*

Shelby had found everything in Cape Cod, not just her two best friends, but her first love, and most of all, a sense of home. But New York City had always been the plan. After a childhood moving from place to place, her only constants were the books she read and her hope of someday writing one herself. And New York was where she'd chase that dream.

"I still can't believe you're both leaving," Colleen said. "I barely remember summers here without you."

They were a threesome because of Hunter. She'd invited Shelby to her parents' beach house the summer after their freshman year. Shelby had jumped at the chance, on the condition that she could find a job. So, Hunter introduced her to Colleen, whose parents owned the town bookstore. That had been the start of their Provincetown summers. And this was the end.

"Just stay," Colleen said, knowing it was impossible. She was the only one who could call Provincetown home, working full-time at Land's End Books. For Shelby and Hunter, the shores of Provincetown could only give so much. And for a time, it had been more than enough. But as she'd learned growing up, there was no sense getting too attached to any one place. The time always came to say goodbye.

From somewhere down the beach, an old Cyndi Lauper song played, something about time after time. Someone was always listening to 1980s music in Provincetown.

"Okay, let's not make this sad," Hunter said, wiping her eyes. "Look up: a crescent moon. A crescent moon represents the cycles of life: birth, death, and rebirth. New beginnings. It's the perfect time to manifest our intentions."

"I know your intentions. To leave," Colleen said dryly.

"Come on—hold hands," Hunter said. Shelby accepted her outstretched hand on one side, and clasped Colleen's on the other.

They faced the sea.

"We have to promise to be back together here next summer." Hunter nudged Shelby. "You have to say it, too."

"I promise to be back here next summer," Shelby and Colleen said.

Shelby said it, but she didn't believe it. If there was one thing she'd learned growing up, it was that goodbye was an ending, not a beginning. That was part of why she loved books so much—they were friends she could take with her wherever she went. And before next summer, she'd write her own novel. She promised herself right there—the crescent moon as her witness—that she wouldn't come back to Provincetown until she'd made that happen.

She wanted books to be more than just the friends she could take with her. She wanted them to be her life. Even if that meant leaving her actual friends behind.

Two

Three Years Later
New York City
May

There was no party like a book party. The Brooklyn bar was packed with Shelby's grad school friends celebrating the publication of her novel.

"What's that saying about putting in ten thousand hours?" one of them said, standing on a chair and raising a glass. "I think Shelby turned that into a hundred thousand. To you, Shelby. You show us all how it's done. So…cheers!"

The group toasted. A group that did not include her boyfriend, Noah. She looked around for him. Union Hall seemed made for a publishing event. It felt like the library of an old estate, with wood-paneled walls, bookshelves filled with leather-bound copies, an old-fashioned standing globe, and worn leather couches. The only telltale signs they were in Park Slope and not Old Westbury were the tin ceilings and the view of bustling Union Avenue out the wide windows. That, and the live music.

Shelby spotted Noah across the room in conversation with a

woman she didn't recognize. He'd been oddly distant all night—all week, now that she thought about it. He'd even forgotten to wish her a happy publication day that morning. It wasn't like he didn't understand what the day meant; he was a novelist, too. An aspiring novelist. They'd met at the MFA program, but unlike Shelby he still hadn't gotten an agent. He'd just sent out a revised manuscript to a few people, and was now waiting to hear back.

Copies of her novel were scattered throughout the bar, some now being used as coasters. It was still surreal to see her book out in the world. *Secrets of Summer* had started out as a short story assignment; Shelby didn't think it would evolve into a novel. And certainly not one that would get published. She hadn't planned to write about her summers in Provincetown, but all during grad school she found her mind returning to it again and again, even as she threw herself wholeheartedly into her New York City life.

Before she reached Noah, she was intercepted by her literary agent. Claudia Linden was dressed in a sharply tailored pantsuit and towering heels and looked every inch the industry power-house that she was.

"Shelby, I must run. But—" she kissed her on the cheek "—I'm proud of you. Just the beginning! And I'm sorry I can't be with you tomorrow, but Ezra will make sure everything runs flawlessly." Ezra, one of the agency assistants, was a man so beautiful he looked like an actor cast in the role for a Netflix series.

Tomorrow, Shelby had a very early trip to Cape Cod for her first event of her book tour: Land's End Books in Provincetown. For the first time in three years, she'd be back in the place that inspired her novel. When she told her friend Colleen that she'd gotten her book deal, Colleen made her promise that Land's End would be her first stop. "Of course! Where else?" she'd said.

Shelby watched Claudia make her way to the exit, then checked the time on her phone. It was getting late. She'd been running on pure adrenaline, but the day was catching up with her.

"Hey," she said, finding Noah. She'd met Noah Beauchamp

during one of her first-year short fiction intensives. As a huge Cormac McCarthy fan, he wrote brooding, hypermasculine prose. His fiction was surprising because he appeared, on the outside, like a typical Brooklyn beta male, with a slight frame and almost feminine beauty to his features that even his carefully groomed facial hair couldn't obscure.

"The lady of the hour," he said, raising his glass. "Shelby, this is Beth—the bass player of the band downstairs."

"Congratulations," the woman said, smiling. "Writing a book must be hard."

"It's just a beach book," Noah said.

Shelby's smile froze in place. The musician looked confused. Either she didn't know what a beach book was, or she—like Shelby—didn't understand why Noah said something denigrating. Shelby waited for him to realize his mistake and self-correct, but he just turned around and set his empty beer glass on the bar. Okay, she'd chalk up the comment to him being a little drunk.

"Noah, we should probably head out. We have an early train tomorrow."

She was so excited for him to see Provincetown, the place where she'd spent the best summers of her life. Noah, a native New Yorker, had never visited Cape Cod. She'd found that was common among people who'd grown up in New York or New Jersey. They had their own beaches and didn't seem especially interested in staking out new ones. But after reading a few drafts of her manuscript, he said he wanted to see the place for himself.

Noah checked his phone. "It's not that late," he said.

The musician drifted off.

"We have to be at Penn Station in…" Shelby did a mental tabulation. "Eight hours."

"Yeah, about that: I'm thinking I'll just stay in the city and catch up with you when you get back," he said.

She took a step back. "You're not…coming?"

"It's just, the timing is bad. You know I've got a lot going on."

What did he have going on? He'd reserved the vacation days from his day job, and he was in wait mode with his manuscript.

"It's only a few days," she said.

"I just feel like, if I get a response from an agent, I should be here, you know?"

He looked her in the eyes and she could see that even through the beer buzz, he was upset. And the excuse that he needed to stay in the city in case an agent called was ridiculous. That wasn't the way the industry worked.

"Noah, what's going on?" She reached for his hand.

"Nothing. But you're not the only writer around here. It's not all about you."

She dropped her hand from his. So that was it: he was upset about her book publishing. He was *punishing* her. She'd thought that being involved with a guy who was also a novelist would make it easier to have a relationship. That he would understand the good and the bad about the writing life. Before Noah, she'd had a boyfriend in Provincetown who was the total opposite: he lived his life outdoors, working with wildlife. He never read fiction. Had never even been to New York! She'd known from the beginning that one wasn't meant to last. But Noah? Their lives really fit.

Or so she thought.

"I know it's not all about me," she said, feeling a little stunned.

He shifted on his feet, looking around the room. Anywhere but at her. "I'm sorry. I need some space."

She didn't know what that meant. Was he breaking up with her? Did he just want to put a pin in it until after her book tour? Either way, deep down, she knew there was no recovering from the moment. If a person couldn't share her happiness, what was she doing with them?

It would be okay. She hadn't moved to New York City to find a boyfriend. She'd moved there to become a writer. Tomorrow was the beginning of her first book tour. Writing was the most important thing.

She'd known that all along.

Three

Shelby would have preferred to go on book tour alone. No—scratch that. She'd have preferred to go with Noah. But after he bailed out, she didn't want company. And she certainly didn't want Ezra, the assistant. She appreciated the support from the agency, but it felt weird to travel with someone who was being paid to go. When the ferry left from Boston Harbor, she kept asking Ezra if he was okay—as if she were there to assist *him*.

The five-hour train ride from New York to Boston had given her plenty of time to get to know Ezra Randall. He was a year younger, from Miami, graduated from NYU, and was ambitious about a career as a literary agent. He told her that when he was in high school, he saw a movie about a famous author and his literary agent.

"I remember watching it," he said, "and thought, okay I can't write, but I *can* do whatever *that* is."

He told her about the recent breakup with his girlfriend, who informed him that she'd decided she only wanted to date guys who could "help support her lifestyle."

"What does that mean?"

Ezra shrugged. "Finance, I guess."

"I feel your pain," she said. "Relationships seem impossible. Too little success, too much success...you can't win."

She was disappointed about Noah, but not heartbroken. She wasn't in love with him—at least not yet. She could tell the difference because she didn't sleep for weeks after her last breakup, and the breakup had been her own choice.

On the plus side, making the trip without Noah would give her more time to reunite with her old friends. That reminded her: she still hadn't heard back from Hunter. Shelby pulled her phone out of her bag and texted her again.

Hey, still hoping to connect. I'm on the ferry now 😊

Shelby hadn't seen Hunter since they'd both moved from Provincetown, and it had been a while since they'd spoken, their communication having dwindled mostly to app messaging. Shelby had planned to visit her in Boston once or twice, and every summer there'd been talk of reuniting with Colleen in Cape Cod. But something always came up. And the next thing she knew, years had slipped by. But Colleen told her that Hunter had moved back to Ptown for the summer.

The ferry hit a bumpy patch and water sprayed the back of her hair. Normally, this wouldn't bother her—she was, after all, on the way to the beach. But getting windblown and damp wasn't ideal; she'd barely have time to change before the book reading.

"I'm getting soaked. Might have to give up the view," she said.

"I'll go below with you. Is it too early for a beer?" he said.

"Don't let me stop you," Shelby said.

"Just kidding. I'm on the clock."

Shelby smoothed down her damp hair and followed the narrow stairs down to the lower cabin. The railing was slick, and she wiped her wet hand on her shorts.

From the cabin window she spotted the Pilgrim's Monument and felt a surge of excitement. *Home*, she thought, then corrected herself: Provincetown was no longer her home. Never had been, really. It had been a waystation on the road to her real life. It had served a purpose, a great one. But ultimately, Shelby had always been just a visitor. And she was fine with that.

It was a lovely place to visit.

Land's End Books was a small space, so Shelby's publicist helped Colleen coordinate the *Secrets of Summer* event at a historic hotel overlooking Cape Cod Bay.

Three years ago, Shelby worked at Land's End with Colleen, side by side almost every day, matching the right book to the right reader. And the entire summer, she'd dreamed of the day when her own novel was on the shelf. Now, that day had arrived.

The dining room of the Red Inn, with its panoramic views of the bay, was filled with tables populated by a mix of Cape Cod readers, some dressed in Tory Burch sarongs and Lilly Pulitzer dresses, others in jeans and Provincetown hoodies.

"Welcome, everyone," Colleen said. Shelby stood beside her, taking in the sight of her old friend. It had been ages since they'd seen each other in person, but she hadn't changed a bit. Her straight blond hair was cut to a sensible shoulder length. She wore denim overalls and a white T-shirt and beaded bracelets on both wrists—the type they sold in shops all over town. The bridge of her nose was a little sunburned, and to Shelby, it was like not a day had passed since she last saw her on that beach. Colleen looked a little heavier, but Shelby had probably just been in Manhattan too long. Some of her friends there seemed to exist on caffeine alone.

She inhaled. It felt good to be back. Well, it felt *mostly* good. She found herself scanning the crowd for her old Provincetown boyfriend. It was irrational; Justin Lombardo wouldn't show up at her book event. They hadn't spoken since the night she ended things just before moving to New York City. She could still remember the way his face looked that day on the beach, the way he seemed sad, but more sad *for* her than sad *because* of her. "I hope you find what you're looking for," he'd said.

Well, she had. She'd become a novelist.

She'd never doubted that she'd done the right thing in ending the relationship. Long distance never worked. Someone, ultimately, would have to give in. And she knew in her situation with Justin, neither one of them could be that person. Still, she was surprised by how long it took for her to stop missing him. After relocating with her family so much in her young life, she thought she'd learned how to move on without looking back.

One person she was more likely to see in the crowd was Hunter. But scanning the rows, she didn't see her, either. She lived in Boston now, working as an editorial assistant at a publisher called Malaprop. But Shelby had hoped she'd come in for the party.

"Welcome, everyone," Colleen repeated to quiet the room, setting off piercing feedback. "I'm Colleen Miller, owner of Land's End Books."

Shelby smiled at hearing Colleen call herself the store's owner. It had been her parents' store, but recently they'd retired and told Colleen they wanted to sell it. Colleen, having grown up in the store, having planned her entire life to continue with the store, begged them for the chance to take it over.

Colleen smiled at the audience, and seemed to be as thrilled with the moment as Shelby. She was lucky, she realized, to be able to share that moment with her old friend. It wasn't so long ago that they wondered if they'd succeed in doing the things they wanted to do, and there they were. Actually, Colleen had never been too uncertain. She'd always known she'd take over the store. Shelby, however, had been less confident she'd actually see her words in print. But it happened.

"I'm delighted to introduce Shelby Archer, whose novel, *Se-*

crets of Summer, published this week. The *New York Times* calls it 'A rollicking tale of family intrigue perfect for any beach bag.' So, please help me welcome Shelby."

The room erupted in applause. Nervous excitement surged through her.

"I'm so happy to be here today," she said, looking at the audience. Her publicist had given her a tip that if she felt nervous, she should look just over people's heads. That way, she didn't get distracted by anyone's facial expression, but she gave the illusion she was seeing the crowd and connecting with them. "Thank you for coming. And thank you to Colleen of Land's End Books for hosting me today." She did make eye contact with Colleen, and her friend's smile made her feel like it was old times. "I'm fortunate enough to be visiting a bunch of bookstores over the next two weeks. All of them will be fantastic, but none as significant to me as Land's End Books. Without this bookstore— without Provincetown—my novel wouldn't exist…"

She was suddenly distracted by a familiar flash of platinum blond hair in the back of the room. Hunter! She'd come after all. Shelby glanced away, focusing back into her speech. She was nervous about speaking and had memorized every single word: how she got the idea for the plot, the most interesting things she learned researching Cape Cod, and her thoughts about the underlying theme of the novel: How well do you really know those closest to you?

Before she knew it, twenty minutes had passed, and it was time to segue to the Q & A.

"I'd be happy to answer some questions," she said, feeling her shoulders relax. This would be the easier part, the fun part.

Colleen had told her that if the audience was shy, she'd ask the first question to get the ball rolling. But it wasn't necessary; several people's hands shot up. Shelby called on the person closest to her, a woman she didn't recognize.

"I was wondering," the woman said shyly. "What do you like best about writing novels?"

Shelby nodded. "That's a great question. I'd say the thing I like best about writing novels is having the ability to deliver the happy endings we don't always get in real life," she said.

The woman beamed at her. The next hand she saw was Hunter's. Shelby knew she probably felt bad for not responding to her texts, and wanted Shelby to know she was there. Smiling, Shelby pointed to her. Hunter stood, and Colleen walked over with a mic so the rest of the audience could hear the question. Hunter took the mic from Colleen's hand.

"I'm wondering," she said, "did you even think twice about the people you betrayed in writing this book? Or doesn't that matter? Maybe getting this book published is just more important than your friends."

The room fell silent. Shelby hadn't realized there had been an ambient hum in the room until everything came to an absolute halt. She glanced at Ezra, who jumped into action, grabbing the mic from Hunter and announcing:

"Thank you, everyone. Now, if you'd please form a single line at the book signing table Shelby will be happy to personalize your copies."

Shelby stood frozen. The audience followed Ezra's direction, forming a line while tittering nervously. But in that moment, she wasn't thinking about her readers. All she could think was: she never should have come back to Provincetown.

Four

Hunter Dillworth felt herself shaking from adrenaline. It would take a few drinks to calm her down, so she walked straight from Shelby's book reading to her favorite bar.

The Bollard was a locals' place, overlooking the bay and originally a fisherman's hangout. On some nights, it still was. The decor included fishing nets nailed to one wall, framed photos of locals with their boats, and a shelf filled with antique Coca-Cola bottles. The few wobbly tables were mismatched. The juke box stopped adding songs circa 1998, but Hunter didn't like much of the music that came after the mid-90s, so that was fine by her. The only food on the menu was fish and chips—also fine by her.

It was a place where there was no shame in drinking alone, and that was exactly what Hunter did: two quick tequila shots at the curved end of the bar.

She thought about the look on Shelby's face when she asked the question. Hunter hadn't spoken her mind so freely since she was let go from her publishing job two months ago. She'd looked the HR person straight in the eye and quoted Kurt Cobain: "You can't fire me because I quit."

Saying exactly what was on her mind always felt pretty damn good. Unfortunately, that in itself never fixed any problems. So although she confronted Shelby—publicly at the reading and privately when Shelby followed her outside afterward—it didn't change the fact that her best friend had written a main character based on some of the most private details of Hunter's life. Not just written, but *published*.

She ordered a beer, trying to avoid the unpleasant truth that Shelby's book was only part of the problem. Maybe she wouldn't be as upset with the fictionalized version of herself if she wasn't disappointed in the real-life version.

Losing her job had been a blow. Her parents didn't understand why she was so upset: she didn't need the job for money. No one in the Dillworth family needed to work. Her mother volunteered at a museum, and her father had just gone back to school for his Masters in Renaissance painting. Her parents' mutual interest in fine art was what drew them to Provincetown, a place that Jackson Pollock, Norman Mailer, Mary Oliver, Eugene O'Neill, Lee Krasner and a lot of other legendary artists had once called home. But ultimately, the Cape house was just another thing her parents collected and then moved on from. They'd spent the past two summers in Italy.

Hunter had always felt a little embarrassed by their wealth, and frustrated with their assumption that she wanted to follow in their footsteps as a socialite. She'd felt, for as long as she could remember, an urgency to earn her own money. It was the only way she'd stop feeling ashamed about her generational wealth. And the truth was, she loved publishing. It wasn't just about proving something to herself, or to her parents. She wanted a career in books, and she'd been on her way when she was laid off.

A guy walked in, catching her eye. She'd seen him earlier at Shelby's book event. He was tall and lanky with straight dark hair and eyes that seemed nearly black. She guessed he was maybe part Japanese; he reminded her of the guitarist James

Iha of the Smashing Pumpkins circa *Siamese Dream*. During the Q & A, he'd rushed over to grab the mic from her after she question-bombed Shelby. At first she thought, okay, this could be the best meet-cute of all time. But then it turned out he worked with Shelby. Maybe her publicist? She didn't get the story straight before she left.

He slid onto a bar stool just a few down from hers. When the couple between them got up and left, the guy noticed her.

"Hey," he said. "You're the woman with the question."

"That's right. And thanks to you, I never got an answer."

He smiled. "Apologies. Can I buy you a drink?"

"No," she said.

She waved at the bartender, who slid another tequila shot across the bar. The guy moved down two stools to sit beside her.

"So, are you Shelby's publicist or something?" she said.

He shook his head, and a lock of his dark hair fell across his forehead.

"No. I work with her literary agent," he said.

"In New York," Hunter said. He nodded.

Hunter hadn't taken the logical next step in her career, which would be looking for a job in Manhattan, where nearly every major publishing company had an office. The thought of New York City intimidated her. She was a tenth-generation Bostonian, and her hometown gave her a sense of security and confidence she just didn't feel anywhere else.

So, she'd spend the summer at her parents' beach house while they opted for two months on the Amalfi Coast. She just needed time to regroup. In the meantime, her own professional setback made Shelby's success even more infuriating.

The flip in the power dynamic of their friendship was a twist Hunter hadn't seen coming. When they met freshman year, Hunter had been the golden girl. She was the Bryn Mawr legacy, her great-great-grandmother's name on more than one building. Shelby had been a wide-eyed farm girl from Virginia—or wherever her family was living at the time; Shelby wasn't from any one place. Hunter had believed, at first, that it sounded exciting to have moved every few years growing up. Then Shelby told her how lonely it had been. Hunter had taken her under her wing, introducing her to all the right people for the rest of the year. Every summer, she brought Shelby to live at her parents' Provincetown beach house. And how did Shelby repay her?

"So, do you know Shelby?" he said. "That question..."

She narrowed her eyes. "Did you read the book?"

"Sure," he said. "I read all the books by Claudia's authors. It's my job."

"As a feminist, I find her characters offensive."

"I think the characters are all interesting women," Ezra said. "They have their issues, but that's what makes the book compelling. It's the way they work *through* the issues."

Hunter found his cavalier take infuriating. "Don't you think the first few chapters of the book are essentially slut-shaming Ashley?"

His brow furrowed. "I didn't read it that way, no."

"Okay, let me put it this way: If the character of Ashley was based on your sister, and you knew it was based on your sister, and you read the book..."

"I don't have a sister," he said, tilting his head back to finish his beer. He had an elegant neck, and artistic hands. Like a pianist.

Hunter put down her beer bottle. "Do you want to come back to my place?"

He looked at her, assessing if she was serious or playing around. After a minute, he said, "Only if you let me take you for dinner first. I'm starving."

She shrugged. "Fine. Just as long as we're clear—this isn't a date."

He laughed. "What's that supposed to mean?"

"It means," she said, leaving a bunch of twenties on the bar. "I don't do relationships."

He stood up and held out his hand. "I'm only in town for tonight."

"*That* is one of my favorite sentences." Hunter slid off the bar stool and pressed against him, Shelby's stupid book forgotten. She wouldn't think about it for the rest of the summer.

She was finished with Shelby Archer.

Five

Colleen made dinner reservations for the two of them. But after the blowup with Hunter, Shelby just wanted to check in to the B and B and hide.

"I'm sorry," she said to Colleen. "You're welcome to come over. I just don't want to be out." She felt raw. Wounded. And also well aware that she had absolutely no right to feel that way. She wasn't the victim. She was the one who'd hurt someone.

"No problem," Colleen said, agreeable as always. "Let's go. We can pick something up on the way."

They walked a few minutes up Commercial to the Beach Rose Inn, a three-story, gray-shingled Georgian with a wraparound veranda, red brick steps, and a mosaic sign out front. On the way in, Shelby dropped off a signed copy of *Secrets of Summer* at the front desk for the beloved innkeeper, Amelia Cabral. She'd known Amelia since her college summers. But considering the way the night had gone, she wished she could ship every book back to the warehouse.

Colleen followed her into the guest room, effusing about the cuteness. It was lovely. The queen-size bed had a white bookcase headboard, sea green sheets and a white down comforter topped with a green-and-blue afghan that was clearly hand-knit. A wooden side table had china knobs painted with cornflowers. A decorative piece of driftwood rested against one wall.

"Let's eat outside," Shelby said. They had lobster rolls from the Canteen.

Glass-paned double doors opened onto a terrace. Shelby and Colleen got comfortable on two lounge chairs. A foghorn sounded in the distance.

"For the record, I think Hunter overreacted," Colleen said, uncapping a bottle of water.

Shelby wasn't so sure. She was second-guessing everything. And she kept replaying the confrontation she'd had with Hunter directly following her outburst during the Q & A. Hunter had stormed out and Shelby had followed her. But Hunter didn't slow down even though Shelby had called out to her over and over again. Finally, half a block away, Hunter had whirled around to face her.

"I don't want to talk to you."

Her expression was so cold, Shelby didn't want to talk to her, either. She wanted to pretend this wasn't happening.

"Hunter, I'm sorry. I didn't mean to upset you. It's fiction—she's just a character I made up."

"Fiction? Imagine the reverse. Imagine I wrote a character who'd never lived in one place for more than two years growing up. The loneliness. The pain of losing friends until she stopped bothering to make them. How she wanted to become famous one day so that wherever she went, people would remember her. Because that's how empty and insecure she is."

Okay, that stung a little. Shelby wasn't perfect, but her writing didn't come from emptiness or insecurity. Then she realized she was missing the point.

"I'm really, really sorry," Shelby said.

"That changes absolutely nothing," Hunter said, and turned

to walk away. This time, Shelby let her go. She walked back to the Red Inn and forced a smile on her face as she finished her event. But she was only half there. She mentally combed over her entire novel, thinking about her main character, Ashley.

Yes, Shelby had borrowed some of Hunter's background. It had started as a creative exercise in grad school: take someone you know and write a thousand words turning them into a fictional character. She'd written about her mother and one of her ex-boyfriends, but the "Hunter" pages were the ones that really came to life. Months later, when she started the novel that would become *Secrets of Summer*, she couldn't shake the character.

Every writer has heard the expression "write what you know." But for Shelby, the creative spark came from writing not what she knew, but *who* she knew. It wasn't a malicious impulse; if anything, Hunter was just so interesting and had made such an impression on her, the urge to write about her was hard to resist. And Ashley was the heroine of the novel, not the villain. But Shelby could see, looking at it now, how some aspects of Ashley hit too close to home: she'd been born into an old Boston family—tremendous generational wealth—but flouted it to create her own wild-child identity. Which landed her in boarding school, where she acted out by sleeping with a lot of guys. It was just background characterization. Ashley didn't look like Hunter or share any of her interests. And the character's big mistake that set the plot in motion was pure fiction. Ashley triumphed in the end. And after two years of writing and rewriting the novel, Ashley had become her own entity. Shelby had all but forgotten the genesis of the character.

She turned to Colleen.

"Did I cross a line with the character Ashley?" She assumed Colleen would have told her.

Like other booksellers across the country, Colleen had read an advanced copy sent out by her publisher.

She waited a beat before answering her. "I recognized some

details. And I understand why Hunter might have been a little freaked out seeing them in black-and-white on the page. But anyone reading your book comes away loving the character in the end. I know you didn't mean to hurt her."

Shelby nodded. She appreciated Colleen's understanding. Still, she was relieved to be leaving in the morning for the next stop on her book tour.

Six

Hunter showed up in front of Town Hall at the agreed-upon meeting time, nine in the morning. Excruciatingly early for a Saturday, but at least it gave her a good excuse to ask her unexpected overnight guest, Ezra, to leave. He was as good in bed as he was good-looking, but when he started making noise about seeing her again, she had to shut things down. She didn't do relationships.

Hunter didn't particularly want to spend a gorgeous Saturday morning in a town council meeting, but she'd been invited by Duke Nestley—unofficial town historian and civic gatekeeper. He, too, felt burned by Shelby's novel, and this gave them a connection. Also, he offered her a job at his small press. So she agreed to go.

"Changes are coming to town," he told her a few days earlier. "I'm worried about our whole way of life getting eroded. Every voice must be heard. Especially young ones like yourself."

In his midfifties, Duke had lived in Ptown since the 1980s in a one-hundred-and-fifty-year-old house on the West End, out of which he ran a small press. Very small. When he learned that she'd lost her publishing job in Boston, he told her he could use an editor on staff. It was a low-paying position she could only afford to take because she had family money as a safety net, and this bothered her. No, her job in Boston hadn't paid a lot, but it was enough to live on modestly. The gig with Duke would be more like an internship. But it would fill the gap on her résumé until she found a new job with a major publisher.

"Good morning," he said, chipper as always. Duke had white hair that had apparently turned that color when he was still in his thirties. He had a mustache and was a fan of Hawaiian print shirts and pleated shorts. He wore glasses and spoke with the faint remnants of a Boston accent. "Shall we?"

"Let's do it," she said, mustering a smile.

Town Hall was a Beaux Arts building in the center of Commercial Street. She'd only been inside once, for a lecture on the environment. That has been boring enough, but the town council meeting? Utter snoozefest. They wanted to raise money to buy a building up for sale on the wharf in order to keep it out of the hands of developers.

The first-floor meeting room had rows of folding chairs and a table in the front where the selectman sat peering out like they were students at a lecture hall. The air was stuffy, an unwelcome contrast to the fresh breeze outside. She looked for an aisle seat.

"You know," she said, fanning herself with the agenda printout, "I could be having brunch right now with a very attractive guy I met last night." That wasn't exactly true. The whole point of a one-night stand was that it was *one night*. So even without the morning meeting, she wouldn't have made an exception for Ezra. She was, as Lady Gaga said, a "free bitch, baby."

Maybe the thing that bothered her the most about Shelby's book was that it was, on the surface, a fairly accurate depiction of how indiscriminate her sex life might look from the outside. But Hunter didn't want to be in a relationship. She didn't see the point. She had no intention of getting married and living like the rest of the Dillworths: kids in all the right schools and homes all over the world filled with all the right stuff. No thanks. She wanted to travel light.

And also—she liked sex. So what? It was totally normal to hook up with a lot of people when you were in college. She had nothing to feel ashamed about. And she hadn't—until Shelby's book.

There was one particular scene in which the main character, Ashley, was called DD behind her back—for Dirty Dozen. Hunter had practically tossed the book across the room when she read that. Had people called her that at school and Shelby never told her? Never told *her*, but announced it to the world?

She couldn't ask. She had too much pride.

"Well, I'm glad that you're here," Duke said. "It's important to be involved."

"If I take the job with you and Seaport Press, that's involvement."

"Civic duty helps the entire town, not just the reading population."

One of the things she liked best about Provincetown was that *everyone* seemed to be part of the reading population.

"And speaking of reading populations," Duke said, "how was Shelby's event last night?"

She'd wondered if he was going to bring it up. "I wish you'd been there. I really let her have it."

Duke's eyes widened. "What did you say?"

Before she could fill him in, Gene Hobart, owner of the hardware store, tapped his mic from his seat at the front table. Gene was in his sixties, with gray hair and a beard, and wore round, wire-rimmed glasses. "This meeting is called to order."

The chatter in the room fell to a murmur and then dropped off completely.

"Welcome, everyone. We have a lot to get to and I know everyone wants to enjoy the day so without further ado…" He shuffled some papers in front of him. "We have one outstanding vote from the last meeting: parade applications. Judy, can you please read the names of our applicants?"

Judy, an art gallerist who wore her strawberry blond hair in a long braid, read a list of local businesses everyone recognized. Someone in the second row stood and said, "I move to approve all the applications as a whole."

After a pause, Judy said, "I second that motion." And then it was passed unanimously.

Hunter checked her phone. At that rate, she might be able to meet up with Colleen for brunch.

"One more bit of follow-up from last month: we do have an applicant for the short-term lease at 629 Commercial." He adjusted his wire-framed glasses and again consulted his paperwork. "It's a Boston company looking for a seasonal outpost: Hendrik's Books."

Hunter and Duke shared a glance. A new bookstore in town? Colleen was going to flip—and for good reason. Hendrik's Books was a huge chain in Boston and Rhode Island. Why would they bother with a place as out-of-the way as Provincetown? There were more convenient places on the Cape.

"I'll handle this," he whispered, then stood up. "We already have Land's End Books. The priority should be supporting *that* business. I don't think another bookstore is a good use of that space."

Hunter pulled out her phone and mapped the address of the proposed new bookstore: 629 Commercial—formerly a store where people bought clothes that said things like It's Better on Cape Cod—was only a half mile away from Land's End.

Across the room, Justin Lombardo stood as well. Justin was tall with dark hair and cheekbones that could cut glass. Everyone turned to look at him, because, well, no one passed up an excuse to stare at Justin Lombardo. No one except Shelby Archer, who'd been selfish enough to break up with him.

"Actually, I think it's a perfectly reasonable use of that space," Justin said. "We have more than one coffee shop, more than one candy store. More than one Italian restaurant. There's no reason to reject an applicant with solid financials and great name recognition."

He sat back down. Murmurs broke out, and Gene Hobart called for everyone to settle down.

"For the record, I agree with Mr. Lombardo," Gene said. "But let's take a vote. Everyone who's for the Hendrik's outpost, raise your hand."

Hunter and Duke glanced around the room as hands shot up.

"And everyone who opposes?"

Hunter, Duke, and someone from the family who owned the boatyard raised their hands.

"The ayes have it," Gene said.

Duke leaned over and said, "We need to warn Colleen."

Seven

Shelby waited outside the SoHo brasserie. Minutes later, a black Lincoln Navigator deposited Claudia on the corner of Spring and Broadway, and Shelby watched her cut through the crowded sidewalk with ease. Wearing her Manolos and a cashmere wrap, she dressed like a certain breed of successful woman who'd conquered Manhattan in the '90s.

"Shelby," Claudia said, giving her a hug. "How's my superstar?"

The lunch was celebratory: *Secrets of Summer* had hit the *New York Times* bestseller list.

"Oh, Claudia," Shelby said. "I couldn't have done it without you. I don't even think it's fully sunk in yet." Reaching the bestseller list was a dream come true. Doing it with her first book was beyond anything she'd let herself imagine. But it was marred by the fallout in Provincetown.

She'd hurt her friend, and she didn't know what to do about it.

The maître d' greeted Claudia by name, leading them to a red leather banquette. The room was full of carved mahogany, with enormous brass mirrors, high tin ceilings, and antique lamps that gave the place a turn-of-the-century candlelight glow.

Claudia tucked the edge of her silver blond bob behind one ear, ordering a bottle of champagne. When it arrived, she made a toast.

"To *Secrets of Summer*," she said. "Your first *New York Times* bestseller, but certainly not your last."

They clinked their glasses together, but before Shelby finished taking her first sip, Claudia said, "So, how's the new manuscript coming?"

That was fast. Her next novel, *Guest Rooms*, was about two competing bed and breakfast owners in Provincetown who banded together when a new modern hotel threatened both of their businesses. And it was taking forever to write.

"Great," Shelby said. She didn't want to admit she was behind schedule. Or that the fallout with Hunter was messing with her head. It was difficult to think about Provincetown every day, knowing that her best friend there hated her. Worse, there was nothing Shelby seemed to be able to do to make it up to her. She'd sent Hunter flowers, apology notes, and a dinner delivery from Liz's Café. Hunter didn't respond to any of it.

"I had drinks with your editor last night," Claudia said. "She's eager to get the next one on the calendar. She'd like to publish a book every summer."

Shelby nodded. She knew this. Her editor planned for Shelby to be part of the ever-growing category of "beach books." Shelby didn't mind labels. One thing they didn't teach her in grad school but that she'd learned from Claudia was that if an author didn't know where their book would go on the bookstore shelf, a publisher wouldn't know, either. And wouldn't want to publish it.

"I'll have some pages for you soon," Shelby said.

"How soon?"

Shelby did a quick mental calculation. She had to finish the story arc and round out the characters a bit. She'd already put in half a year, and according to the legendary Stephen King, a first draft should only take three months. And who would argue with Stephen King?

"August 1?" she said.

"Great. Looking forward to seeing what you've got for me," Claudia said.

The server appeared with their smoked salmon tartine and Belgian waffles. When he left them alone, Claudia leaned forward, elbows on the table.

"I know you're busy, but I might ask for a little favor and have you do an 'in conversation' with a new author of mine. Her book pubs in July—a fabulous debut."

"Oh?" Shelby said.

Claudia nodded. "She's just out of Iowa." The Iowa Workshop was the best MFA program in the country. "Her book is also set on Cape Cod—Martha's Vineyard. It's called *Summerset*. Beach town, drama…you'll love it."

"Sounds like something I would write," she said. Actually, it sounded like something she should have written already. Damn, she'd really fallen behind. She'd thought the second novel would be easier. But unlike most things in life, when it came to writing fiction, practice didn't necessarily make perfect.

She looked across the table at Claudia, who was momentarily distracted by an incoming text. Maybe she should be more honest with her. Shelby didn't have to pretend to be perfect. After all, Claudia had responded to her early draft of *Secrets of Summer*, back when Shelby was just an unproven writer. Claudia had believed in her then. Surely, she could admit that she was struggling a little now.

"A friend of mine got mad at me for things I wrote in the book," Shelby said carefully. "I used some real life details for the main character."

Claudia refilled Shelby's glass of Perrier. "I'm sorry you're dealing with that, but it comes with success. I've heard all sorts of negative reactions from writers' friends and family: they wrote about them, they didn't write about them, this was true, this wasn't true. It comes with the territory. You're an artist. You have a right to draw inspiration where you find it. And like the saying goes—better to beg for forgiveness than ask permission."

Shelby nodded. But what happened when she begged for forgiveness and didn't get it?

"I know that in many ways, writing the second novel is harder than the first. You've lost a sort of creative innocence. That's normal." Claudia leaned forward. "But Shelby, do get cracking. You don't want to miss publishing next summer. Readers have short memories."

Shelby swallowed hard. It was time to get back to work.

Eight

Freshly motivated from her lunch with Claudia, Shelby walked a few blocks to one of her favorite SoHo coffee shops, aptly named Back to the Grind. Actually, writing wasn't a grind. Not even with the pressure of a deadline.

She'd always wanted to be a writer. Maybe every book lover felt that way at some point, and for Shelby, it just stuck. She suspected it was because her family moved around a lot when she was a child. Until high school, she was never in the same place for more than two or three years because of her father's job. Since she couldn't keep friends, books were her only constant and reliable companion. In sixth grade, marooned in yet another new school where no one talked to her, she read Sarah Dessen, Ellen Hopkins, even the Eragon novels by Christopher Paolini even though fantasy wasn't her thing. It didn't matter: a book was a book. A book was company. A book was belonging.

It was funny, though. She thought once she found a literary agent, she'd have "arrived." Like she'd reached the finish mark— from wannabe to *being*. But then, the mark moved: she would feel like she belonged once her agent sold her manuscript. And after that, she'd feel it once the book was published. And after that, she'd feel it if the book became a bestseller. Well, now she had a bestseller. But the mark, that tricky little thing, had moved again: she had to write another one.

Her phone rang. She still half expected it to be Noah, but they hadn't spoken since the night he came over to pick up his things from her apartment. Instead, it was Colleen. Shelby resisted the urge to send it to voicemail.

Although they'd been messaging back and forth as usual, she hadn't actually spoken since Shelby left town.

"Hey, Colleen," she said, trying to sound upbeat.

"Hi! Is this an okay time?"

"I'm at a coffee shop. It's a little loud. But I can talk for a sec. What's up?"

There was a long silence. Shelby checked her phone screen to make sure the call dropped. "Colleen?" she said.

"Yeah, yeah—I'm here. Um, I was wondering: Can you come back to Provincetown?"

Shelby frowned. What did that mean? Was she worried she'd never come back because of the blowup with Hunter?

"Of course I will. I just feel like I should give Hunter some space. Maybe in the fall." She resisted the urge to ask if Hunter had said anything more to her, to gauge if Hunter had softened towards her even a little. But didn't say anything. She had to focus on work.

"I was thinking more…immediately," Colleen said.

Shelby picked up on the urgency in her voice. She hadn't noticed at first.

"How immediately?"

"This week? For the summer. To run the bookstore."

So, she was teasing her. "Very funny," Shelby said.

"I'm serious."

Shelby froze. At the table next to her, two women passed their phones back and forth with loud TikTok videos.

"Hold on a second, okay?"

Shelby stood from the table, scooped up her laptop and bag, and walked outside. Spring Street was hot and crowded and she squinted at the sunlight that hit her from above. She had the urge to walk, as if movement would ward off whatever Colleen was going to say to justify such a request. As a friend, she'd listen. She'd take the time to talk Colleen gently down from whatever ledge she'd climbed onto.

She crossed the street to the shady side, the cobblestones knobby through the thin soles of her sandals. She leaned against the building on the corner, out of the way of people rushing along the sidewalk.

"Colleen, what's going on?"

"I just found out I can't work right now. And you're literally the only one I can reasonably ask to manage the bookstore. You worked here for three summers, my parents love you. They trust you."

"I don't understand: Why can't *you* work in the bookstore?"

"I have to restrict my activity," Colleen said. "For at least a few weeks."

Shelby pressed her hand to her mouth. Was she ill? Recovering from an injury Shelby didn't know about? She closed her eyes, hating herself for being so self-absorbed that she hadn't noticed something was wrong. And Colleen probably hadn't wanted to tell her because she didn't want to ruin Shelby's book tour. That was so like Colleen!

"Are you okay? Are you…sick?"

Colleen didn't say anything for a beat, and Shelby's heart raced.

"I'm not sick," she finally said. "I'm pregnant."

Hunter found out the new bookstore was opening by the end of June. She walked to Land's End to tell Colleen.

"Hey, Mia. Is Colleen around?" Hunter asked the part-timer,

a local high schooler on summer break. The girl had to pull her Beats headphones off to hear what Hunter was saying. Colleen would *not* be happy to find Mia just hanging around listening to music. Colleen was under pressure to make the bookstore work. Her parents were looking at the summer as a test run. If it went badly, they were likely to go ahead with a sale.

The eighty-year-old bookshop had barely changed since Colleen's great-great-grandfather, Augustine Miller, first opened its doors. Much of the wood shelving was original, and the tables stacked with books were in the same spot as in the old family photos. One wall had framed vintage, sepia-toned photographs of beachgoers at Herring Cove. Customers could still find a pay phone in one back corner. Handwritten signs, faded from years and bleached from the sun, directed customers to various sections, and an antique iron chandelier hung above the check-out counter. The only thing that changed were the titles on the shelves. And Land's End customers liked it that way.

"Colleen didn't come in today," Mia said.

"Not at all?" Hunter frowned. That was unlike her. Since the day Colleen dropped the shock of the millennium with her pregnancy news, she seemed to be in denial that she'd ever slow down.

"What about managing the store?" Hunter had asked. At the publishing company, one of her colleagues had a baby and went on maternity leave for months.

"I've got it all figured out," Colleen had said, clearly unfazed. "My parents will come in the fall to help with the babies. And while they're here to help, I'll hire and train a part-timer. I just need to have a strong sales summer so that I can afford it."

Now, thinking about that conversation, Hunter felt more uneasy about Colleen being absent. Every day counted towards making or breaking the summer season. That was true for all Ptown business owners. But Colleen's situation made it seem especially true for her.

Hunter checked her phone for the time. In a half hour, she had a meeting at the Seaport Press office (aka Duke's living room). Talking to Colleen would have to wait until after work.

She turned to leave, and a familiar blue book cover caught her eye. There it was: Shelby Archer's damn book on the *New York Times* bestseller shelf.

Hunter walked out.

Nine

At first, Shelby said no. There were so many legitimate reasons not to go back to Ptown, she didn't even have to make one up: she was on a deadline. She still had a few book events scattered throughout the summer. She didn't want to live in the same town as her now ex–best friend. Not to mention her ex-boyfriend. Provincetown was tiny—just three miles long and two streets wide. There was nowhere to hide.

But then Colleen told her more: not only was she twenty weeks pregnant, she was expecting twins. And she was experiencing bleeding.

"I'm not in pain or anything," Colleen said. "But the doctor put me on modified bed rest."

It was a lot to absorb. The pregnancy alone was a lot.

"Your parents can't help?" The Millers had retired and were now spending summers in Maine and winters in San Diego. But surely, they'd change plans if Colleen asked.

"If I tell them about the bed rest, they'll use it an excuse to sell the store. That's what they wanted in the first place. I'm the one who promised to make it worthwhile to keep it in the family."

After decades in the book business, Colleen's parents worried that the best years were behind the store. Still, Shelby couldn't believe the Millers would actually sell. It was unthinkable. Land's End Books seemed as intrinsic to Provincetown as the jetty, or MacMillan Pier. Personally, she felt it was as much a part of her literary education as her graduate degree. In some ways, maybe more so. Her MFA program helped her develop the craft of writing, but Land's End taught her about the relationship between books and readers. She'd seen firsthand how people responded to book covers, observed what they came in asking for, noted when a book's rave reviews didn't match customer feedback. The bookselling experience made her think as much about the reader as she did about the story she was telling, and that this set her apart from her classmates.

Shelby wanted to agree to help—to say yes right there on the spot. But Claudia's directive, still fresh in her mind, held her back. Instead, she told Colleen she just needed a day to think about it.

Now, out for drinks with her grad school friend Eve, it was *all* she could think about. And unfortunately for Eve, all she could talk about.

"It's not that I don't want to help Colleen with the store," Shelby said. "But I can't take off from my own job. And it's already questionable if I'll make the deadline on my next book. Claudia will kill me."

They were sharing a bottle of pinot noir at a wine bar near Union Square. Eve had tried to change the topic twice asking about Noah. But there was really nothing to talk about there: he'd messaged her a bunch of times, and she'd ignored them. There was no getting past her disappointment in him.

God, she wondered if that was exactly how Hunter felt about *her*. She gulped her wine.

The server, a tall, broad-shouldered brunette who talked with a Scottish brogue, checked in with them. Eve opened her menu and pointed to the rosé section.

"I'm going to try that orange one," Eve said, looking up at her. "You want one, too?"

Shelby declined, even though the server assured her it didn't have an orange flavor. She wasn't in the mood to be adventurous. After the server left, Eve said, "Do you want me to cancel my order? We can get out of here if you want."

"What? No," Shelby said, shaking her head. "Sorry. I just don't know what to do." She meant what to do about Colleen, but Eve clearly thought she meant the novel, because she said, "Maybe a writer's retreat would help. I did the Woodstock one—just went off the grid and pounded out a first draft."

Shelby had to get off the grid; that was for sure. She just wasn't sure which one: either she stayed in New York City and let down Colleen, or she went to help Colleen and let down her agent. *And* herself.

And then it hit her: she was looking at the summer all wrong. What was her biggest excuse—to Colleen, and to herself—for not going to Provincetown? Her deadline. But her new book was once again set in Ptown. Maybe going back would actually give her a creative boost. And she'd help Colleen in the process.

Hunter went to Colleen's straight from work.

A month ago, Colleen moved in with her boyfriend, Doug MacDougal, leaving behind the apartment above Land's End where she'd grown up and where she'd returned after college. Colleen and Doug had known for a while that they'd ultimately move in together, but the pregnancy had turned "at some point" into "immediately."

Doug's one-bedroom was on the ground floor of a classic Cape cottage on the East End that had been converted into four apartments. The entrance to the unit was on the side of the house. In the back, a pebbled path led to a shared flower garden with a few iron benches. It was lovely. She'd take it over her parents' sprawling, modernist house anyday.

"It's open," Colleen called out when Hunter knocked.

She followed Colleen's voice to the living room. Colleen was alone in a corner of the sectional couch, her arms around a needlepoint pillow decorated with a starfish made by her mother Annie. She held the pillow like a shield around her midsection.

"Hey," Hunter said. "Doug still at work?"

Colleen shook her head. "He ran out to get a few things."

"I hope that doesn't include dessert." Hunter had picked up lemon cake from Connie's Bakery, and placed the box on the coffee table. She sat next to Colleen. "So, a little update: I found out that the new bookstore is opening in a few weeks. I didn't want to text you because it's not great news, obviously."

Colleen reached for her eco-friendly water bottle. "Well, I guess we knew it was coming."

Hunter appreciated the sanguine response, but she knew how Colleen really felt. When Hunter first told her about the bookstore a weeks ago, she'd burst into tears.

"Really, I almost feel sorry for Hendrik's," Hunter said. "Everyone in town loves you—will be loyal to you. And anyone who visits here summer after summer knows *you're* the Ptown bookseller. Hendrik's might have half a dozen locations, but they don't have you." She leaned forward and pulled the cake box from the paper bag.

Colleen sighed. "Well, as you can see I'm sitting here so Land's End doesn't fully have me right now, either."

Hunter stopped messing with the bag. "Yeah. I stopped by the store today to talk to you. You feeling okay?"

The door to the apartment opened and closed, and a moment later Doug strolled into the bedroom with two cups of take-out ice cream from Lewis Brothers. Doug was over six feet tall, with light brown hair, kind brown eyes, and the hint of a beer belly.

He was like a big teddy bear. "Hey, Hunter," he said. "Didn't know you were coming by. I would have brought more."

"I'm good, thanks," she said. "I'm just checking on Colleen."

"I'm fine," Colleen said unconvincingly before glancing at Doug.

"I'm going to put these in the freezer," he said.

Hunter watched him walk out of the room, then turned to Colleen.

"Okay, what's going on?" Hunter said.

Colleen pulled the butterfly clip out of her hair, then clicked it open and closed, open and closed. "I found out I have a complication. My placenta is blocking part of my cervix."

That sounded bad. But Hunter was embarrassed to admit she had no idea what that meant. She didn't actually know what a cervix was supposed to do.

"Are the babies okay?"

Colleen nodded. "But I can't spend much time on my feet, or lift boxes, or basically do anything I have to do at the bookstore. Exertion puts me at higher risk for bleeding."

Doug walked back in. "I'm calling Liz's for takeout. You wanna stay, Hunter?"

"Um, sure. Thanks," she said, distracted. What was going to happen with the bookstore? Mia was a part-timer, but she couldn't run the place. "So what are you going to do? Can one of your moms help out?"

Colleen pulled a second pillow onto her lap. "No. I haven't told them. You know how skeptical they are about me taking over in the first place. I can't give them any more reasons to doubt the plan. So I asked Shelby to manage the store for the summer—her old job."

"Very funny," Hunter said.

"That's what she said when I asked her," Colleen said.

Wait—this was for real? Doug sat next to Colleen and put his arm around her. Together, they faced her in a way that made it clear it was, in fact, for real.

"Hunter, we really need for you to put your beef with Shelby aside for now," he said.

"My *'beef'*?" Hunter felt a flash of annoyance. She knew Colleen was having a rough time, but they were totally invalidating her. How would Colleen feel if Shelby had written about *her* personal life? Maybe she was getting upset about nothing: Shelby was a big-shot writer now. She wasn't going to leave her book tour to work at Land's End. "So Shelby agreed to this?"

"Not yet," Colleen said, but her expression told Hunter she believed that ultimately, she would. And that was the difference between the two of them: Colleen hadn't learned yet that Shelby's only concern was Shelby. Which was why Hunter wasn't going to stress about it.

There was no way Shelby Archer was coming back.

Ten

The entire ferry ride, Shelby wondered if she was making a mistake. Sitting on the upper deck, exactly where she'd been sitting four weeks earlier with Ezra Randall, she felt panicked. She should be in the city working on her book. How could she have agreed to this? Was it some elaborate form of procrastination?

She went straight from the ferry to Doug's apartment. Inside the front door he kept well-worn water boots lined up and a shelf that displayed vintage brass sea lanterns. In the living room there was weathered wood furniture, and she saw Colleen's decorative touches: needlepoint pillows, a plush pale green throw, and a ceramic pitcher filled with fresh hydrangeas.

Colleen rested on the couch, looking so obviously pregnant, Shelby wondered how she could have missed it a month ago. Had she been *that* consumed with her book launch?

She bent down and hugged her gingerly, recognizing the scent of Colleen's familiar lavender-and-apples shampoo.

"You can give me a real hug," Colleen said into her shoulder, tightening her arms around her. "I'm not going to break."

Well, apparently that wasn't completely true. Or Shelby wouldn't be there.

"Do you feel okay?" Shelby said, sitting next to her.

"I feel fine. That's the frustrating part. I'm fighting the urge to run around and do things." She opened her laptop. "I typed up a list of instructions for you just in case you forgot how to use the inventory system."

Shelby smiled. Colleen had been making her "lists" for as long as Shelby could remember. "I haven't forgotten anything. Once a bookseller, always a bookseller."

The printer across the room spit out pages.

"Better to be safe than sorry," Colleen said. "Mia's not great with the computer. But the customers love her."

"Mia?" Shelby said.

"Yeah. Surprising, right? With most kids her age, it's the opposite. But she reads *everything*. More than anyone I've ever known."

"Mia Lombardo?" Had Colleen forgotten to mention that her part-timer was Justin's sister? But she was only fourteen. Wait—no. She was now *seventeen*. Wow. It was hard to believe she was going to be a senior in high school.

"Yeah. I told you that," Colleen said. No, she definitely hadn't.

"That's a detail I would have remembered," Shelby said gently.

"I'm sorry. I have total brain fog." She frowned. "Wait—it's not a problem for you, is it? I didn't think you'd care one way or another."

Shelby waved her hand. "Totally fine. I'm just surprised. Actually—now I get it. This is all just a ploy to get Justin and me back together," Shelby joked. When she broke up with Justin, Colleen had told her she was making a big mistake.

Colleen laughed. "You busted me, Shelby. I got pregnant just so I could lure you back to Justin Lombardo."

Shelby laughed.

"Actually," Colleen said, "I think he's with someone new."

"Oh. Well, that's great." And she meant it. Good for him. She wanted him to be happy. Maybe they could even be friends. She checked her phone. It was almost noon. "I can hang out some more or I could get started…"

"Go! Definitely go. You didn't come all this way to babysit me. And thanks again. I feel so much better already just having you here." Her eyes filled with tears. Shelby was surprised and reached out to squeeze her hand.

"Colleen, you're going to be fine."

She nodded and sniffed. "I know. But it's not just about me anymore." And that was when it hit her. A baby. Colleen was bringing another human into this world. Two! She'd known that, of course. But now that she was actually there with her, it was more real.

And she knew, from the scared look in her friend's eyes, that she'd made the right decision returning to Ptown.

Land's End Books occupied one side of a white wooden house that had once been a two-family fisherman's cottage. The second floor was a two-bedroom apartment where the Millers used to live. Colleen had lived there until she moved in with Doug, and for the next two months, it was Shelby's. But she'd wait to go upstairs and unpack after the workday.

Inside, Shelby was met with the familiar scents of salt water, cardboard, and the handmade beeswax candles for sale near the register. Her stomach did a little flutter; she hadn't realized how much she'd missed it.

A very grown-up-looking Mia Lombardo stood behind the counter, unpacking a box of books. She was a pretty young woman, with the same thick, wavy dark hair as her brother. She was dressed in cutoff jeans and a gold-and-black Nauset Regional High T-shirt.

Mia looked up, and from the look of confusion on her face,

Shelby realized Colleen hadn't just forgotten to tell Shelby about Mia: she hadn't told Mia about Shelby.

"Hey there," Shelby said, as if it had been three months since she'd last seen her instead of three years. She wasn't just taller; her face had filled out, losing some of its baby roundness and looking more chiseled, like her brother's striking bone structure. "I'm just here helping out Colleen."

Mia blinked at her with big, skeptical chocolate brown eyes. Her brother's eyes.

"She didn't say anything to me about it. Where is she?"

"She has to rest for a few weeks," Shelby said.

"And so she called *you*?"

Shelby was taken aback by the rancor in her voice. Looking back on it, she'd never said a proper goodbye to Mia. She'd been so concerned with Justin, she hadn't thought about the fact that she was also "breaking up" with his family. And they were a great family. She'd been especially close with his mother, Carmen. Shelby had a challenging relationship with her own mother, who made no secret of the fact that she'd given up her own career to move around the country with Shelby's father. She was resentful, and somehow, her attitude towards Shelby was collateral damage. But for Carmen Lombardo, who worked long hours beside her husband at the family restaurant, being a mother was her number-one job. She doted on Justin and his sister. And when it became clear to Carmen that Shelby made her son happy, she began treating her like an honorary daughter.

The thought of running into Carmen—of seeing the same look of displeasure as the one on Mia's face—made Shelby uneasy.

A customer walked in, saving Shelby from the awkward moment. While Mia helped her in the memoir section, Shelby walked behind the counter. She found the usual smattering of Post-its, worn composition notebooks, piles of books with names scrawled on lined paper and strapped to them with rubber bands. The bookstore had a computer system for inventory and reading publisher catalogs and scheduling author events, but everything around the edges of that was remarkably low-tech.

More customers walked in. A woman wearing a khaki vest and shorts that made her appear to be on her way fly fishing. She browsed the front tables, then wandered deeper into the store.

"Can I help you find something?" Shelby asked. The question was like flexing an underused muscle. How many hundreds of times had she asked it in summers past? It was often the same: she'd ask a customer if they needed help, they'd say no, then a minute later ask her for a recommendation. In four summers of bookselling, she could only remember a few times when she couldn't find a book match for someone. And that was essentially what bookselling was: matchmaking.

"No, thanks," the woman said, then turned to look at her. "Wait… Are you that author?"

Shelby froze. Somehow, it hadn't crossed her mind that someone would recognize her outside of her own book events.

"You are!" she said, grinning. "Irene," she called out, beckoning to another woman browsing the nonfiction shelf. "Look who's here." She turned back to Shelby. "We just picked your book for our next book club. Irene won a copy on Goodreads and loved it."

Irene glanced up and her eyes widened. She had dyed red hair, wore green glasses and had another pair of glasses on a chain around her neck.

"Shelby Archer!" she exclaimed. "We came to Provincetown after reading your book. I had to see this place for myself. I was sure it couldn't live up to the way you portray it in the book, but it actually does."

"Well, I'm so glad you're enjoying it," Shelby said, touched that her book had inspired a ladies' trip. The woman retrieved copies of *Secrets of Summer* from a front table and brought them over. "Would you mind signing these?"

"Of course."

"Can we take a photo?"

Shelby still wasn't used to people wanting her to sign books, or take a photo with them. It was still surprising that her book was actually *out there*—that strangers were spending their time reading it. But whenever someone asked to take a selfie or for her to sign their book, it became more and more real. And the more real it became, the more secure she felt. Even her parents, who had expressed doubts about her less-than-practical career choice, were coming around. She'd always believed that becoming a writer would be the antidote to everything that bothered her growing up: not having control over where she lived, not being able to keep friends, the nagging fear of being forgotten as she school-hopped from one state to the next. The loneliness.

The ladies threw their arms around her and one another and, holding the camera above their heads at a practiced, bird's-eye angle, snapped photos.

"Can you believe Shelby Archer is here today?" Straw Hat said to Mia, who watched the spectacle from the middle of the room.

"No, I can't," Mia said. And then she walked out.

Eleven

Justin Lombardo got the call late in the afternoon: hundreds of fish washed up on Herring Cove beach. He worked for the Center for Coastal Studies in marine research and coastal conservation. His team was on-site within twenty minutes.

"They're Atlantic saury," said his boss, the director of research. She stood from her crouched position. A species of *Scomberesocidae*, the saury were needle-nosed fish that swam in large schools. In the summer and fall, they migrated to continental shelf waters.

Dead or alive, marine life was washing ashore more frequently. Every incident raised questions and it was his job to answer them: What caused the event? What could be done to prevent it from happening again? What was the environmental impact?

"Looks like a red tide situation," Justin said. Red tide algae sucked the oxygen out of water, a harmless part of the underwater ecosystem at normal levels. But contaminants that made their way into the water or that were dumped there could cause the algae to reproduce in dangerous quantities.

"We'll do some sampling," his boss said. "As soon as Doug gets here."

Doug MacDougal was their chemical oceanographer. He was also one of Justin's close friends.

"I'm here, I'm here," Doug said, running down the beach. They'd been casual, friendly coworkers until Doug started dating Colleen Miller, who was best friends with Justin's ex, Shelby Archer. When they all started hanging out three years ago, he never imagined that Doug and Colleen would be the ones whose relationship lasted. He'd been so blindsided when Shelby ended things, it had been hard for him at first to even hang out with Doug and Colleen anymore. But he eventually got over it.

Doug was prepared with his testing kits and seemed to have his usual let's-get-'em energy. But Justin knew he'd had some sleepless nights lately. Colleen was unexpectedly pregnant, and while Doug always intended to end up with her, things were moving a lot quicker than he had anticipated. He'd missed a few days of work for her doctor's appointments, but Justin doubted anyone else in the office realized how distracted he was.

They got to work, anticipating that soon the seagulls would descend en masse, turning the blanket of dead fish into an all-you-can-eat buffet.

His phone buzzed with a message from his sister.

Why aren't you picking up?

He ignored it. Mia had been high-maintenance lately. She'd gotten terrible grades last semester of junior year, refused to talk about college, and seemed to be pushing back against their mother over everything. His parents had asked her to pitch in at the restaurant—they were having a problem staffing up that summer because housing in town had become so expensive—but she'd turned them down. She was fixated on working at the bookshop.

Doug handed him a clipboard.

"I'm going to do some sampling here and then let's get out on the water," he said. From a boat, they would collect water for testing and try to put the puzzle pieces together. Their colleagues busied themselves photographing the site and taking notes.

"Whenever you're ready," Justin said, just as he noticed his sister walking through the sea grass, making her way towards them. So much for ignoring her phone calls.

"What's up?" he called out. "Kinda busy here."

"Yeah, I can see. But you're not answering your phone."

She traversed the uneven sand quickly in her Converse shoes, holding her hand up against her forehead as a sun visor.

"So you thought I'd have more time to talk in person?" he said.

"Trust me: you want to hear this," she said, a little out of breath when she reached him.

"Mia, stop being so dramatic. And look around: this isn't a good time."

She glanced at the dead fish and turned back to him. "Well, I hate to break it to you, but those fish aren't the only things washing ashore. Shelby's back in town."

Okay, that was news. And yes, something he appreciated hearing from his sister instead of finding out by running into Shelby on the street. But the truth was, while there was a time this would have bothered him, he was over it. He'd finally moved on.

He'd met his girlfriend, Kate, at a fund-raiser in Boston, an event to raise awareness of the threat to sea life caused by off-shore wind turbines. Things moved quickly (they affectionately dubbed their relationship a "whirl*wind* romance"). Sure, it had been long-distance. But that was changing now. He'd convinced her to take some time away from Boston, to give summer on the Cape a try. She had a business to manage, but they'd even worked that out. She was going to use the summer to test Provincetown as a potential new market for her family business. Kate Hendrik was opening a summer bookstore.

The lease was short-term, and she viewed the shop as exploratory. But he couldn't help but hope that once she'd spent the summer there, she'd find a way to make it permanent.

"Thanks for the heads-up," Justin said to Mia. "But it's irrelevant. I haven't thought about Shelby Archer in a long time."

"Really?" Mia said with a shrug. "Okay. But you don't have to say that, you know."

"Mia, look around," he said, glancing pointedly at the beached fish. "I've got work to do here." Also, she was wrong: of course he had to say that Shelby meant nothing to him.

If he didn't say it, how else would it become true?

Twelve

The Millers' apartment above Land's End looked the same as the last time Shelby had been there. The space was cozy, with wide wicker chairs, hardwood floors decorated with colorful Turkish rugs, and eggshell-colored walls decorated with black-and-white photography of Cape Cod wildlife. The main bedroom had robin's-egg blue walls, an antique iron bed, and a view of the beach.

Shelby sat on the sofa and opened her laptop. After a quick pizza dinner, she was determined to get some pages written. Why wasn't the book clicking? She'd been so frustrated she kept looking back at early drafts of *Secrets of Summer* to remind herself that writing a bad first draft was normal. No, more than normal—it was necessary.

Maybe part of the problem was that she'd had her MFA program as a support system for *Secrets of Summer*. Now, she was writing in comparative solitude and a creative bubble. Without the academic structure for sharing work and getting feedback, Shelby hesitated to ask anyone to read her pages. It felt like an imposition now that they were all out in the real world. So she couldn't get the same outside perspective to keep her on course.

But none of those things were the reason Shelby was writing so slowly. She suspected it was a much deeper problem: she didn't feel connected to the story. When she wrote *Secrets of Summer*, she felt an urgency. She simply had to *get the story out*. Now, she had a contract, a deadline. And she'd do her job. But writing felt more like a waning marriage than a passionate love affair—not that she'd ever been married and, well, her passionate love affair didn't end very well.

Someone knocked on the door. Startled, she stopped typing. It was something that never happened in New York; friends didn't stop by unannounced. The only time her doorbell rang unexpectedly was when food delivery had the wrong apartment.

Shelby checked through the peephole and saw Duke Nestley. He wore a Hawaiian shirt and salmon-colored linen pants. His white hair was longer than when she'd last seen him.

"Duke," she said, opening it. She'd anticipated seeing Duke at her Land's End reading and had been disappointed when he didn't show. He was one of the most passionate readers she'd ever known. The summers she'd worked at Land's End, he stopped in nearly every day. Before *Secrets of Summer* was published, she'd considered sending him an early copy of the book—what the publisher called an ARC. Then she decided not to, thinking the friendly gesture might feel more like a burden to someone with so much reading to do for work. But she left a signed copy for him at Land's End. Now that she thought about it, she'd never heard back. Maybe he felt bad about missing her event, learned she was back in town, and decided to talk to her in person. Made total sense.

"Come on in." She closed the door behind him.

"Hunter told me you're helping out with the bookstore," he said.

She nodded. "Yes. Crazy, right?" Through an open window she heard a neighbor's music, the unmistakable synth of New Wave. Her summers in Ptown were like an auditory time machine. If she hadn't lived there all those summers, would she have ever listened to New Order? Depeche Mode?

Duke played a part of her cultural education, too. Shelby, as Colleen's friend, was included at his occasional dinner party or reading salon. She particularly recalled one enchanting night, before she moved to New York City, when the literary salon stretched until two in the morning. The house flickered with candles, the backyard was strung with lights, and Shelby basked in the company of writers, imagining the day when she'd be a real published novelist.

Her four summers in Provincetown shaped her more than any other time in her life. Surely, she would find enough to draw on to finish her second book.

Duke sat on the nearest chair.

"I haven't said anything to you about your book because I haven't known what to say."

Shelby looked at him, startled. "Oh?" So that was it: he thought the book was bad. She felt her face flush.

"I have to admit I'm surprised—no, I'm hurt—with the way you wrote the character Royce."

Wait—what? Shelby needed to sit down now, too.

Royce Jones was a secondary character in her book—part of what she thought of as the B storyline. She'd used some details from an old breakup Duke had told her about: a few years ago, he went to a party during Carnival week—the Mardi Gras of Provincetown—and mistook one of the masked revelers for his boyfriend. He realized his mistake as soon as they kissed, but also was quite drunk and things got carried away and before he knew it, he'd left with him. His partner found out and ended their long relationship. But in *Secrets of Summer*, she changed Carnival to a Halloween party. And not a single detail of the characters resembled Duke or his ex.

"Duke, I'm sorry," she said, leaning against the couch armrest, her arms hugging herself. How had she so completely misread her own writing? How many other people had she offended with the book? "I would never intentionally upset you. And no one would ever connect you to the character in the book. It's fiction and Royce is nothing like you."

"The bumper sticker," he said.

"What?"

"Royce has a truck with a bumper sticker saying, Gut Fish Not Houses."

"Okay. And?"

"That's my bumper sticker. On my truck."

Shelby felt the color drain from her face. She'd only seen the truck parked in town. She liked the bumper sticker. She imagined she'd like the person who owned the truck. She used it in her book. As far as she'd known, that was the end of the story.

"I didn't even know you *own* a truck," she said. Locals didn't drive in Provincetown during the summers. They biked; they walked. Fine, the occasional trip to Stop n' Shop. But she couldn't place a single one of her friends with a specific car, except the Millers' blue Subaru. "I saw it on a car parked on Commercial," she said slowly. "Out on the street. Not at your house. Not with you."

Neither of them said anything. Shelby felt like she was holding her breath. He seemed sad, as if he wanted to believe and understood how much she *wanted* him to believe her.

"Even if that's true, you did know the Carnival story was mine. And changing it to Halloween doesn't make it any less mine." He shook his head.

Shelby swallowed hard. Had she lost perspective after moving away? Had she imagined more distance between her friends and her characters than there actually was?

"Duke, I feel terrible. I never, ever intended for that storyline to be connected to you. Is there anything I can do to make it up to you?" she said.

Duke shook his head, avoiding eye contact. Shelby's stomach tightened. What could she do to fix this?

"Duke, maybe I can revise it for the paperback." She didn't know if that was actually an option, but she'd ask her editor.

"I appreciate the offer, but sadly, the damage is done," he said, his blue eyes crinkled with disappointment. "That was a very painful time for me, and to see it in print like that—commodified for entertainment…"

Shelby covered her eyes with her hands. "Duke…"

"But I didn't come here tonight to complain. At least, not *just* to complain."

Hearing a hint of levity in his voice—more like his old self—she looked up.

"You didn't?" she said, hopeful.

"One of my authors is coming to town in August. Can Land's End host a reading?"

"Of course! Absolutely," she said, relieved to be able to offer him something.

"Great," he said, standing up. "We can do it in my backyard. As you well know, the bookstore has limited space."

Shelby nodded. As lovely as her event at the Red Inn had been, she wished they'd had space to host her at the actual bookstore. "I know. I wish the store could host more events, but it's too small."

"I said the same thing to Colleen. Land's End needs event space. Outdoor space. But in her condition, she obviously can't take that on this summer."

The beach behind Land's End wasn't zoned for commercial use—a source of frustration for Colleen every summer they worked together. But Colleen's parents, Annie and Pam, had no interest in changing the way the store had operated since the beginning. They'd only reluctantly replaced shelving and floorboards when needed, trying to preserve as much of the original aesthetic of the space as possible.

"I just don't think that's something the Millers ever planned for," Shelby said. "They've done fine without it. I think they like to keep their in-store events intimate."

"Well, they've never had competition before. Now Land's End has to step up its game. And it seems you're the only one who can do that at the moment."

She didn't know what he was talking about. "What competition?"

"A new bookstore is opening this summer. Hendrik's Books from Boston. And no offense to your ex-boyfriend, but his the-more-the-merrier attitude is short-sighted."

Okay, Duke lost her there. What did Justin have to do with the bookstore? Before she could ask, he said, "We need to support the long-standing businesses here so we don't see our entire way of life and our community erode. It can happen, you know."

She couldn't imagine another bookstore in town. And how could Colleen fail to mention that to her? Forgetting to tell her about Mia was one thing. But a competing bookstore?

"Of course I want to help. But I don't see what I can do," Shelby said.

"Come to a town council meeting. Petition for beach access. Someone has to get the ball rolling. And apparently, you're our bookseller for the summer. So that someone is you."

"I want to help. I do. But I'm only here temporarily," she said. "I don't think I'm the right person to—"

"Shelby, may I offer some words of wisdom? As someone who has had his fair share of experiences and mistakes?" he said. "This is a special place. And in order to hold on to it, we need to give more than we take."

Ouch. Okay, message received. She'd "taken" his story for her book. And now it was time to do something positive.

Maybe managing Land's End was more than a chance to help Colleen. It might be her chance to redeem herself.

Thirteen

Justin's parents, Carmen and Bert Lombardo, lived in a middle Georgian built during the whaling era, complete with a widow's walk. A fence bordered the property, and he opened the gate to the stone walkway leading to the rear of the house. No one used the front entrance, and considering his family's entire world centered around their restaurant, entering the home through the kitchen was fitting. The windows were wet with condensation from his mother's cooking, and the air was pungent with fresh garlic.

Tuesday night was the Lombardo family dinner night. It was the slowest night in town, after the weekenders left and before the next crop of visitors arrived, and therefore the only time his parents were willing to leave the restaurant in the capable hands of the managers.

"Hello?" he called out, checking his phone for the time.

He was a few minutes late, and everyone was already at the dining room table. He planted himself in one of the craftsman chairs, opposite his father. The long table was covered with food from end to end. His mother served linguini in a bowl hand-painted with roosters—Portuguese pottery that had been part of their meals for as long as he could remember. The crusty garlic bread in a basket was his sister's contribution, the only thing she ever "cooked." His father was busy decanting the red wine. Two big platters of chicken parmesan rested between his parents, and he knew his mother would send him home with leftovers to freeze.

"Sorry I'm late. Work was busy."

"Mia mentioned. All those fish! Is it a red tide situation?" his mother said. She had initially been disappointed when he said he didn't want to take over the family business, but she respected his choice in vocation. She understood the value in the work he was doing. It was impossible to live on the Cape and not experience the fallout from water pollution, climate change, overfishing, and countless other threats to their beloved home.

Justin shook his head. "We don't think so. Not this time."

Mia, busy eating, offered a distracted wave. He wondered if she'd told their parents about Shelby Archer's return, and decided no, she wouldn't. Why give them another reason to push back on her bookstore job? They'd argued for weeks about her decision not to work at the restaurant.

He wasn't surprised that Colleen needed help managing the store. When Doug confided in him that Colleen was pregnant and said "nothing will change," Justin thought he was being naive. He still had a vague memory of being ten years old and the arrival of his baby sister—how it turned their family of three into something exponentially different. But what did surprise him was that a) the person she had asked for help was Shelby and b) Shelby had actually come back to Provincetown. She'd made it clear when she left three years ago that she didn't plan to be back, and certainly didn't want any obligation to be. That was what their relationship had been reduced to in the end: an obligation she couldn't meet.

He'd never understand why she moved to New York without even trying to make it work. It made him wonder if it had been a one-sided relationship all along. But he had to hand it to her—she'd done it. She was a published novelist.

For a while after Shelby, he couldn't get emotionally invested in anyone. But he'd come to realize that timing was everything in life. That was why he was optimistic about the way things were going with Kate. They'd met through a shared interest, a passion project. They were geographically compatible—especially now that she was opening a store in Ptown. And they wanted the same things out of life: meaningful work. Life on the Cape. Someday, a family of their own.

He never imagined he'd be thinking of the future in such permanent terms at just twenty-eight years old. But the way Doug and Colleen had escalated things so quickly, it changed his perspective. No, he couldn't say for sure that Kate was *the one*. But he did hope to someday have a marriage like his parents'. Carmen and Bert had met in their twenties while vacationing separately in Sicily. They'd grown up an hour away from one another in Boston, but it took a trip across the ocean for them to cross paths. They'd been together ever since. They married, had Justin, and opened their first pizza place on the Boston waterfront, all by the time they were thirty. Could Justin fill in so many blanks in his personal and professional life within the next three years? Did he want to?

"I had a beer with Bill Hockney last night," his father said. "He was fishing over in Yarmouth, had a striper on the line, and a seal snatched it right off."

"I'm not surprised," Justin said. *Halichoerus grypus*, gray seals, were the most common species of seal found in Cape Cod waters during the summer. The males could grow larger than ten feet long and weigh over eight hundred pounds.

"Well, we didn't have this problem thirty years ago. Now folks like your boss are passing all these laws that do more harm than good."

"Dad, look at what the Marine Mammals Protections Act did for whales and manatees. I don't hear you complaining we have too many of *them*."

"Well, they're not the ones attracting sharks."

His dad had a point there: the increase in white sharks was a problem. Justin was working in a program that captured sharks and tagged them with accelerometers to track their movement. They'd logged hundreds of miles so far.

"Nature is a delicate balance," Justin said. Another reason why he'd chosen to work in Ptown was that he understood the balance there innately, almost instinctively. He felt it was his life's purpose to be its steward. And it wasn't just about marine life; the change in climate was affecting every aspect of their lives on the peninsula, with more and more damaging storms that were hurting businesses and threatening their way of life.

But he wasn't in the mood to debate that tonight. The news about Shelby was bothering him more than he wanted to admit. "Mia's workday was actually more eventful than mine," he said. She set down her fork down and shook her head.

"Oh?" his mother said, turning to Mia, who shrugged.

"Shelby Archer is working at Land's End for the summer," Justin said, trying to sound nonchalant. But it felt wrong to say her name aloud, as if he were welcoming her back into his thoughts. And the last thing he wanted was to think about Shelby. So he brought it up to get the news out of the way.

"*That one's* back?" his father said. Ever since Shelby left, he'd referred to her only as "That one." His parents had taken the breakup almost as hard as he did. They'd adored her. But while his father dealt with it by never mentioning her again, his mother took the opposite tack. "It's hard when you're young," she'd said at the time. And then continued to ask about her for months until she finally gave up.

"Well, that settles it, Mia," Bert said. "No more wasting time at the bookstore. We're short-staffed and you can earn more money with tips."

"The bookstore job will look better on my college applications," Mia said.

"She's right," Justin said. "But Mia, if you want to work at a bookstore, work at the new one."

"What new one?" Carmen said. His mother had selective memory.

"I told you, Ma: Kate is opening up a Hendrik's here for the summer. And hopefully, longer." He wasn't surprised his mother had conveniently forgot the news. She didn't seem to like Kate. He wasn't sure why. It wasn't her fault she had a gluten allergy and couldn't eat pasta.

"Work for a competing bookstore? I would never do Colleen dirty like that," Mia said. "And I can't believe Doug isn't totally pissed at you."

"Mia, you know I don't like that expression," Carmen said.

"Why would Doug care?" The truth was, Justin only considered the new bookstore as competition for Colleen's business after the fact. He hadn't considered it until Duke brought up the issue at the board meeting. But the way Justin saw it, Land's End was an institution. Hendrik's was just a little summer bonus catering to the massive wave of visitors. There was so much summertime foot traffic, he was sure both bookstores could successfully coexist.

He wasn't so sure about himself and Shelby Archer. It had taken him a long time to get over her, and the one thing that helped was the fact that they lived three hundred miles apart.

His father muttered something he didn't catch, and his mother laughed. The big belly laugh that made everyone around her smile, too. Shelby laughed like that. He had a memory of Shelby and his mother leaning in towards one another, shaking with laughter at that very table.

He pushed the thought away.

The problem, he realized, was that his mother simply hadn't spent enough time around Kate. He'd have to do something about that.

They had their routines, Carmen and Bert. It varied from season to season, but in the summer, it went something like this: Tuesday was their weekend. It was the only night they trusted their kitchen and the front of the house to run smoothly without them.

After dinner with the kids, they drove their open-topped Jeep to Herring Cove beach, parked in the lot, then walked their oversize blanket to a spot near the water. The blanket was one of her favorites, Turkish cotton, purchased at a now-defunct store called Loveland. Stores came and went in PTown, just like people. She and Bert were among the few who stayed, year in and year out.

Sunsets on Herring Cove were like a magic trick in the sky. Relaxing on the beach among her neighbors and watching nature's light show was usually enough to make her forget any worries. Not tonight.

"You're quiet," Bert said. She knew it was his way of asking what was wrong. If he just came right out and said, *What's wrong?* she'd reflexively reply, *Nothing.*

"I'm thinking about Mia," she said. "Every time I try to talk to her about college, she shuts down. We're running out of time." Summer went quickly. In the fall, she'd have to start doing her applications. She had friends whose children were already working on their essays.

"She mentioned it tonight—how the bookstore job would look good on her application."

"That's a smoke screen. She just wants any excuse to work there."

"There's time," Bert said, reaching for her hand. He wasn't necessarily the calmer of the two them, but he did tend to see things in reductive terms. As far as he was concerned, there was time until the applications were actually due.

"At this point, I'd settle for an opinion about where she'd like to go." Carmen didn't understand why this was so much to ask. Mia loved books. So why did she hate school?

"Frankly, I think the more immediate worry is Justin," Bert said.

She knew why he felt that way. Shelby Archer. As Justin's father, Bert was more of a confidant to their son. He'd no doubt heard a lot more about their son's heartbreak three years ago than she had. Around her, Justin always put on a brave front. So maybe it was easier for her not to feel cynical about Shelby. They'd been so young! But whenever she said that in Shelby's defense, Bert replied, "*We* managed to make it work."

It was true. They'd met at the same age as Justin and Shelby. But unlike Carmen in her early twenties, Shelby had professional dreams—and the maturity to know that a serious relationship might not be compatible with her ambition. She wished her own daughter had some goals for the future.

"Maybe having Shelby back is a blessing in disguise," Carmen said. "She sets a good example for Mia."

The truth was, Carmen had enjoyed getting to know her that one summer. She was able to talk to her in a way she didn't connect with her own children. Justin was good kid, but as a boy he'd always been closer with Bert. And Mia, once such an easygoing child, saw her now as someone to rebel against. But Shelby had seemed to genuinely enjoy Carmen's company, asking her about cooking and the restaurant business and her early years on the Cape. Shelby confided in her about her rootless childhood, admitting that she didn't have a great relationship with her own parents but hoping that might change one day. Carmen had been impressed by how focused she was on having a career and financial independence.

Carmen liked to think of herself as having been mature for

her age when she met and married Bert. But she didn't think she'd ever had such concrete goals. She'd just stumbled along, lucky to find the right partner and willing to figure it out from there. Shelby wanted to figure it out first, then find the right person. She couldn't blame her. Really, it made Carmen respect her.

Bert cast her a sideways glance. "*We* set a good example for Mia. Things might be bumpy with her right now, but don't lose sight of that."

He leaned over and gave her a kiss. She hoped he was right. But just in case it turned out he wasn't, she was keeping her eyes open for another way to reach Mia. And she couldn't help feeling that might have something to do with Shelby Archer.

Fourteen

The day was muddled from the start. A customer was already waiting outside Land's End when Shelby unlocked the door. She'd overslept. Last night, just as she was drifting off, Noah called to say he missed her. He didn't exactly apologize, but he made it clear her wanted to see her and get back on track.

"I'm away for the rest of the summer," she'd said, as if distance was the only problem. She didn't have the energy to get into it late at night, to explain that she could never look at him the same after he acted like a jealous child. But even without having a whole long conversation, the call kept her awake for hours. She didn't know what upset her more: the fact that Noah blew up their relationship for such a ridiculous reason, or the fact that she missed him so little, she had to wonder what she'd been doing with him in the first place. But then, she handled most breakups with ease. Justin had been the most difficult. Ironically, distance *had* been the only problem. Ultimately, a breakup was a breakup, no matter how easy or heart-wrenching. It was an ending.

The first customer in the store was a man in his forties, sunburnt and balding, dressed in a striped shirt, denim shorts, and suspenders.

"Let me know if I can help you find anything," Shelby said.

He walked to the new-release table, then turned to her.

"There's a book... I don't remember the title."

Shelby nodded. "Okay. Is it recently published?"

"I'm not sure, but the cover is blue."

Shelby waited for more information to go on, but that was apparently all she would get.

There were countless books with blue covers. When he realized she had no idea what he was looking for, he said, "Is Colleen here? She'll know what I'm talking about."

No, Colleen was not there. But she'd already texted her a few times that morning with reminders and details she'd forgotten to tell her yesterday, the most important of which was the event that night for a nonfiction book about revered local poet Mary Oliver.

"Colleen isn't here today. But I'm sure I can help you find it." Shelby walked to the fiction shelf, scanning the blue spines. *The People We Hate at the Wedding* by Grant Ginder? Or maybe *When We Were Bright and Beautiful* by Jillian Medoff? Oh—maybe it was *Seven Days in June* by Tia Williams.

Mia finally breezed in, her curly dark hair in two pigtails, a short-sleeve T-shirt under a strapless sundress, and Birkenstocks. Shelby thought back to the time when she'd first met her, barely a teenager, obsessed with old episodes of *Hannah Montana*, and determined to be a singer. She hated school, and already knew she didn't want to go to college. "But don't tell my brother. He'll tell my parents."

As someone who'd never been able to confide in her own parents, Shelby said, "Your secret is safe with me." Still, she thought Mia was underestimating Carmen. She'd always found her easy to talk to.

Mia greeted the man as "Walter," and after conferring with

him for thirty seconds, walked to the *S* section of the shelves. She pulled out a copy of *The Light Between Oceans* by M. L. Stedman.

After Mia rang up the sale, Shelby said, "I guess it'll take me some time to remember all the customers. Things have probably changed since I last worked here."

Mia shrugged.

"Mia, I'm sorry I left without saying goodbye. Or keeping in touch," Shelby said. "I just had a lot going on, and it was also sort of a gray area after your brother and I broke up."

"You mean, after you broke up with him."

Shelby nodded. "Yes, okay. That's right. But I didn't break up with *you*, and I'm sorry if it felt that way."

Mia shrugged. "Don't worry about *me*. You should be saying you're sorry to my brother. Maybe you can do that tonight."

The book event was being held at Lombardo's upstairs patio bar. Not ideal, but she couldn't change it at the last minute. And certainly not for a reason as ridiculous as it just made her uncomfortable. She expected Carmen would be there, but not necessarily Justin. After all, he didn't work there. Mia was probably just being provocative. Shelby had forgotten what it was like spending time with a teenager. But she hadn't forgotten what it was like to spend time with Carmen. The truth was, she'd missed her.

Shelby couldn't help but think that if Mia had soured towards her, Carmen would feel the same way. Or maybe, none of the other Lombardos had given her a second thought in the past few years. There was no way to know, and really, it didn't matter. She was back in town for Colleen, and that was all.

By early evening, she was so busy writing last-minute introductory notes for the visiting author and making sure all the books and chairs had been delivered to the restaurant, she didn't have the headspace to think about her ex-boyfriend or his family. Still, she felt a little pang walking across the street to the restaurant.

Lombardo's had classic red-checked tablecloths, wide bay windows, plank wood floors, and whirring ceiling fans. The front patio was full and the sound system pumped out Billy Joel songs. Servers passed colorful cocktails, and she spotted her favorite brick-oven pie: prosciutto, arugula, and fresh mozzarella. Shelby caught sight of her reflection in the window on her way inside and realized wearing her hair long and loose in the heat had been a mistake; she put down the extra box of books she was carrying and pulled it back into a messy ponytail. At least she'd been smart enough to wear a lightweight dress.

Carmen Lombardo stood at the host stand to the side of the entrance, talking animatedly with her hands while a server nodded intently. She was a handsome woman, with thick salt-and-pepper hair, high cheekbones, and wide-set dark eyes that looked nearly black. She wore a pastel boat-necked floral dress that showed off her deep tan. Shelby hesitated for a moment, unsure whether she should stop and say hi or just go straight upstairs. Before she could decide, Carmen spotted her.

"Welcome back," she said, walking towards her with open arms.

Surprised, Shelby leaned into Carmen's embrace. She smelled the same, like rosemary. The scent memory was a punch to the gut; she was twenty-two all over again. And Carmen was the mother she'd always wanted and never had.

"So good to see you, Carmen. I'm…well, I'm not really back. I'm just helping Colleen Miller for the summer."

Carmen held her by the shoulders, beaming. "You look good. You're a big shot now, eh?"

"No," Shelby said, embarrassed. "I'm actually… I'm working upstairs tonight. The book party."

"Of course. Go…go. You know your way around." She gave her a wink. "Don't be a stranger."

"I won't," Shelby said with an awkward wave.

She was in a nervous sweat, her dress clinging to her back. If she felt that way about seeing Carmen, she could only imagine the stress of running into Justin. Hopefully, she had a lot more time before she'd have to contend with that.

Justin held one end of the tape measure, and Kate Hendrik pulled the stiff plastic measuring tape parallel to one wall.

"Do I need another shelf here?" Kate said, glancing around at the space that would soon be a fully operational bookstore. Her blue eyes, an icy shade, settled on him. Those shocking eyes stood out because the rest of her was so understated: her shoulder-length straight hair was neither brown nor blond but somewhere in between—a sandy color. She dressed in neutrals and linen and ballerina flats. There was something soothing about her, no surprises. He liked that.

"If it fits, why not?" Justin said.

He was disappointed by his family's apathy towards Kate's new bookstore—towards Kate in general. Again, he told himself that they simply hadn't had the chance to get to know her. That was one problem with their long-distance relationship. Most of their time together had been in her town, not his. It meant something to him that she was making such an effort to remedy that for the summer. And, if things went well with the store, maybe longer. His family would have to get with the program eventually.

"Are you hungry?" he said. He knew his mother was working the front of the house tonight because they were short-staffed.

"I'm getting there," she said, pulling a paper towel from the roll on the counter and wiping her hands. "What do you have in mind?"

"Brick-oven pizza."

She smiled. "Do you have a reservation?"

"No," he said. "But I think I can pull a few strings."

Fifteen

Lombardo's upper deck, with its long bar and view of the bay, was crowded. It was set up for the event with rows and rows of folding chairs. Now, half the seats were taken and the people milling about would certainly fill the rest.

The bartender served glasses of prosecco, and a Harry Styles song played in the background. Shelby surveyed the crowd and recognized the author from her jacket photo. Dee Dee Tattinger had dark skin, close-cropped curls, and was dressed in a denim jumpsuit. Shelby gave a wave, and Dee Dee made her way towards her.

"Thank you so much for hosting," Dee Dee said warmly, smiling and shaking her hand. "And congrats on *your* book. I feel like, of course Provincetown's bookseller is also a bestselling author!"

A woman with a pixie haircut and wearing a pin-striped pantsuit inched between them. "I'm Patricia, Dee Dee's agent. You're the bookseller?" she said.

"Yes—Shelby Archer. Good to meet you."

"Is there a way to rope off the stairs? I think we're at capacity." She swept her around, as if Shelby might have failed to notice the crowd.

"I'll talk to the owner and see what I can do."

She didn't want to talk to Carmen again. While she appreciated the warm welcome, she felt more comfortable leaving it at that. But she dutifully headed back to the front of the house.

"Everything okay up there?" Carmen asked with a smile, passing menus to a server.

"Great. I think we're full, though. Do you have a—"

She'd lost Carmen's attention to something over her shoulder. Shelby turned to follow Carmen's gaze and saw Justin directly behind her. He wore faded jeans, work boots, and a white button-down shirt with the sleeves rolled up to his elbows. His dark hair was on the longer side—the way it looked when he was too busy to get it cut.

He held the hand of a slight, pretty woman wearing a bone-colored Burberry trench.

"Shelby," he said. His expression was neutral, his expression unsurprised. Of course, Mia had to have told him she was working at the bookstore.

"Hey. How *are* you?" she said, smiling.

"Look at this! A reunion," Carmen said, waving Justin and Burberry Trench inside. "Give me a sec—I need to seat some people."

Shelby, Justin, and Burberry stepped to the side. With Carmen gone, the vibe shifted from friendly to awkward.

"I'm just here for a book event," she said. "Upstairs." She pointed, as if Justin and his lady friend didn't know where upstairs was located.

"Mia told me you're working at Land's End," he said.

"Just for the summer," Shelby said quickly. "It was unexpected."

"This is Kate," he said, putting his arm around the woman. "Kate Hendrik, this is Shelby Archer."

"Of course," the woman said, reaching out to shake her hand with a smile. "Congratulations on your novel."

Kate *Hendrik*?

"You're not...the same Hendrik as the bookstores?"

"I am," the woman said, offering a small, modest smile.

"She's opening a location here this summer," Justin said.

Shelby was speechless, and aware her silence was creating a socially awkward moment. But... Justin's girlfriend was Colleen's competition? It was too much. It was like something out of a novel.

Like something out of a novel. She realized, in that moment, what was wrong with her new book. She didn't feel emotionally invested in the story. She couldn't relate. And if *she* felt that way, how could she expect her readers to connect to it?

Maybe she was just avoiding the discomfort of the moment, but her mind started racing with ideas. What if she changed the competing bed-and-breakfasts in her novel to sparring bookstores instead? And maybe add some kind of romantic tension—not that there was romantic tension between her and Justin. But seeing him with his new girlfriend, the irony of the bookstore situation—it gave her the idea for raising the stakes in her novel. For the first time since she started writing *Guest Rooms* (the title would have to change), she felt it had a heartbeat.

Her return to Provincetown was already paying off creatively. And, as Justin wished her a good night and went to be seated in the restaurant, she felt it was paying off emotionally, too. Closure was important.

But the thing with Kate Hendrik. The stakes had been raised in real life, not just her work in progress. As Duke said, Land's End had to up its game. And she was ready to swing big for Colleen.

After running into Shelby at the restaurant, the night never fully recovered. At least, not for Justin. He had to hand it to

Kate—she kept it classy. Clearly, she wasn't the type of woman to be threatened by an ex. And she didn't seem to notice that Carmen was clearly more interested in talking to Shelby. But hours later, he was still riled up and decided to stop by the Bollard before heading home.

He spotted Doug at the bar. If anyone would understand why the night left him feeling off-kilter, it was Doug. But when Justin walked over and tried to fist-bump, Doug left him hanging.

"Everything okay, buddy?" Justin said.

"They'd be better if your girlfriend wasn't opening that bookstore. Colleen's taking it hard."

So he *was* pissed. Mia had been right. "I honestly didn't think of it that way. I'm sorry."

"Is there any other way to think of it? I mean, it's direct competition."

Justin realized he should have been more sensitive. But he'd lived in Provincetown his entire life, and knew that when it came to retail, Commercial Street was like Noah's ark: two of everything. Especially in the summer, when the year-round population swelled from under three thousand to up to sixty thousand people.

Feeling bad and unsure what to say, he stood with his back to the bar and watched two guys throw darts across the room. Shelby came to mind again—the first night he'd brought her to the bar. She'd never played darts before, and he could still remember the gingerly way she'd held them at first, and how by the end of the night she was throwing them with precision and let out a delighted laugh when she hit the bull's-eye. They hadn't stopped playing until the lights flickered at closing time.

He turned back to Doug.

"And *you* could have given me a heads-up about Shelby coming back to town."

Doug furrowed his brow. "Fair enough. The truth is, Colleen didn't want me talking about it to anyone."

"Why not?"

"Because she doesn't want to broadcast her situation. She sees it as some sort of failure. She was determined to prove to her parents that keeping the store open was worthwhile, that she had the energy and focus to make it work. Now she's not allowed to do much more than walk inside."

"Look, I'm sorry about the bookstore," Justin said. "I know what it seems like from your end. But if Colleen was working, if it were a normal summer, I don't think Hendrik's would bother you. And I had no way of knowing it would be like this."

Doug signaled for two beers and nodded.

"Don't let Shelby get to you, man," he said.

"I'm not. Things with Kate are solid."

Doug took a swig of his fresh bottle of Modelo. "So why are you here with me?"

"Why aren't *you* home with Colleen?" Justin said.

Doug touched his bottle neck to Justin's. "Touché," he said. "Let's just get through this summer."

Sixteen

The only downside to working in a beautiful beach town was that Hunter had to go to the office when almost everyone else was going to play.

She passed couples walking hand in hand, men jogging with dogs on leashes, groups laughing on restaurant patios over breakfast cocktails. It was warm, and sunny, and to her right, the bay was in near constant view the entire stretch of Commercial. Hunter had to remind herself that the people behind the counter at Joe Coffee and the front desk at the Anchor Inn or selling trinkets at the Shell Shop were also working. That many of the people biking, sailing, and brunching were only there on vacation, while she got to *live* there. For the summer, at least. She was lucky to have a publishing job at the beach. She might not be where she wanted to be professionally, but at least she was somewhere she loved geographically.

And she had to admit, her office in Duke's house—a lavender Queen Anne's cottage on Franklin Street—was a lot nicer than her cubicle at her last job.

Still, Hunter stalled that morning by going out of her way to stop at Scott Cakes, a bakery that only made vanilla cupcakes with pink frosting. She ordered a dozen, and she could feel through the box that they were still warm even by the time she reached Duke's.

The front door was open.

Duke's entrance hall floor was all handmade tile, and the walls were decorated with paintings by local artists. The living room featured chinoiserie and wood furniture with Queen Anne details and cabriole legs. She walked through to the library, where they both had desks. The large, sun-filled room had oriental carpets, Japanese fans, and porcelain figurines on every surface.

"I brought snacks," she said, walking the box over to him.

"Oh, Hunter." He shook his head. "I swore I wouldn't eat dessert during the day anymore. Things just get so decadent this time of year. It's like, the temperature rises above seventy and all the rules go right out the window."

"Suit yourself," she said, setting the cupcakes on her desk. She opened the box, plucked one out, and peeled the wrapper from its base. Her mouth watered just thinking about biting into the icing.

She sat in her chair and looked out the window at Duke's back lawn. His birdfeeder attracted a constant stream of finches. Most were brown, but when an occasional redhead appeared, it was the highlight of her workday. Last week, a red one had set to work on a tree stump and its determination put her own work ethic to shame.

Duke walked over and handed her a pile of manuscripts.

"These are slush, but you never know when you'll find a gem. So please read at least the first few chapters."

Oh, how she'd love to find something special. But she wasn't optimistic. The odds of finding a publishable novel in the slush pile had been slim even at her old job where award-winning writers were published. At a start-up press like Seaport, it was like picking up oyster shells on Herring Cove beach and expecting to find a pearl inside.

"Okay," she said dutifully.

"By the way, I stopped by Shelby's the other night."

Hunter was surprised. And irrationally irritated. Duke was free to talk to her. Maybe their solidarity on the issue of Shelby had been partly in her imagination. "Why didn't you mention it before?"

He sighed, glancing upward then back at her. "I've been trying to figure out how I felt about it. She did apologize. And I know how myopic artists can be—it's part of their charm. Also, she's helping Colleen..."

"Don't tell me you're fine with what happened," Hunter said, crossing her arms.

"I wouldn't say *fine*. But I'm trying to be my best self and turn it into something positive. And I think I did: Shelby agreed to petition for beach access by Land's End. If she can get that done, her bookstore will have a competitive edge over Hendrik's. Their location doesn't have outdoor space."

"I think if any of us are depending on Shelby, we're really in bad shape."

Duke let out a sigh. "Colleen is trusting her with the store. That must count for something."

Hunter reached for another cupcake. "It just seems unfair to me. Shelby uses our secrets to write a bestseller, then just glides right back to her spot here in town like nothing ever happened. She gets away with it!"

"What would make you feel better?" Duke asked.

Hunter knew the answer. She'd thought long and hard about it. "I want to edit a bestseller. I want my own success."

Duke patted the manuscript pile. "Success *is* the best revenge. Now pass me one of those cupcakes."

Shelby stood behind the counter, scrolling through the Land's End calendar. She must be missing something. Colleen had barely scheduled any author events.

"Excuse me," a woman said, approaching the counter. She had long red hair and carried a bicycle helmet. "Do you have a local interest section?"

Shelby led her to a shelf stacked with Michael Cunningham novels, design books by Ken Fulk, and yes, copies of *Secrets of Summer*. "Are you looking for fiction or nonfiction?" she asked.

"Nonfiction," the woman said.

She handed her Mary Heaton Vorse's *Time and Town*. "This is a local classic. She writes about Provincetown like no one before or since."

Shelby read the book twice during her first summer in Provincetown. One line stayed with her for a long time: *"I am not the only person who came here to spend two weeks and remained a lifetime; I am not the only one who if exiled would feel as though my taproot were cut."* Thinking of the words now, she felt nostalgic. That first trip with Hunter, she'd fallen in love with Provincetown. Until that point, when she heard people use the expression "falling in love" to describe a feeling for a place, she felt it was hyperbole. And then she experienced the Cape. But unlike Mary Heaton Vorse, she'd always known the time would come to leave.

Shelby returned to the computer, looking again for any events on the schedule she might have missed. Was it possible Colleen hadn't scheduled more than three events over the next eight weeks?

Author book readings had never been a huge priority for Pam and Annie. But things were changing in town and Land's End should change with them. They'd sold out of the Mary Oliver biography last night. That might have happened over the course of the summer, but in one night? That could only happen with a book event.

There wasn't that much she could do about it now. Summer book tour schedules would be set by now. Still, she logged into a program that listed touring authors. The interface was surprisingly basic, as if it had been built in the 1990s. It featured a single field to request an author, then two fields asking how many readers you expected for the event and how many books you expected to sell. There was a small text field for additional comments so bookstore owners could pitch themselves and their store.

"I found a few more copies," Mia said, emerging from the stockroom and depositing three Mary Olivers on the counter.

"Mia, why are there so few authors events scheduled?" Shelby asked.

"I think Colleen requests a lot of authors but gets denied."

"Denied?" Shelby hadn't thought too much about how her publicist decided what bookstores to send her to on tour; she assumed it was a combination of which stores requested her and what made sense geographically. She'd never imagined a bookseller requesting her and being told no. They even sent her to one store where literally the only one in the audience *was* the bookseller. Shelby performed her presentation anyway. The bookseller's sad little clap at the end made her want to curl up in a ball.

Standing in front of a room full of empty chairs had been a terrible feeling. It brought her back to the days of being the new kid at school, the last one picked for the team or the group project. She knew bad turnouts were a normal rite of passage for debut novelist, but it hadn't felt that way.

"And also, you have to decide what to do with these," Mia said, dragging a box close to her feet. "They're coming out in paperback this month. So are we keeping them or returning them?"

"I'll look through and decide." It was tricky when books came out in paperback and they still had hardcovers in stock. She could lose money mailing a return for a fraction of the book's retail value, or she could lose money by not selling the book at all because readers could go for the paperback.

Sometimes, making a living selling books seemed like pushing a rock up a hill. Pam and Annie probably thought there were more practical ways for their daughter to make a living. Practical, yes. But special? No.

Shelby hadn't realized how much she missed the feeling of finding the perfect book for someone. It was one thing to suspect it when she made the sale, but then when they came back and told her they loved it? Or emailed her all of their thoughts and she'd had the exact same feelings about it? In some ways, it was even more rewarding than writing a book—at least, most of the process of writing a book. So much of her time was spent alone, creating a story she could only hope would connect with readers. But when she sold books, she had a finished product in her hands and got the immediate gratification of sharing it with another person. For the most part, bookstore owners were in it for the love of books.

She knew Colleen certainly was. And she wasn't going to let Kate Hendrik move in on her territory.

Seventeen

Hunter faced the ocean from a chaise longue on the deck of her parents' house, a manuscript on her lap.

No one else she knew in Provincetown had a home like hers, nearly all glass and sprawling with six bedrooms and ten bathrooms. Her parents built it on a lot overlooking the famous jetty that stretched from Pilgrim's Landing Park to Long Point and the Wood End lighthouses. Her parents bought the view, but they never actually walked out onto the jetty, over a mile of uneven, slippery rocks. But Hunter had done it a few times and was thrilled by the feeling of being suspended between land and sea. She enjoyed extremes. Maybe that was part of the reason she preferred one-night stands to relationships; they never got boring.

She took the manuscript off her lap and set it aside. Fifty pages in, and she knew it was a DNF—Did Not Finish. Instead, she picked up the novel she'd bought weeks ago, and turned to the acknowledgments page. She liked reading the names of the people who'd helped get the book published. One day, her own name would be in there. She couldn't wait.

Although, what was the expression? "Be careful what you wish for." Ironically, her name *was* in the back of a book; Shelby had thanked her in *Secrets of Summer*. She'd mentioned her and Colleen both, writing something like, "This book wouldn't exist without you." *Yeah, for real. You stole my life.*

It pained her that while her future career would get a boost by discovering a publishable manuscript, one of the best "discoveries" of the past few years had been written by her best friend. Was that what made her so angry? Not just that Shelby had written about her, but that she'd become successful first? Hunter hated that she felt so competitive with her. It hadn't always been that way. In fact, she'd always rooted for Shelby. Hunter was an only child, but she imagined having a sister was exactly the way she felt about her best friend. Until their last summer together.

The sunset was giving shades of purple; the people on the jetty had a spectacular view. Hunter stood up. In that golden moment, the vision of the life she wanted was so clear. But in a few minutes, the light would be gone and she'd be alone with piles of fiction that wouldn't help her one bit.

Duke had made his peace with Shelby. Maybe he had the right idea; she didn't trust Shelby anymore, but she was a good connection in the book world. Why spite *herself* by freezing her out? Better to just be friendly towards her. Friendly *with* her. But they couldn't be the way they were. That was over.

Shelby heard the pulse of techno music, laughter from the beach, and the occasional car honk on Commercial Street. She was probably the only person within a five-mile radius who was sitting at home. But then, she wasn't on a vacation.

Her work-in-progress was open on her laptop, and she stared at the blinking cursor.

She was stuck, and she didn't have time to be stuck.

Crafting a novel was a delicate balance of asking the right questions, but not waiting until she had all the answers to begin writing. In fact, it was the opposite. Writing a novel was a leap of faith. If a novelist waited to know everything they would need to get from page one to the final sentence, they would be paralyzed. Still, with the new book, Shelby expected to be able to skip over the "driving through the fog with no head-lights" feeling. But the uncertainty was just as strong this time around—if not stronger.

Someone knocked at the door. She set her laptop aside. This had happened last night, too. A friend of Colleen's stopped by, not realizing she'd moved. Shelby needed a sign on the door with an arrow pointing in the direction of Doug's place: This Way for Colleen Miller.

"Hold on," she called out, making sure her laptop didn't tee-ter on the edge of the couch. The door was locked—one habit of hers that marked her as an out-of-towner. She unlatched it and pulled the door open.

"Hunter," she said, more surprised than when the stranger showed up last night. "Colleen isn't here."

"I know," she said. "I came to see you."

Shelby anticipated the moment would come. She'd been anx-ious about it, but figured running into Hunter couldn't be worse than what happened the last time she'd seen her.

Hunter walked in, not waiting for an invitation. She had her full '90s aesthetic going strong, with a vintage black-and-purple lace dress (Anna Sui?), combat boots, and silver heart choker necklace. Her hair was loose, her roots dark as always against her bleached blond hair. It was all very Courtney Love by the sea.

She plopped down on the couch and Shelby jumped to move her laptop.

"Writing a new book?" Hunter said.

"Uh, no," Shelby said. She didn't know why she lied, but it felt right. It felt safer. She really did want to make amends with Hunter. She hadn't realized, living her life in New York, how much she missed her. Or really, she missed what they'd had.

College friendships were different than those she'd found in adult life. They were almost like love affairs, with their intensity. She would never spend as much time with a new friend as she'd spent with Hunter, living together, taking classes together, partying together, summers together. She'd have to be married for years before she'd clocked that much intimacy with someone else. That was why it had seemed so natural to write bits and pieces of her into the heroine of *Secrets of Summer*.

"Well, thank God," Hunter said. "Maybe *some* of my secrets are safe."

Okay. She probably deserved that.

"I really am sorry," Shelby said. "About the book."

Hunter waved away the comment; she didn't want to talk about it.

"No, I mean it," Shelby said. "I was an idiot. I didn't mean to hurt you. I'd never do that." She meant it. But she could tell from the look on Hunter's face, something faraway in her eyes, that it wasn't that simple. It might be a long time before Hunter was able to let it go. If ever. The one difficult thing about Hunter was that she saw everything in black-and-white. Good or bad. Madly in love or indifferent. A lot of people tended to think that way, but it felt more extreme with Hunter. She'd seen Hunter turn on people in the past who let her down. And while Hunter always insisted she avoided relationships because she didn't want to get married, Shelby suspected they would simply require too much emotional compromise.

"Anyway, we owe it to Colleen to get along this summer, right?"

Hunter said, "Yes. We do."

They looked at each other. Hunter's blue eyes, outlined in smudgy charcoal liner, were wary. Shelby wanted to just reach out and hug her, but she refrained. A few seconds ticked by. It was awkward.

Finally, Hunter stood and said, "Let's go get drunk."

Eighteen

Tucked away on a side street off Commercial, the Atlantic House—better known as the A-House—was over a hundred and fifty years old and looked more like a twentieth-century schoolhouse than a bar. Inside, it pulsated with pop music and was crowded with a makeshift dance floor. Britney Spears videos played on a big screen. It smelled like beer and old cigarettes and something musky and damp, and the familiar scent brought Shelby back to past summers.

Shelby and Hunter found spots at the bar. She recognized the bartender, Chris. He'd been there forever. She never knew for sure if he was a few decades older than they were or if he was just weathered-looking from the sun. He was bald, with a full sleeve of tattoos on both arms. Behind him the bar was strung with Christmas lights, and decorated with a wooden bust of a merman.

Shelby had grown up with strict parents. She never drank during high school. So the first time Shelby ever went to a bar had been with Hunter. It was their first week of freshman year. Bryn Mawr College was an all-women college in a suburb

of Philadelphia, a leafy campus with Gothic architecture de-
signed like the buildings at Cambridge. The nearby thorough-
fare, Lancaster Avenue, was lined with bars, drawing students
from nearby Haverford College and Villanova University. That
was why Hunter was eager to go off campus. It wasn't for the
drinking; it was for the guys.

Hunter never would have chosen an all-girls school, but she
was a third-generation legacy and her mother insisted. Shelby
hadn't necessarily been looking for a Seven Sister school, but
Bryn Mawr had an exceptional English program. So while they
came to the school from different upbringings and for different
reasons, the hands of fate (and roommate assignments) brought
them together. Shelby, with her military father, wasn't a big rule
breaker. She'd been nervous to go out with a fake ID. Maybe
that was what drew her to Hunter: opposites attract.

Hunter ordered two shots of tequila. When Chris slid them
across the bar, Shelby said, "Remember Flannery's?" Once
they'd both turned twenty-one, they'd stopped going.

Hunter touched one of the multiple piercings in her ear, a
silver hoop. "Gotta love Flannery's," she said, raising her shot
glass. Shelby touched hers to it.

"To Flannery's," she said. They both knocked them back.
Hunter signaled to Chris for another round.

"So…we haven't discussed the Colleen situation," Hunter
said, turning her empty shot glass around and around on the bar.

No. They hadn't.

Shelby still couldn't believe it: the first of their threesome was
becoming a mother. It seemed like just a few months had passed
since they'd stood together on the beach, wondering what life
would look like after college.

"Colleen's going to be a *mother*," Shelby said. Colleen would
be the world's best mom—Shelby had no doubt. Personally,
she couldn't imagine being ready for such a responsibility. Her

career came first, and lately it felt like she couldn't even manage that. "I think it's amazing. It's just a lot to absorb. Babies…"

Hunter pulled a vape out of her pocket and took a drag, exhaling away from Shelby's face. "Colleen's upset about the timing," she said. "But it was going to happen eventually. The way I see it, if you're going down that road, just…go. You know what I mean?"

Shelby wasn't so sure about that. It was important to be ready for things when they happened. That was the problem with her relationship with Justin; she hadn't wanted to fall in love at age twenty-two. She couldn't handle a long-distance relationship. Looking at Colleen's situation, she saw the trade-off she was facing: motherhood might come at the expense of losing her dream to take over Land's End. To Shelby, it seemed like a terrifying trade-off.

"It's just mind-blowing that Colleen is going to be a *parent*, and I guess get married and buy a house. And I'm, what— working out of Duke Nestley's living room and crashing at my parents'?" Hunter said.

"What do you mean? You don't even want a serious relationship."

"How do you know what I want?" Hunter snapped. "Besides, what I mean is—at least her adult life has started. I feel stuck in this way station."

"It's not a way station, Hunter. You're here on your own, working for Duke's press, living your life. This summer would have seemed pretty good to both of us when we were in college. Or even that last summer here. It was hard to leave—for both of us. But now we're back. I hope we can find a way to enjoy it." She reached out and touched Hunter's arm.

Hunter didn't reply, but ordered a glass of Patron Silver over ice with a lime. Shelby frowned. They should slow down.

"For you?" Chris said, but Shelby shook her head.

"Just water, thanks."

The song "Shape of You" by Ed Sheeran played, and Hunter smiled. Shelby knew exactly what she was thinking: they'd gone to see him live in Center City Philadelphia sophomore year. On the way home their phones had died, they had gotten off on the wrong exit, and had ended up in a neighborhood called Manayunk, a small hipster town built on a canal. They'd parked and asked a group of people their age for directions, and ended up at a house party where they spent the night. Shelby was anxious, but Hunter had loved the adventure, and her calm helped Shelby roll with it. It was always that way between them: Hunter ran towards the unknown and the novel, while Shelby yearned for comfort and stability.

Hunter got up to use the bathroom and was noticeably wobbly.

"Be right back," she slurred. While she was gone, Shelby called Chris over and said, "We need to cut her off."

It was time to get her home. That was what friends were for.

Half a block down Commercial, Hunter sat on the curb and refused to get up.

"You have to walk," Shelby said, holding out her hand. Hunter ignored her and pulled the vape pen from her bag. Shelby grabbed it away. "Not till you're home."

A breeze blew off the bay and the night was comfortable, but Shelby felt perspiration on the back of her neck. She also felt a sense of déjà vu; like they were back on campus, dragging themselves back to the dorm after a bar crawl on Lancaster. But they weren't college kids anymore, and she wondered if Hunter always got that wasted.

Hunter sat on the curb, and Shelby searched the street for a pedicab. She saw one half a block away. It had a bright blue, open-topped passenger cabin and the driver appeared to be wearing a top hat. Shelby waved down the cab, but a group of men spilling out of 1620 Brewhouse got it first. Behind it, she spotted Justin behind the wheel of his trusty old Jeep Wrangler. He pulled over.

"Everything okay?" he called out. Shelby was relieved to see him, and immediately recognized this was a vestigial feeling. Justin was someone she'd once counted on and cared about, but it wasn't appropriate to involve him in her messy evening.

"Everything's fine," she said. Hunter lay down on her side, as if she were on her bed and not the sidewalk.

"You sure about that?"

"Hunter's a little wasted. I'm trying to get her home."

He reached over and opened the passenger door. "Hop in." He put the car in Park then walked over to lift Hunter to her feet and into the back.

Justin knew the way to Hunter's house, having driven Shelby home many times that last summer. By the end of July, she started sleeping at his place. And in August, he told her that she didn't have to worry about where she'd stay when she visited during the fall and winter: she was welcome at his house anytime. He'd give her a key.

She pushed the memory away and looked out the window. Cruising into the West End, restaurants and bars gave way to quiet houses and closed retails shops. It was dark enough down that way to see the stars in the sky.

The Coldplay song "Clocks" came on the radio and with it, she felt the undeniable intimacy of a car ride late at night. With a quick, subtle glance at Justin, she told herself it was normal to have mixed feelings. She'd done the right thing three years ago when she ended it, but at the same time, she hadn't really had to confront the ramifications. When she moved to the city, everything was different all at once. Missing Justin had just been part of the mix. But now, in the setting of the place where they'd been together, it stung a little. On some level, she'd known it would. Maybe that was why she never returned to visit Colleen or Hunter. It wasn't only because she was busy in New York.

They turned right before Pilgrims' First Landing Park and headed up Creek Round Hill Road, passing marshes and dunes. Justin turned down the music and she heard the hoot of an owl. If she'd been with anyone else it would have felt strange not to talk, but Justin was someone who was comfortable in silence. It came from a place of deep confidence, and was one of the many things she'd liked about him.

He pulled into the Dillworths' driveway.

"Thanks so much for doing this. Sorry for taking you out of your way," she said.

"No problem," he said, turning off the ignition. He turned to look at her. A painful few seconds of silence ticked by until Hunter interrupted with, "Oh, fuck off, you two."

Shelby shook her head. "I'd better get her inside."

Nineteen

Colleen made it clear that even though she was physically sidelined, she still intended to be involved with Land's End. So Monday morning, Shelby picked up coffee and croissants from the Wired Puppy and went to Doug's for a meeting.

She found Colleen sitting out back in the garden on a cushioned wicker bench shaded by a standing umbrella. The garden was mostly leafy hosta plants, irises, and daisies, with one stalk of bright pink hollyhock blooms. A bumblebee buzzed around it.

"Don't forget you're meeting with the publisher of Malaprop Books today," Colleen said, handing her a printed catalog of their fall titles. Part of her job as a bookseller was to meet with sales reps—or in the case of small presses, the publishers themselves—to learn about the upcoming list and figure out what books to stock for her customers.

Malaprop was the Boston-based book publisher where Hunter had worked before losing her job. The company was small but prestigious, known for its signature book covers, which featured the title in white against a solid cobalt blue background. Their authors were so widely acclaimed, that was really all they needed. Malaprop Press won so many literary awards that the list on their website felt like an infinite scroll. Shelby became familiar with their books in college, and she obsessed over a particular novella called *Opaline*, back when she aspired to write the type of debut they might publish.

"I know. I got your text. Don't worry about it."

Colleen had planned on taking the meeting herself—sitting and talking was one thing she could still do. But her doctor's office rescheduled her appointment for the same time and she was hoping to hear that there was some improvement in her condition—that the doctor might ease up on the restrictions.

"It's so frustrating," Colleen said.

Shelby nodded. "Of course it is. I'm really impressed by how you're handling all this." She reached over and squeezed her arm. Colleen's expression clouded.

"So, what else is on the agenda?" Colleen said.

Shelby checked her phone for notes. Top of her list was the issue of getting beach access. But there was something else she wanted to talk about first.

"I saw Justin at the book event the other night," she said.

Colleen raised an eyebrow.

"How was that?"

"Fine," Shelby said. "And Carmen was very sweet."

"I sense a *but*…"

"I met his new girlfriend. Do you know who she is?" Shelby said. It was hard to imagine Colleen didn't know. But then why not mention it?

"Yes," Colleen said. "And to be honest, until this very second, I didn't think about your history with Justin. I only see Kate Hendrik through one lens, and that's as a threat to my store. But it doesn't bother you, does it? That he's with someone new?"

"No, of course not," Shelby said. "It's just ironic. Or maybe just…strange. Honestly, it doesn't matter who the new bookseller is. We need to focus on making things pop for Land's End this summer. Duke thinks we should petition town council for beach access. I know you don't have a lot scheduled, but I'd like to wrangle some more events. The Hendrik's location doesn't have outdoor space. It's just one way to be competitive."

Colleen nodded. "Yeah, he's been on me about that for a while. There's just so much to do and I feel like event management is an entire job in itself. Are you sure you can take that on?"

No. She wasn't even sure she could manage the bookstore inventory. Or write her novel. And she certainly wasn't confident she could do all of it at once.

"Yes," Shelby said. "I got you."

Mondays were beach days for the Seaport Press staff. All two of them.

Hunter and Duke settled side by side on folding lounge chairs on Herring Cove beach.

At nine in the morning, the air was still cool enough for her to wear a long-sleeved T-shirt. They sat under a big red umbrella that said Carnival 2017. Carnival was one of biggest celebrations of the entire Ptown summer. Tens of thousands of people from all over the world descended on the town for a week of parties, parades, costumes, and overall revelry. Every year had a different theme. Her favorite had been a few years earlier, Gods and Goddesses. Hunter had dressed as Aphrodite, the goddess of sexual love.

"What's the Carnival theme this year?" she said.

"Somewhere over the Rainbow," Duke said. "Prepare to get your Dorothy on."

Noted. Hunter pulled a manuscript from her Land's End tote bag and dug around on the bottom for her red Sharpie. She'd started reading the submission the night before, the fourth she read over the weekend. After drinking way too much with Shelby, she'd spent the next two nights staying in and working.

She felt a little better after spending some time with Shelby.

It was easy to demonize someone you didn't see, but sitting at a bar like they'd done a million times before, looking her straight in the eye, Hunter couldn't stay angry. She believed Shelby when she said she never meant to hurt her. But she *had* hurt her, and there was no going back to the way things used to be. That sense of absolute trust was gone. The worst part was that Shelby was one of the first real friends Hunter had ever made—real in the sense that she knew for sure Shelby wasn't hanging out with her because of her family fortune. While everyone at her Boston high school knew what being a Dillworth meant—the name on three banks, a museum, and a wing at the Boston Children's Hospital—Shelby didn't. She'd never even been to Boston.

Duke reached over and handed her the latest issue of *Ptownie* magazine.

"Check out page ten," Duke said. "An article by *moi.*"

"Oooh," Hunter said. "Is it a gossip column?"

If anyone could write one of those in town, it was Duke. For a few years during the end of high school and early summer, she routinely heard her parents talking over evening cocktails on the deck about a scoop from Duke: the bed-and-breakfast owner who had two granddaughters she never knew show up on her doorstep. The time when the Barros family, owners of Barros Boatyard, exiled one of their elders—shipped off to Florida—because she was such a troublemaker. One summer, a woman moved to town and ended up in a love triangle with one of the Barros brothers and her own ex-husband.

Gossip was fun when it wasn't about you.

"No, it's a bit more serious: the housing situation." He reached over and flipped the pages to his piece.

"'No Rest for the Weary: Restaurant Staffers Sleep in Cars Amidst Housing Shortage,'" Hunter read aloud. "Are people really sleeping in their cars?"

Duke held up his hands. "Fret not: we're working on it. There's a building for sale on the marina. The community trust is trying to buy it to turn into subsidized housing for workers. In fact, there's a meeting this afternoon if you can come."

Hunter passed the magazine back to him. "I'm not sure what help I'd be. I don't know anything about housing or zoning or whatever it takes to make that happen."

Duke pushed his Ray-Bans to the top of his head and they held back his white hair like a headband.

"Well, I'm working on that angle. What we really need is donations."

Hunter's stomach tensed. She sat straighter in her chair.

"I think you of all people know I have a pretty meager salary," she said, trying to give him a graceful exit from the conversation. She still hoped he wasn't asking what she thought he was asking.

He laughed appreciatively. "You're getting paid in experience," he said. "No, I meant your parents. I know they're abroad this summer but maybe they—"

"No!" Hunter said. "I don't ask my parents for money. Not like that. And I never will. So if that's why you hired me this summer, I'm happy to resign right now." Yet another person using her for the fortune. She never expected it from Duke, and it was like the breath had been knocked out of her. She pressed her hand to her chest to calm herself.

Duke's face paled. "Of course that's not why I hired you. And I didn't mean any offense. Forget I mentioned it."

Hunter blinked rapidly behind her sunglasses. She certainly would *not* forget he mentioned it.

Twenty

Shelby met publisher Max Walder outside Liz's Café on Bradford Street. He was a slender Black man who bore a strong resemblance to the actor Stanley Tucci. He wore wire-rimmed glasses and carried a spiral notebook and had a brown leather man-purse strapped across his torso.

"Great to meet you," Shelby said. "I'm a big fan of your books."

The host seated them outside at a table for two, and they arrived just in time because minutes later a line formed at the front door. Max pulled sunglasses from his bag and perused the menu.

"I haven't eaten here since last summer," Max said, then looked up, eyes narrowed, scrutinizing her face. "Have we met before? You look familiar."

"We haven't met. But I'm a novelist. I'm just helping out at the store temporarily."

He snapped his fingers. "That's how I recognize you. I saw your photo in *Publishers Weekly*. They featured your book in their Must-Have Beach Bag Books list. That's you, right?"

Shelby shifted in her seat. "That's me. But today—bookseller."

Max ran through a short list of titles he guaranteed were "absolutely made for the Ptown readership," and then a few that he said were a "stretch, but worth a copy or two just to broaden your offerings." Shelby took notes, then wondered how many of their titles the store had ordered for the summer.

"Do you have anything publishing in July or August I should know about? Just in case for some reason Colleen missed it?" She doubted Colleen had missed anything, but wondered if there was an author or two she could somehow convince to stop by the store if they were on book tour.

"I know Colleen ordered *Harvest Town* by Jessup Crane and *Plow* by Daryna Anichka—July and August respectively."

"Would they visit Land's End?"

"I'll put you in touch with our publicist."

"Thank you. I'm trying to expand our event schedule."

Max snapped his fingers. "Where is my head? Anders Fleming is teaching here this summer. Just a thought…"

Anders Fleming was a Booker Prize–winning novelist. His last few books had published with Malaprop. It would be a coup to have him at the store. "I'd be honored to host him for an event. Could you ask him for me?"

"Does Land's End have space for the crowd he'll draw?"

"I'll make sure it does," Shelby said. Another reason to petition for beach use: if she didn't get Anders Fleming on the calendar, it would just be a matter of time before Hendrik's Books did.

"In that case, why don't you join us sailing tomorrow? You can invite Anders to Land's End yourself."

She smiled. "I'd love that."

"Excellent. Bring a friend if you'd like."

The first person who came to mind was Duke. He loved to sail, and he loved to talk all things book publishing. Shelby felt hopeful. If she was able to do enough good that summer, no matter how small, it might make up for the very big thing she'd done wrong with her book.

★ ★ ★

Walking back to Land's End, her phone rang with a call from her literary agency.

"Hey there," Ezra said. "I saw on Instagram you're back in Provincetown?"

"I am." She remembered, for the first time, that he'd met a mystery lady. The morning they left Provincetown together, he'd mentioned that he met an "incredible" woman the night before, but that she didn't want to see him again because she didn't "do relationships." That was all he would say about her.

"Have you heard from your hookup?"

"Not really," he said. "She's a woman of few words. And even fewer texts."

"Sorry to hear that. How's the city treating you?" she said.

"I'd say at this point it's an abusive relationship," he said. "But then, I'm used to that. Oh—here's Claudia."

"Hey, hey, superstar," Claudia said. "I hear you're back on the Cape."

"Yes! I decided to spend the summer in Provincetown to finish my manuscript."

"Love that for you," Claudia said. "Just don't forget you're speaking at the Boston Arts Club the first week in August."

Shelby hadn't forgotten. The Boston Arts Club was one of the oldest art institutions in the country and she was honored to have been invited for their summer reading program.

Now that she had Claudia on the phone, she had an idea. "While I'm out here I'm helping my friend who owns the bookstore. Any of your authors coming to the Cape? I'm sure she'd love to have them swing by the bookstore to do a signing." Shelby didn't want to admit how very much she was helping with the bookstore. Claudia might think she wasn't taking her deadline seriously when actually, the opposite was true. She was cranking.

She'd started rewriting her book the night she ran into Justin and Kate Hendrik. Once she had the idea about two competing bookstores, she couldn't go back to her original plot idea. She scrapped it entirely, and began writing about a thirtysomething single woman who owns a bookshop. She called the character Emily, which was her own middle name. Emily was preparing for the big summer season when wham—she's diagnosed with breast cancer. At the same time, a competing bookstore owned by a newcomer named Jackson opens shop. The storyline followed Emily and her friends as they rallied around her shop. Shelby was also playing around with a romance subplot between the two competing bookstore owners, but she wasn't sure yet. The one thing she knew was that the words were pouring out of her. The story was flowing much more naturally than the one she'd been laboring over. It was a huge relief.

Now she just had to make sure the real-life bookstore stayed competitive.

Twenty-One

Shelby hesitated outside of Town Hall. After spending the night before prepping with Colleen, it was time to make her case for beach access for Land's End. Shelby borrowed Duke's car and stopped by the apartment to pick her up, but Colleen was asleep. Doug refused to wake her.

"I don't want her pushing it," Doug said. "Please, just handle the committee meeting the best you can."

So she drove back to Duke's, parked the car, and they walked to Town Hall together.

She told him she didn't feel right about petitioning without Colleen.

"Maybe we should wait for another night, when Colleen can make it."

He shook his head. "You've got this." Reluctantly, she followed him inside.

Town Hall smelled like wood chips and cherry incense. She went for the first time four years ago, the summer between junior and senior year. Colleen's mother Pam brought them to hear an ecological lecture that their friend's son was giving. The auditorium was full and she'd been impressed that the speaker, Justin Lombardo, was just a few years older and already had his master's in Marine Science.

"The waters of the Gulf of Maine, an ocean basin that spans from Cape Cod to the southern shores of New Brunswick and Nova Scotia, is one of the fastest warming regions of all the planet's oceans," he said. He was tall, with broad shoulders, dark wavy hair, and a penetrating gaze that she felt from the third row in the audience. "For fifty years, researchers observed the area's water temperatures slowly warming, but in the past decade, that gradual trend sharply accelerated to the concerning scenario we see today."

After the talk, Carmen Lombardo invited Pam out and during dinner, Shelby found herself watching him across the table. She listened to everything he said even as she went through the motions of other conversation. Every time he happened to glance in her direction, she offered a smile and when he returned it, she felt it like an electric shock. For the next week or so, she hoped to run into him on the beach. She even went to Lombardo's restaurant hoping to spot him. But the summer ended, and she and Hunter drove back to Pennsylvania for their senior year at Bryn Mawr.

The next summer, their first night back at the Dillworth house, it was unusually hot with a stifling humidity. They were eating dinner on the deck when a flash thunderstorm hit. Within minutes, trees and power lines toppled over, blocking roads and knocking out the electricity. The entire town was without power on one of the hottest nights on record.

Colleen rushed over: volunteers were meeting up at Lombardo's restaurant to help elderly residents who lost their air-conditioning. Some homeowners had generators, but many people didn't and the concern was that the elderly would suffer over the long hot night. The couple who owned Harbor

Lounge and several properties in town offered up a house on Pearl Street as a shelter.

Two dozen people convened on the front porch of the restaurant, where Mr. and Mrs. Lombardo assigned search and rescue zones. Shelby and her friend split up in opposite directions. Shelby was tasked with checking a three-block radius on the West End. Before she reached the first house, it started pouring again. Dressed in sneakers and a T-shirt, she was drenched through in seconds. Still, she pushed forward.

She knocked on a few houses but didn't get any response. She kept moving, making a note to check them one more time before moving on to the next street. When she knocked on a door and saw it begin to open, she felt a rush of adrenaline. She imagined an elderly couple who'd been huddled in the dark, relieved to see a friendly face in their hour of need.

But the person behind the door wasn't a vulnerable neighbor. It was the handsome marine biologist she'd met last summer.

"Can I help you?" Justin Lombardo said. If he recognized her, he showed no sign of it.

"Oh—I'm sorry. I thought this house was on my route." She glanced down at her phone for the text she sent herself with the radius she was supposed to cover.

"You must be off course. I've got this block. But come in so the cat doesn't run out."

Shelby stepped inside, and he closed the door behind her. The house was already overheated and had a strong floral smell. "I could use some help, actually. I've been here for fifteen minutes trying to get the woman who lives here to leave." He turned on his flashlight and she blinked against the bright beam.

"I don't care how many of you show up, I'm not going," a female voice said from the darkness. The beam from Justin's light danced near the woman, not directly on her, but close enough for Shelby to make out a long green robe and the fact that the woman resembled actress Maggie Smith.

"Ms. Brier, this heat is dangerous. Just come to an air-conditioned shelter until the power comes back." Justin leaned close to Shelby and whispered, "She won't go without her cat."

"Understandable," Shelby whispered back.

"How are you with animals?"

"Great," Shelby said. The truth was, she'd never even had a pet. But she found herself volunteering to find the cat and bring it to her owner at the shelter. Shelby and Justin exchanged phone numbers to get in touch if needed.

Later, when she reconvened with Hunter and Colleen at the Dillworth house, she told them both about her little adventure. Hunter seemed particularly interested and asked her a million questions. But Shelby didn't confide in them that she hoped to see Justin Lombardo again. It was embarrassing to have a summer crush. She was an adult now. There were more important things to think about.

Then, a few days later, Justin texted her. Then they spoke on the phone, and he invited her for a hike. He picked her up in his truck and they drove to Dune Shacks Trail. The mile walk led up and down steep hills to the ocean. They talked about their families. He was soft-spoken and serious and for a while she wondered if he was even interested in her as more than a friend. And then he kissed her at the edge of the ocean.

Now, in the Town Hall room where she'd first seen him, it took her less than thirty seconds to spot him in the front row. He'd been so kind the other night with Hunter. She hoped she'd at least have his vote today.

The town selectman, Gene Hobart, banged a gavel on top of the table where he was seated alongside five other members of the council. The room silenced itself. "The first item on to-night's agenda is the sale of 16 MacMillan Pier, the current site of the Pirate Museum. Now, as a reminder, we're looking at three thousand square feet with a twenty-five-foot boat slip. Prime real estate," he said. "At issue is whether or not we expand the zoning to allow for residential use."

The crowd erupted in chatter.

"Order, please," Gene said, banging his gavel again. "Bert Lombardo has the floor."

Justin's father stood and turned to look at the room. When they first met she'd liked him immediately. He was a man who did his job without fuss or drama, with a determined "do it right or don't do it at all" ethos. She'd sensed from the beginning how important it had been to Justin that she and his father click, and they had. So it hurt now to see his deep-set brown eyes skip over her like she was a stranger.

"Every summer we have less and less affordable housing for seasonal workers," Bert said. "We're failing the people who help us service the tens of thousands of tourists spending the money that, for most of us, makes our entire year. If it weren't for generous neighbors donating their guesthouses for my line cooks, I don't know if I'd be operational right now." He spoke quickly, obviously uncomfortable with public speaking, but making an effort for something about which he felt strongly. When he finished, he glanced at Justin, who stood just as his father sat back down.

"I'm sure everyone in this room knows that Lombardo's Restaurant isn't the only business in this situation," Justin said. "So let's do something about it: a building's for sale on the wharf. It could be turned into affordable housing. I'm asking that the town trust put together an offer to try to buy it."

Shelby knew all about the town trust from her summer with Justin. The group had formed a decade ago, when the general store closed and the town missed it so much they decided to find a way to bring it back. An offshoot of the town council created a Provincetown Community Trust, raising hundreds of thousands of dollars to reopen the store and subsidize its continued operation.

The room erupted in conversation. Gene banged his gavel for silence, then called the vote. It appeared everyone raised their hand to vote yes.

"Do we have any nays?" he asked.

The room was silent. Satisfied, Bert Lombardo sat down.

Next, it was her turn. She stood, squared her shoulders, and glanced at Duke. He gave her a thumbs-up.

"Hello, everyone," she said, clearing her throat. "I'm Shelby Archer, and I'm working with Colleen Miller at Land's End Books. One thing we're trying to do to keep the store competitive is host more author events. But our floor space is less than two thousand square feet and a lot of that is taken up by permanent shelving that can't be moved to make room for an audience. I'd like permission for temporary use of the beach behind the shop, just to set up folding chairs and host events once a week."

Justin languidly unfolded himself from his seat and once again faced the room. "As head of the Conservation Commission, I'd like to remind everyone that we voted to cap the commercial bay beach usage at forty percent, and we've reached that ceiling since the Buoy opened their outdoor seating." He sat down without so much as a glance in her direction. She felt her face turn red.

What was he doing?

"Land's End is an institution," Shelby shot back. "The book industry has changed since the store opened and, respectfully, I think this town should help Land's End to change with it. It's a beloved bookshop, and it needs our support."

Justin stood back up. "We need to draw the line somewhere to protect our beaches."

Gene Hobart took it to a vote. Shelby lost by three.

Afterwards, as everyone filed out, she marched over to him.

"What was that all about?"

He stopped walking and ran his hand through his hair.

"I think I made myself pretty clear." His dark eyes regarded her with detachment. People filed past them. Duke touched her arm and mouthed, *See you outside.*

"Are you doing this to get back at me? Is this about what happened between us?"

He shook his head, looking infuriatingly amused.

"I hate to break it to you, Shelby: not everything is about you." He turned and walked out before she could find the words to respond.

She wished she hadn't come to the meeting. She wished she hadn't seen him. She wished… Actually no, she didn't wish either of those things.

The exchange would make for great dialogue in her novel.

Twenty-Two

Hunter walked along the bay side of Commercial Street, already late for work.

She just hadn't felt right since Duke tried to hit her up for a donation. It was disappointing—as it always was when a friend looked at her and saw dollar signs. But with Duke it was also surprising. She knew he didn't mean any harm, that it was for a good cause. But it hurt because she'd convinced herself that while her friends in Ptown knew her family was extremely wealthy, it never crossed their minds. One of the things she loved best about her summer life was that it made her feel just like everybody else. So when one of her Ptown friends treated her like, well, like she was rich—it was upsetting.

And it was why the character in Shelby's novel was so triggering. It wasn't just that she was promiscuous; it was that she was a stereotypical rich girl.

Hunter stopped walking. A man sitting on a bench on the bay side of the street caught her eye. He was reading a newspaper and smoking a cigarette. Not a vape—an actual cigarette. The way he held it drew her attention, the casual elegance. He had a mop of brown hair, long limbs, and was dressed in long pants, canvas shoes, and an all-weather jacket.

It was Anders Fleming, the acclaimed British novelist.

What an incredible turn of luck! She'd been so busy feeling bad about losing her job, exiled from "real" publishing for the summer—and there she was, ten feet away from her fiction-writing idol.

She'd been reading his books since she was in high school, when—bored on vacation with her parents—she borrowed her father's copy of *Nowhere Land*. When Hunter was a junior in college, Anders Fleming spoke at Bryn Mawr just after winning the Booker Prize.

Did she dare go over and say hello? Really, why not? She was already late, but Duke wasn't going into the office today. He was going sailing with a sales rep from Malaprop. He said he could see if there was room for her, but she wasn't in the mood to hobnob with the publisher of the company that let her go.

But now, Anders Fleming. Of course she had to say hello. She waited for two cyclists to pass and then crossed the street.

"Excuse me, Mr. Fleming?" she said. He glanced up, regarding her with curious gray eyes. "Sorry to bother you, but I'm a huge fan," she said. He appeared skeptical, and she realized that in her black Paramore T-shirt and her hair pulled back in low pigtails she probably looked like a teenager. "You spoke at my college a few years ago, Bryn Mawr."

"Well, hello, huge fan," he said. "What's your name?"

"Hunter," she said. "Are you in town doing a reading?"

He stood, and she realized he was remarkably tall. Probably six foot five. He reached out and shook her hand. "Nice to see you. Actually, I'm teaching at the Fine Arts Work Center."

The Fine Arts Work Center was a famous Ptown institution on Pearl Street, over fifty years old. It was an incubator for artists that provided housing. Every summer it offered courses in everything from visual art to playwriting and literature. If he was teaching, it meant he'd be local for weeks.

"Amazing," she said.

"Are you a writer?" he asked.

"No, but I work in publishing. I was actually at your publisher for a while, but now I'm working for a small press here in town."

"Well, good for you. We need our small presses. I don't think I'd be here today if it weren't for the indie that first published me."

She smiled, suddenly feeling like a warrior for the arts instead of a corporate failure.

He checked his phone and stood, folding the newspaper under his arm. "It was lovely to see you, Hunter. I'm afraid I have to go meet up with some friends." He turned and Hunter watched him stroll away. When he was out of sight, she pulled her phone out of the messenger bag on her shoulder and logged onto the Fine Arts Work Center site to check the class schedule.

The summer was finally looking up.

Shelby forgot how exhilarating it felt to leave land behind—even just on the rocky little water taxi transporting her and Duke to the sailboat waiting on its mooring. She'd also forgotten how much cooler it was out on the water, and was underdressed in a T-shirt and jeans. At least she'd remembered a hair tie, and pulled the rubber band from her wrist to contain her hair from blowing wildly in the breeze.

She inhaled, fighting the dizzying combination of too much coffee and too little sleep. She'd been up all night writing, and then, when she'd finally closed her eyes, her phone rang with a call from Claudia.

"Remember that debut author I told you about over lunch at Balthazar?" Claudia said. "She had an event canceled in Nantucket over the Fourth of July. Can you host her at the bookstore in Provincetown?"

"Sure," Shelby said groggily, wondering if it was a mistake to schedule an author who might lure Claudia to visit town. Shelby didn't want to see her again until she had the manuscript finished. Having her in town was the type of thing that could mess with her head at that delicate stage of writing. "Will I get to see you, too?"

"Unfortunately, no. I have plans that weekend. But I'll be at your August event in Boston."

That was fine with Shelby. By the date of her scheduled reading at the Boston Arts Club, she should have a first draft finished.

The skiff drew closer to Anders Fleming's sailboat, an impressive white Beneteau. She admired the towering mast and sleek lines of the hull. The water taxi driver helped her onto the boarding ladder. She used her upper-body strength to climb, and once she reached the deck level, Anders Fleming himself was there with an outstretched hand to help her get her footing.

He looked different in person, older than his book jacket photo, but also more handsome. His brown hair, threaded slightly with gray, poked out from underneath a Cambridge University baseball cap. He wore a navy blue hooded waterproof jacket, trousers, and brown deck shoes.

"Thanks," she said, making sure she was steady on her feet before shaking his hand. "Shelby Archer. Honored to meet you."

"The honor is all mine," he said.

Max Walder helped Duke aboard, and then Anders gave them a tour of the lower cabin with a table, a sink, and a comfortable wraparound couch.

"I'm afraid you might be chilly," Anders said to her, and pulled a pilled hunter green cardigan with wooden buttons from a narrow closet.

"Oh—thank you," she said, placing it over her shoulders.

"Shall we?" he said, leading the group back up the stairs to the deck. The sun peeked out from behind clouds, burning off the early-morning fog.

A woman was at the helm, someone she recognized from the boatyard but didn't know personally. She wore a red windbreaker and a Helltown baseball cap and asked Anders if he wanted to stop at Long Point, a fifteen-minute sail. Long Point, the former site of a Civil War battery, was a 150-acre peninsula that attracted tourists looking for a perfect picnic spot.

They sat on benches, facing each other in pairs—Shelby with Duke, and Max next to Anders, who uncapped a thermos of coffee. He asked Duke about his work with Seaport Press, saying that small publishers were the lifeblood of the industry, "Saving us from a bleak hellscape of the corporate monolith that is publishing today."

Shelby wasn't so sure she agreed with that. She felt lucky to be published by a big corporate publisher. They were giving her a way to make a living doing what she loved.

"Well, I appreciate that, Anders," Duke said. "It means a lot, coming from you. But I must admit, distribution is a real challenge."

"Agreed. And more so every season," Max said. "Do you know I had to explain to a bookseller last week who Anna Garréta is? I told him one of my fall debuts is like a current day *Sphinx*, and he looked at me like I had three heads."

"I mailed out dozens of copies of a debut mystery," Duke said. "And not one store responded. Actually, that's not entirely true. One store did respond: they sent me a form letter offering to donate the book to the local library."

Max sighed in solidarity. They turned to Shelby.

"I can't complain about publishing," she said, almost sheepishly. "I've had a great experience with my imprint, my team. I feel very fortunate."

"A *New York Times* bestseller right out of the gate. Fortunate? I think you're being modest. That type of success only comes with talent and hard work," Anders said.

Shelby felt herself blush. The sales of her book felt more like luck or good marketing than they did a barometer of her ability. She'd read countless brilliant books that published with little notice. "Well, thank you."

"Are you working on something new?" he asked.

She nodded. "I'm writing a new novel, yes. But I'm here in town to manage the bookstore this summer. I'm friends with the owner. Actually, we'd be honored to host you at the store. For a reading…signing…whatever works for you."

He slapped his knee and smiled. "Now *that's* the best offer I've had in a while."

She smiled at him gratefully. He'd made it so easy for her.

"Well, that's just amazing news. Our customers will be thrilled. You can put me in touch with your publicist to work out the details. I'm going to find a venue for the event because our store is small, as I'm sure you know."

Anders waved away the suggestion. "You'll never hear back from my publicist. Deal with me directly, please. We're neighbors now."

"I'd be happy to host a reading at my house," Duke said, glancing at her in excitement.

She smiled at him, and a fragile hope filled her chest. Maybe by the end of the summer, Duke would not just forgive her missteps with *Secrets of Summer*, but also forget.

In the meantime, she couldn't wait to tell Colleen the good news.

Twenty-Three

Shelby and Colleen met up at the small bay beach on the West End. It was a lesser-known gem of a spot next to a boat slip. The stretch of Commercial nearby was dotted with pastel-colored Queen Anne and Victorian homes. Shelby's favorite had a wildflower garden in front overrun with stalks of lavender and black-eyed Susans. "You were right. It's not too crowded," Shelby said, following Colleen to one of two wooden benches at the edge of the lot facing the water.

"It never is," Colleen said. "Doug and I come here all the time. It's so peaceful."

Shelby carried a take-out bag from the Canteen. When they were situated on the bench, she unpacked it and handed Colleen a warm lobster roll with a side of coleslaw and a pickle. Detecting food, two seagulls wandered over and paced near their feet.

Colleen exhaled with a heavy sigh. She'd told Shelby on the ride over that her last checkup didn't show any improvement. She still had to follow activity restrictions.

"I know you're frustrated," Shelby said. "But this is temporary."

Two men wearing neon wet suits pushed a paddleboard into the water. A golden retriever ran after them, and a teenage girl ran after the dog.

"The physical part is. But I'm not so sure when it comes to impact on the bookstore. My parents called this morning and they're freaking out, just like I knew they would. They're angling to take the bookstore 'off my plate.' That's what they said—like it was an extra side of fries."

"Why do you think your parents are so hyped about selling? Is it purely a financial decision?" Shelby said. Colleen shook her head.

"It's a big part of it," she said, her blue eyes blinking fast to hold back tears. "Sorry, I'm a mess." She pressed a paper napkin to her face. Shelby reached out and put her arm around her. "They think publishing is changing, Ptown is changing, and that I'm playing it safe instead of being, quote, 'open and ambitious about my own future.'"

"I'm sorry. That sucks."

Shelby knew how it felt to have to defend choices to parents who had their own ideas about what was best. Her father still wouldn't acknowledge that writing was a "real job." They'd come to one of her book events near their new home in the Outer Banks, and her mother suggested now that she'd gotten the book "out of her system" she should consider teaching. But unlike her own parents, she believed Pam and Annie would come around.

"I think the store's going to do great this summer, and maybe that will help them see things differently."

Colleen shook her head. "I'm not saying all this to put pressure on you."

"I know." She adjusted the box of food on her lap and angled herself to face Colleen. "I have some good news, though: Anders Fleming is going to do an event at the store."

Colleen perked up. "Really? I reached out to his publicist

when I heard he'd be teaching here. But she never got back to me. How did you reach him?"

"Max Walder introduced us. And Duke offered to host at his house."

"Or…maybe you'll have beach approval by then."

Shelby swallowed hard. She hadn't told her yet about the town council rejecting her petition, partially because she was embarrassed by the failure and partially because she wasn't ready to give up on it yet. She'd have to regroup.

And in the meantime, maybe she could plan something for *Colleen*, not just the store. Maybe…a baby shower? That would give Colleen something to look forward to—all the cute little baby things would get her excited about the prize at the end of this struggle. Nothing like an adorable little onesie or big stuffed animal to make her condition seem less like an affliction and more like a pit stop on the way to something beautiful.

Should she surprise her with it? She'd run it by Hunter. She hadn't heard from her since the night at the A-House. Maybe planning a shower together would be a good way for them to continue to mend their friendship.

Twenty-Four

Kate wanted to keep the grand opening of Hendrik's on the Cape low-key. Justin offered to help plan a party for her, but she said it wasn't her style to "make a big fuss."

After closing, he took her to celebrate at Fishtail, a seafood restaurant on the East End. It had a beachfront deck, and they provided cozy Pendleton throws when it was cool outside. Their table was the closest one to the water, and the bay reflected off Kate's pale eyes. She was dressed in a flowy gray dress and pearl earrings. He ordered a bottle of prosecco, and the server set it next to their table in a standing bucket of ice.

"To Hendrik's," he said, raising a glass. "Congratulations."

She touched her glass to his, smiling. "I'm already having fun with it."

He hoped the store was so successful that she would see Ptown as a viable place to spend more time. They'd only been together a few months. But he knew right away that there was something special about her. This wouldn't be another Shelby Archer relationship.

He was a fool to let Shelby distract him for even a minute.

The fact that he had to grapple with it made him angry. He wanted to use her unwelcome return as fuel for disliking her, but he couldn't even do that because she was only back in town to help a friend. He thought again about her accusation that he shot down her beach-access request for Land's End out of spite. But why focus on the negative? The overall meeting had been a success.

"Did I tell you the town council is looking at a building for sale on the wharf?" he said to Kate. "It could be turned into affordable housing. We're putting together a coalition to raise money and buy it," he said.

"Oh, that's such a good idea. I can talk to my family and see if they'll contribute," Kate said. "They were involved in something similar on the Boston waterfront a few years back."

He reached for her hand. She was good for the town. And she was good for him.

"Listen, I know you wanted a soft launch today," he said. "But maybe you'll reconsider by next weekend. The town will be so packed for Fourth of July. It's an opportunity to make a little noise."

Kate sipped her wine, then set the glass back down. "Actually, I was hoping we could spend the Fourth in Boston."

"Boston?"

She nodded. "I don't want to miss the Boston Pops Fireworks. It's one of my favorite traditions. I go with my parents and brother every year."

This was news to him. But then, he was still getting to know her.

"Okay, we'll figure it out," he said.

"Oh, but that reminds me; there *is* something I want to do while we're here. Did you know Anders Fleming is in town?"

"No," he said. The name sounded familiar, but if pressed, he wouldn't be able to say who he was.

She nodded, her lips curled in a subtle smile. "I remember

reading *Down with Dust* my sophomore year at Wellesley and thinking, okay—so this is what literature is. This is the bar. Anyway, he's doing a reading with Land's End at a private home next week. Let's go?"

"Sure," he said. "Let's go."

Justin had told Kate that the woman he'd introduced to her the night at Lombardo's was his ex, and that she was running Land's End for the summer. Kate was utterly unfazed by it. He knew he shouldn't be, either. But one thing nagged at him: If she could come back for Colleen, why had she refused to come back for him?

When Shelby told Hunter her idea for the baby shower, she invited her to the house to discuss it. The Dillworths' beach-front home was cavernous, with muted colors and minimalist furniture. Floor-to-ceiling glass windows overlooked the sea, and the flawless acoustics softened the sound of steps across the hardwood floors.

Shelby had her own guest bedroom when she lived at the house all those summers, but they often ended up falling asleep side by side, talking into the earliest hours of the morning in Hunter's room. Or dozing off on the deck only to wake up in the middle of the night and move indoors. Shelby knew there wouldn't be any such casual intimacy tonight, and it was sad. Maybe it was a natural evolution, simply part of getting older.

"I can't talk for long. I have a ton of reading to do," Hunter said, leading her out to the back deck.

Shelby had work to do, too. She needed to keep putting down words. Sometimes, it helped her to think of her manuscript as a lump of clay. No matter how much of a jumble it seemed to be, chipping away at it bit by bit would lead to a shape, and then that shape would turn into something readable. It seemed impossible, but she would get to the end.

She'd thought about that on the way over; her book would

eventually get finished, and she'd go back to New York. But Colleen might still be on bed rest. And when she was finally off bed rest, she'd have two babies to take care of. What would happen to Land's End when Shelby returned to Manhattan? No wonder Pam and Annie were pessimistic.

"I was thinking," Shelby said. "Maybe you can help out with the store when I go back to New York? I'm not sure what Colleen is going to do."

Hunter frowned. "Um, I have to get back to work, too, Shelby. This summer is just a regroup for me. You're not the only one with big plans." She uncorked a bottle of Kim Crawford.

She wasn't implying that Hunter didn't have plans. She just thought it was possible to do two things at once, at least for a little while. When had their friendship become full of land mines? Had it begun before *Secrets of Summer* published?

They sat on brushed metal chairs on either side of a small table. They faced the ocean, the sun just beginning to set and turning the sky into a swirl of pastels.

"Okay, we don't have to talk about the bookstore," Shelby said. "Baby shower: What do you think?"

"I'm down for it. I've never been to one, but I guess we'll figure it out. Did you tell her we're planning this?"

Shelby shook her head. "I wanted to run it by you first. So, I figure we can get a guest list together, maybe cater it from Liz's Café? And I don't think she has a gift registry, so she'll have a reason to start one now."

"Sounds simple enough. We can have it here."

"Amazing. Thank you!" Shelby had hoped she might offer, but didn't want to be pushy about it. Her hesitation was another reminder of how things had changed between them. There had been a time when she could say anything to or ask anything of Hunter. "And do you have ideas about who to invite? I'm sort of out of the loop in terms of who she's closest with now."

"Sure. I can put together a list." She leaned forward. "You're quite the hostess this summer. I heard about the Anders Fleming reading at Duke's house."

Shelby nodded. "Great for Land's End, right?"

"Do you remember when he spoke at the library?" Hunter said.

Somehow, she'd forgotten about it. After years and years of attending book readings, she had lost track of who she'd seen in person. Back in school, going to hear authors speak was something they did together all the time. Their other friends would be out drinking and the two of them would be in line to meet Alice Hoffman.

"You should come to the reading," Shelby said. "We can all go out to dinner after."

Hunter's eyes lit up. "Sure! Okay. Sounds good."

Shelby smiled. Between the baby shower, book events, and keeping Colleen company, maybe they'd spend enough quality time together that summer to get close to where they used to be.

Twenty-Five

After a fruitless weekend reading submissions for Seaport Press, Hunter decided she couldn't spend all summer just waiting for a good manuscript to drop into her lap. And she had an idea: What if she took Anders Fleming's creative writing class to scout for talent? If she discovered the next Jennifer Egan, Seaport Press would go from a somewhat obscure press to a major player. And she'd be its star editor.

It was a long shot. But she felt hopeful walking into the Fine Arts Work Center building on Pearl Street, where Anders stood in the front of a lecture room greeting people as they filed in. He seemed to nod in her direction, and she wondered if he recognized her from meeting on the street. She purposefully didn't tell Shelby about running into Anders. There wasn't anything really to tell, but for some reason she didn't want to even mention it.

Planning the baby shower with Shelby gave her mixed feelings. It was the right thing to do for Colleen, but she was unnerved by how utterly natural it felt. It was like she'd never stopped spending time with Shelby in the first place, as if nothing had ever changed. She needed to remind herself not to let her guard down. It was just a détente, not a friendship renewal.

"Welcome, everyone, to the exquisite endeavor we call creative writing," Anders announced. He wore khaki pants, a blue button-down shirt rolled up at the sleeves, and brown loafers, and tortoiseshell glasses. His British accent seemed more pronounced than when she'd spoken to him on the street.

"I'm honored to embark on this literary journey with all of you. Over the course of this class, we'll plunder the depths of our imaginations and harness the magic of words. In this class, there are no limits to your creativity. We'll learn to evoke vivid landscapes, breathe life into unforgettable characters, and craft narratives that transport readers into worlds of our choosing. But remember: the essence of all good writing already lies within you: your life experience."

As he went on to speak about story craft, she realized that studying creative writing would boost her editing skills, a benefit she hadn't considered when she registered.

After class, she waited for everyone else to leave and walked up to him. He was shuffling papers into a worn leather briefcase.

"Ms. Dillworth," he said, looking up. Hearing her name on his lips gave her a rush.

"I decided to take the class."

"So I see," he said with a kind smile.

"I can tell already it's going to be amazing," she said. "But I have some questions that are more related to publishing than the craft of writing itself."

"Well, I hope whatever you're looking to get out of it, that I have something to offer."

"I'm sure you do. And actually, I wanted to ask you few questions that are sort of outside the realm of the curriculum here. Do you have time for coffee?"

"Now?"

She nodded. He consulted the steel watch around his wrist. "Sure. But I do have an early dinner so just a quick chat."

"Very quick," she said.

The nearest café was the Wired Puppy. They ordered at the counter and Anders paid for the lattes even when she tried to insist that she had invited him out. The tables were taken so they sat outside on a wooden bench painted red. It was a busy corner, and with all the foot traffic, she wondered if anyone would notice him. And then she realized people were, in fact, looking at him. But she couldn't tell if it was because they recognized him, or if his rakish handsomeness simply caught their eye.

On the way over, he told her he was going to be teaching a semester at Harvard in the fall. "You're not one of the Boston Dillworths, are you?"

"No," she said, looking away. The lie could be quickly dispelled with one look at Wikipedia, but she doubted he'd give her that much thought.

One of the town librarians passed by on her bike and gave him a wave. Anders checked his watch again.

"Thanks for taking a minute to talk," she said. "I'm in your class probably for a different reason than everyone else. I'm an editor, not a writer. I'm looking for manuscripts to publish—not trying to write one myself."

"Oh. That's interesting. Where do you work?"

"Seaport Press. My boss is hosting your reading with Land's End."

"Ah, Duke Nestley. Wonderful chap. How long have you worked there?"

"Just this summer. I'm hoping to get a job at a larger publisher in the fall. Actually, I used to work at your publisher, Malaprop. But I got laid off in the spring."

"Their loss, I suspect," Anders said. "Will you be joining us at the reading Duke is hosting at his home tomorrow night?"

She nodded. "I'll be there."

"Wonderful. And for the record, I'm all for helping you discover talent."

"Thanks so much," she said.

He nodded, looking thoughtful. "The artist's life is not for the faint of heart."

"I'm not an artist," she said.

"Maybe not. But you're a facilitator. And what would we artists do without you?" He stood and extended a hand to her. She stood, too, and reached out to accept his handshake. "Lovely chatting. See you tomorrow evening, Ms. Dillworth."

Hunter watched him walk across the street and down Commercial. She realized, in her reluctance to look away, that her interest in him wasn't purely professional. She smiled. She'd never slept with a famous person before. Maybe it was a long shot. But thanks to Shelby, she'd get another chance to talk to him tomorrow night.

Their détente was already paying off.

Twenty-Six

An hour before the Anders Fleming event, Colleen called Shelby for help. "I haven't worn anything but sweats and T-shirts in a month. I've forgotten how to dress like a normal person," she said.

"You *are* a normal person." But she was happy for the excuse to run over and help her pick an outfit. It felt almost like the old days, when the best part of their night was the hour right before going out, dressed to impress, pre-gaming with some wine or Hunter's specialty margaritas, blasting "Delicate" by Taylor Swift and "Whatever It Takes" by Imagine Dragons.

Shelby realized now that she'd taken the bond between the three of them for granted. She'd known some things would change when she moved to New York, but hadn't realized that nothing would ever be the same.

"You look so pretty," Colleen said. Shelby wore a mid-length blue gingham dress with short sleeves and a flared skirt. She paired it with her Keds, and left her hair loose.

"And you're going to look beautiful. I know you've got something in here that's perfect. Oh—what's this?" Shelby said, pulling a navy-blue-and-white polka dot sundress with an empire waist from the closet. Colleen took it off the hanger and held it in front of herself, looking in the full-length mirror behind Doug's closet door.

"Carmen Lombardo gave it to me when she found out I was pregnant. She said she loved her own pregnancies but never felt she had anything to wear."

That was so like Carmen.

Once Colleen was dressed, they went out back into the garden to take a selfie for the Land's End Instagram. When Shelby checked the photos after to find one to post, she saw that Colleen appeared melancholy in every single one.

"Tonight's going to be a success," Shelby said to her. "The store is going to be fine. You'll see. And your parents will see. And by the fall, this rocky summer will just be a memory."

Colleen gave her a smile, but Shelby could tell she didn't quite believe her.

Anders Fleming, looking dapper in a light herringbone jacket, spoke for forty minutes against the pastel backdrop of the setting sun. Earlier in the evening, Mia set out a few dozen white folding chairs and strung fairy lights on the trees. The book-signing table was off to one side, decorated with a Land's End Books banner. In the back, Duke's fancy teak picnic table was designated for wine and cheese.

Shelby sat in the front row along with Duke, Mia, Hunter, and Colleen and Doug. Behind them, every chair was full. People trickled in even after Anders started speaking. Colleen reached over and squeezed her hand.

"Thank you," she said.

Shelby leaned close to her and whispered, "I got you."

She sat back and listened to Anders's melodic voice read his own prose. A nearby bird, invisible in the thick of Duke's trees, let out a staccato chirp. The air smelled like the garden honeysuckle. Shelby made mental note of it all, certain she could use some of it for her novel. One of the downsides to being a writer was that it was sometimes hard to be fully in a moment without storing details of experiences away for later, like a creative squirrel.

When it was time for Anders to sign books Mia tended to the line, taking people's names and writing them on Post-its for when it was their turn to have their book personalized. When Shelby was confident everything was under control, she crossed the lawn to get a glass of wine.

Justin and Kate Hendrik stood together at the refreshment table. Shelby couldn't believe his nerve. He'd tanked her chance to get an outdoor space for Land's End, and he'd brought the store's competition to the event she'd had to hold off-site.

Kate noticed her before Justin and smiled, greeting her with "Congratulations! Wonderful event."

Justin turned around and offered her a nod.

"Thank you," Shelby said. "And congratulations to *you*. I hear you're officially open for business." She'd walked by on opening day. The balloons had irritated her. She'd crossed to the other side of the street.

"Yes, well, a rising tide lifts all boats, right?"

"Absolutely," Shelby said.

"Great spot for an event," Justin said.

Was he for real? "I guess I have you to thank. If you hadn't shot down my request for a beach permit, we'd be at Land's End instead." She turned to Kate. "Enjoy the rest of your night."

She slipped away, carrying a glass of white wine. Her dress clung to her back with perspiration. She pulled a rubber band from her wrist and tied her hair up in a high ponytail, letting a much-needed breeze reach the back of her neck. *A rising tide lifts all boats? Spare me!*

Shelby spotted Duke chatting with Shireen Glenn, the head

of the Fine Arts Work Center. She ambled over just as the conversation seemed to break up.

"Hey," she said to Duke. "Thanks again. This was perfect."

"My pleasure. After all, I have an empty house. So much space to myself. It feels good to share it."

She checked the time on her phone. "I made a reservation at Sal's for a bunch of us, including Anders." She'd invited Colleen and Doug, but she said she had to go home and get her feet up.

Duke rubbed his jaw. "I'd love to. But I already have dinner plans. With Max."

"Oh, I included him in the reservation. No problem," she said.

"Actually, we were planning to go out just the two of us."

"Oh?" she said. Then *"Oh."* She smiled. He gave a little wave as if batting a fly.

"It's just a friendly... Oh, never mind."

She reached out and touched his arm. "Have a great time. I'll entertain Anders."

A quick look over her shoulder showed the signing line dwindling. She headed over, but was intercepted by Hunter.

"So what's the plan?" Hunter said. She wore a white satin shift dress, Doc Martens, and a Swarovski crystal peace sign around her neck.

"Duke can't do dinner but I'm going to check with Anders now. Give me a minute."

She made her way to the signing table just as Anders was getting up, shaking one last hand, posing for his umpteenth selfie. His face brightened with a smile when he saw her.

"You were fantastic," she said. "Thank you so much."

"Thank *you*," he said. "Great crowd."

Shelby couldn't necessarily take credit for the phenomenal turnout, but smiled graciously. The audience included several acclaimed authors who spent their summers in Ptown, including Michael Cunningham and Julia Glass. The entire board of

the Fine Arts Work Center showed up, as well as the town librarians, Land's End's regulars, and people she didn't recognize
at all but who lined up to buy books.

"We have wine and cheese," she said. "Can I get you anything?"

"You've done far too much as it is. And I appreciate it. May
I take you to dinner to thank you?"

"Oh!" she said. "I actually made reservations for a bunch of
us."

"To be honest, after an evening like this, I can't handle more
than a quiet dinner. I'm an incurable introvert. It takes discipline for me not to just run home to be alone."

She smiled. She understood. There had been nights on her
book tour when she felt completely drained after a reading and
couldn't wait to get back to her hotel room. Hunter would be
disappointed, but it was, after all, a Land's End event and he
was the guest of honor.

"Dinner sounds great," she said.

Twenty-Seven

Hunter nodded politely to the head of the Fine Arts Work Center, hearing her incessant chatter, but not listening to a word. Instead, she watched Shelby talking to Anders, trying hard to look like she wasn't.

Something familiar churned in her gut, something feral and unpleasant. The way Anders and Shelby interacted, it was like they were the only two people at the party. Shelby had always been a man-magnet. And in college, Hunter was all for it. She herself never had any problems getting guys. And she'd certainly never had a problem with her best friend. Until the summer after senior year. Their last together in Provincetown.

Shelby crossed the lawn towards her. Hunter glanced at the folding chairs where she'd left her handbag, and politely extricated herself from the arts center administrator.

"I just need to get my bag," she said when Shelby reached her.

"Actually, change of plan. I'm so sorry, but Anders doesn't want to do a group thing."

Hunter felt a pounding in her ears. Her mouth was suddenly dry.

"Oh, it's what *Anders* wants?"

"Yeah. I spoke to him and—"

"You are so fucking predictable," Hunter said. She backed away, then stumbled over a rock on her way to get her bag.

It was impossible to say who met Justin Lombardo first. They'd all been together that night four years ago—Shelby, Colleen, and herself. But Hunter was certain she'd had the initial conversation with him. They'd gone to a big group dinner after Justin gave a lecture about warming oceans or fish migratory patterns or something else to worry about. Honestly, it had been a little boring. But he was great to look at, the proverbial tall, dark, and handsome with a seriousness that bordered on brooding.

Justin was different than most guys she knew. He was older, he clearly had his life together, and most impressive of all, he seemed completely unaware of his own hotness. At dinner, she'd been seated right next to him. By the time the server cleared the metal pizza trays and Carmen ordered a gelato sampler for the table, she couldn't take her eyes off him. But she got the sense he saw her as just a college kid. He wasn't condescending, but he'd made a few offhand comments to that effect. She'd wondered who he was sleeping with, what woman had somehow found herself worthy of his attention. Hunter imagined she was brilliant and obsessed with the environment and pretty but not beautiful and possibly in her thirties.

She didn't say anything to her friends about her crush on Justin. It felt a little ridiculous. And she was certain by the time she was into the groove of senior year, he'd be forgotten. In some ways, he was. But as a new summer approached, she found herself thinking about him again. Checking his social media. Imagining when and how she'd run into him back in Ptown. As a college graduate, she was an adult worthy of being taken seriously. She briefly contemplated removing her nose piercing.

But in the end, all the fantasizing and analyzing was a waste of time. A few weeks into their new summer, she and Shelby were outside late at night on the deck of her parents' house, sharing a bottle of wine and settling into their end-of-night download—something they'd been doing for the past four years. Hunter had gone to a dance party with Colleen at the Boat Slip, but Shelby had been MIA.

"Where were you tonight?" Hunter asked.

Shelby let out a sigh, a dreamy sort of exhale that made Hunter sit up straight in her chaise longue.

"I met someone. Actually, I met him last summer. We both did. Remember that guy who gave a lecture at Town Hall?"

Hunter's heart began to beat fast. She couldn't form the word *yes*. She didn't have to—the question had been rhetorical.

"We met again during the night of the blackout, when we were both helping out. We've started…spending time together. So that's where I was. He's…amazing."

Hunter had no right to be upset. She'd never shared her feelings about Justin with Shelby. And so she swallowed her jealousy and willed herself to be okay with it. And that became easier as she saw Shelby and Justin together, how they clicked. How right they seemed. And she could live with it because some things were just meant to be.

But then, at the end of the summer, Shelby dumped him. Her move to New York City was more important. Her writing was more important. And it seemed to Hunter like such a waste. Like growing a beautiful garden and then refusing to water it. But then, that was Shelby: nothing was sacred. Not a boyfriend. Not a best friendship. All she cared about was her own success.

Of course Shelby was going to dinner with Anders Fleming alone. He was a major literary figure. He could probably help her career. For Shelby Archer, that was all that mattered.

All that had ever mattered.

★ ★ ★

The restaurant was a new Greek place with only six tables, tucked away on a side street off Bradford. Over a bottle of surprisingly potent red wine, Anders told Shelby about his upper-middle-class upbringing, his time at Oxford. She shared her rootless army brat childhood and the feeling, during four consecutive summers of undergrad, that Provincetown was the first "home" she'd ever had.

"But I'm curious," he said. "You have a bestselling novel out this summer. What made you decide to work at the bookstore instead of focusing on promotion?"

She didn't want to get too much into Colleen's personal business, so she just said, "I'm helping my friend. The woman who did your introduction tonight. Colleen Miller."

They talked about literature and New York City and the vagaries of the publishing industry. In the glow of flickering candlelight and the buzz of alcohol, Shelby couldn't deny how attractive she found him. He was older, accomplished, distinguished. Worldly in a way the guys she met in New York didn't seem to be. Maybe it was the accent. She didn't care to over-analyze it.

And the way he asked questions! He looked at her with such focus, it was as if *she* were the literary giant.

"How do you like working with Claudia Linden?" he said.

"I feel lucky she's my agent," Shelby said. "Claudia's the best."

"You know, she rejected me when I queried her. Fifteen years ago almost to the month."

"No! I find that very hard to believe." How could an agent take her on as a client but reject a talent like Anders Fleming?

He laughed. "Don't look so shocked. Though I admit, it was a blow. But we all have those moments, don't we? And I realize now, it wouldn't have been a good fit. Claudia was savvy enough to know that. She's always had a commercial eye. And it's all about commercial fiction these days, isn't it?"

"Well, I can only speak for myself," Shelby said. "I grew up reading Emily Giffin, Adriana Trigiani, and Jennifer Weiner. I wrote my senior thesis on friendship and class in the books of Anne Rivers Siddons."

"And one day someone will be writing about your books," he said.

She shook her head. "Well, I don't know about that. But… thank you."

His eyes focused on her.

"You know, I've been so busy teaching that aside from that one boat ride, I haven't taken enough time to enjoy the incredible natural beauty here. It feels a bit criminal. I've heard the sunsets on Herring Cove are quite spectacular. Would you like to join me one evening this week?"

She didn't see that coming. She was flattered. She wanted to say yes, but she had so much writing to do. She wasn't there meet a man. Still, it was summer. And how could she write a fun novel if she wasn't having any herself?

"I'd like that," she said.

Twenty-Eight

Carmen Lombardo didn't spend a lot of time at Land's End Books. She wasn't much of a reader. In fact, the only book she read that year had been Shelby's. (She'd been surreptitious about it knowing her husband and son wouldn't understand.)

She wondered if that was part of the bookstore's appeal for Mia. Teenagers always leaned towards whatever was opposite of their parents. And Carmen was fine with that—to an extent. But she was getting concerned.

Two nights ago, Carmen and Bert had been in bed watching an old episode of *Beat Bobby Flay*, debating whether or not they should add beer-battered cod to the menu, when Mia walked into their bedroom. Carmen found it endlessly irritating that her children never bothered knocking on the door before walking in. As if Carmen and Bert couldn't possibly be doing anything that might be embarrassing to interrupt. (Which was entirely off base, thank you very much.)

"Mia, I'm happy to see you, but please, for the hundredth time…"

"I heard your TV on so I knew you were awake," she said,

sitting on the edge of the bed. Carmen looked at her husband and he shook his head: he gave up.

"How was the book party?" she said, turning back to Mia.

"Amazing. I'm actually good at this. The bookstore thing."

"I'm sure you are," Carmen said, smiling at her.

"Yeah. So… I've decided this is what I want to do after high school. I'm not going to apply to college."

Carmen turned to Bert. She didn't trust herself to speak without having an emotional outburst.

"Mia, don't upset your mother with this nonsense," he said. "If you want to work in the bookstore, work in the bookstore. But you're going to do it with a college education."

"I just don't understand why you see this as an either/or decision," Carmen said. "Colleen went to college. Shelby went to college." Where was this coming from?

"I'm not Colleen. I'm not Shelby. And I'm not Justin. And I'm *not good at school*." Her face turned red, and her eyes teared. "Why don't you understand anything I say to you?" She walked out, slamming the door behind her.

"*What* is going on?" Carmen said to Bert. Really, for most of the last school year she'd felt something was off. But she'd hoped that over summer break, Mia would relax a little. Cheer up. But she was barely going out with her friends. In fact, with all the hours Mia was logging at the bookstore, she was spending more time with Shelby than with anyone else. "Maybe I should talk to Shelby," she said.

"Why would you do that?"

"All the time Mia's spending at the bookstore. Maybe she knows something we don't."

Bert conceded it might be worth a try, but not to get her hopes up.

"I just need your help with one thing," Carmen said. "Ask Mia out to lunch so I have a window of time alone with Shelby."

★ ★ ★

Carmen found Shelby busy with a customer. And when Shelby noticed her walk in, her face registered surprise. As soon as she finished with the sale she walked right over to where Carmen stood browsing the new releases.

"Hi, Carmen," she said. "Good to see you."

"Good to see *you*," Carmen said. Shelby was adorable as usual, dressed in denim shorts and a short-sleeved button-down shirt with a Peter Pan collar. "How's your summer going so far?"

"Great," Shelby said. "I didn't realize how much I missed this place."

"Are you writing a new book? I really enjoyed *Secrets of Summer*. The ending was just... It made me smile."

"Oh, that means a lot to me," Shelby said, beaming. "I always want to write happy endings."

A silence settled between them. Carmen knew she should get to the point of her visit, but now that she was standing there, she was second-guessing her visit. Maybe it was inappropriate.

"Mia's been a big help around here," Shelby finally offered.

Carmen nodded. "Glad to hear it." That was her opening. She glanced around the store to make sure no one could overhear them. "That's actually why I'm here. I'd like to talk to you about her."

"Oh?" Shelby said, frowning. "Sure. Is everything okay?" A boisterous group of men filed in, dressed in swim trunks and T-shirts and carrying shopping bags from Tea by the Sea. "Excuse me for just a minute," she said to Carmen.

"Of course. Please, no rush."

Shelby asked the group if anyone needed help, and one of the men asked her to recommend a memoir or essay collection that would make good beach reading. Shelby directed him to the nonfiction section and Carmen heard her mention a book called *The Andy Cohen Diaries*. That sounded fun. She really should try to read more.

Just as she was thinking that she should leave and let Shelby do her job in peace—that it had been a mistake to go in the first place—Shelby returned to her side and suggested they talk behind the counter where they'd have a little more privacy.

"So, something is going on with Mia?" Shelby said in a low voice.

"I'm not sure," Carmen said carefully. "But I'm concerned. She's telling her father and me she doesn't want to go to college. Do you know anything about this? I only ask because of all the hours you spend working together. And also, she was so fond of you that last summer you were here."

Shelby sighed. "To be honest, I'd say she's considerably less fond of me. So I'm probably not the best person to ask."

Carmen couldn't hide her disappointment—not just that Shelby didn't know anything to help her, but that it seemed Mia was closed off to her, too. And she didn't believe it was just because of the breakup.

Something was going on.

The front door opened again, and Duke Nestley walked in. He gave Shelby a wave, then stopped to talk to one of the men in the bathing suit group. When he made his way over to them, he greeted Carmen with notable coolness.

"Mia told me your house was just perfect for the book event," she said.

He put his hands on his hips. "Honestly, Carmen, it would be even more perfect if Shelby could use the beach. But thanks to your son, that's not happening anytime soon."

What was he talking about? She turned to Shelby.

"What did Justin do?"

Shelby shook her head. "It's fine."

"It's not fine," Duke said. "Shelby petitioned at town hall to get temporary use of the space out there for book events, and

Justin led the charge voting it down. It seemed a little personal, if you ask me."

That didn't sound like Justin.

By the time she walked out of the bookstore, she had more unanswered questions than when she'd walked in. At least with Justin, she could just ask him directly what was going on.

As for Mia? She didn't know what she was going to do.

Hunter, sitting in the front row of Anders's Tuesday-morning class, refused to let Shelby's careerist dinner maneuver get to her. It was just one night, whereas Hunter saw him twice a week. They had a genuine, creative rapport. And she couldn't help but wonder if it could lead to something more. He was proper and sexy at the same time—like Hugh Grant in that old movie *Four Weddings and a Funeral*.

From a few rows back someone asked, "What are your thoughts on beta readers?"

Hunter knew from her job at Malaprop that some authors had a writing group or even just one reliable friend who read their work before they delivered it to their editor.

"They can be useful," Anders said. "It's not always possible, but if I have someone who can give my work a quick read? Sure. But it's important to choose that reader wisely, and to not have too many cooks in the kitchen, as they say."

Hunter stopped typing notes and looked up. She'd love to read his manuscript. It would be a great experience—not something she could necessarily put on her résumé, but she'd know she'd done it. It would boost her confidence, make her feel closer to her ambition of making it in the big leagues.

When class was over, she lingered. People trickled out, and just when she thought she was in the clear, a classmate monopolized Anders for five minutes of name-dropping from his experience working at the Newburyport Literary Festival. She stayed in her chair, pretending to be busy on her laptop. When the guy finally left, she packed her things.

"Hello there, Hunter. I apologize for not getting to your question earlier. The class seemed to have stalled on the topic of the unreliable narrator and we needed to move on."

"Oh, that's fine," she said. "I just wanted to say that if you need someone to read your work in progress, I'd be happy to take a look."

Anders rubbed his jaw thoughtfully. "Well, that's a generous offer. I might very well take you up on it."

Hunter walked out of the classroom feeling better than she had all summer. And she realized it wasn't just because of the manuscript. It was because of Anders.

She wanted him.

Twenty-Nine

Anders picked Shelby up in a gray Land Rover with the top down. He parked and walked around to open the door for her. She climbed into the front seat, dressed for the beach in denim shorts and a cropped Madewell T-shirt over her two-piece bathing suit. It could get windy near the water so she pulled her hair back in a low ponytail and tossed sunglasses into her tote bag along with flip-flops.

The Smiths played on the radio.

"I'm glad we're doing this," she said, smiling at him. "I've been spending most nights writing. It's good to get out of my head for a few hours."

It would be a nice change to spend time with someone who didn't have anything to do with her past in Provincetown. Everything felt so weighted lately. Like the visit from Carmen Lombardo. She combed through her own conversations with Mia looking for any clues that something specific was wrong. The only thing that stood out was an incident a few days ago. Shelby got an ARC—an advanced reader's copy—of a novel that HarperCollins was publishing in the winter. One of the perks of being a bookseller was getting to read books early. ARCs helped booksellers decide what books to order for the store. But sometimes, the ARCs she was most excited to read were new books from authors whose work she already knew and loved and had no doubt belonged on the Land's End shelves. That was the way she felt about the HarperCollins book that arrived in the mail, and she gave it to Mia, knowing she felt the same way about the writer. "Let me know what you think," Shelby said to her, expecting Mia would be as excited as she was to have an early look at a book that was sure to be a bestseller. Instead, she accepted the ARC with something that Shelby could only describe as reluctance. Very odd.

Shelby hadn't been on a beach date in a long time. She'd forgotten how to dress for it, and after much deliberation settled on faded jean shorts and a white cotton button-down top. It could get windy, so she brought her cashmere wrap just in case. She felt nervous.

Anders picked her up in a dark green Land Rover, the top down. They couldn't have asked for better weather. She said as much when she climbed into the passenger seat.

"That's what I was thinking," he said. "But I'm trying not to put too much pressure on the sunset to live up to its reputation."

"Oh, as someone who spent every college summer here, I can guarantee it will."

It was a ten-minute drive to Herring Cove, and they didn't talk much because of the wind whipping through the car along Route 6. His hair was tousled in the breeze, and she noticed a touch of silver in the stubble along his jaw. He certainly was handsome. But then, for some reason, Noah popped into her mind. This time last summer was when they'd started hanging out. A year later, they were completely done. And she also couldn't help thinking about Justin. They used to drive the same route, under the same early-evening sun, a night of possibility ahead of them. She glanced over at Anders and thought, *This too shall pass.* She didn't know why some people found it so easy to have lasting relationships. She was just certain she'd never be one of them.

Anders pulled into the crowded beach parking lot. Once again, he came around and opened the door for her, then retrieved beach blankets and a cooler from the back.

"Ready?" he said.

"Let's go." She smiled and they walked close together but not touching as they made their way across a tarp-covered path towards the water.

The beach was lively, filled with groups of friends and couples set up for their own sunset viewing. There was a festive vibe and she felt happy to be sharing it with Anders.

"I wasn't sure what you like, so I brought a bit of a mobile buffet," he said, unpacking crusty breads and cheese and fruit from the cooler. She liked the way he said "mobile" with a long *i.*

He uncapped a chilled bottle of Pellegrino and poured some into a paper cup, handing it to her.

"My editor told me that beach culture is very different in the UK," she said, searching for small talk.

"How did that come up?" he said.

"Well, we were talking about foreign rights before the London Book Fair, and she said beach books that succeed here don't always translate."

He nodded. "Interesting. And yes, I can see that. My family used to holiday in Cornwall. The water was always quite chilly, and if I recall, the pebbles and stones made it a bit inhospitable."

She glanced at his profile, his fair skin and the way his hair flopped boyishly across his forehead. It was strange to spend time with someone whose face you'd known from photographs, whose work you'd read for years.

The sun dipped, and magical shades of gold and rose and

lavender painted the sky. When they'd finished eating, he suggested they take a walk.

At the shoreline, where the water met the sand, he reached
for her hand just as the tide washed over their feet. She felt a
shiver, and she didn't know if it was from the water or his touch.

Then she spotted something in the sand a few feet away. She
stopped walking.

A sea turtle was stranded. It was a large one—about two
feet long and probably a hundred pounds. It had a triangular-
shaped head and a hooked beak that made it look somewhat
angry. The top of the shell was grayish-green. She knew, from
her summer with Justin, that it shouldn't be on the beach like
that. Sea turtles spent most of their time underwater, surfacing
only to breathe. They crawled ashore at night just to lay their
eggs. Once, Justin took her to see the hatchlings. She watched
the tiny baby turtles race to the water on pure instinct. Justin
told her they wouldn't return to land until it was time for them
to lay eggs of their own.

"Look at that," she said, her voice hushed.

He turned, following her gaze. "What is it?"

"A sea turtle. It shouldn't be on land like this." She dropped
Anders's hand to reach for her phone. She needed to report the
stranded animal.

There was only one person she knew to call.

Justin invited his family out for Tuesday-night dinner instead
of going over to the house. He figured it was a more diplomatic
way to include Kate instead of imposing on his mother to cook
for one more person.

His parents and sister were already seated at an outdoor table
when he arrived. His mother didn't get up to kiss him hello,
which was out of character. He wondered what was bothering
her, and figured it was just the restaurant being short-staffed.

At least, he hoped that was what had her on edge, and not the dinner with Kate. But no, he was being sensitive.

"Mia, take off your headphones, please," Carmen said.

Kate turned to his sister. "That was such a lovely book event the other night." Mia thanked her, but she seemed as lackluster as his mother. What was with everyone?

"Mia, have you been to Kate's store yet?" Bert asked, turning to give Kate an encouraging smile.

"Uh, no. Because—and no offense, Kate—it's the competition."

Justin and his father exchanged a look.

"So," Bert said, changing topics, "are we all set for the Fourth of July?"

Justin pressed his fingers to his forehead. He'd rather spend another hour talking about the bookstore issue than get into Fourth of July.

"Yes! Let's discuss," Carmen said, looking more animated. The Fourth of July was his parents' wedding anniversary and every year they had a party. She turned to Justin. "How many of your friends do you think are coming this year? I need to start getting a headcount."

"Actually," Kate said, placing her hand on his forearm. "Justin and I decided to spend the Fourth in Boston."

Carmen closed her menu.

"What?"

A server stopped by the table.

"We just need another minute—thanks," Justin said to him.

This wasn't just news to his mother—it was news to him. Technically, "they" hadn't decided. She'd suggested it, and he'd said something along the lines of "We'll figure it out."

Carmen looked at Kate as if she'd just announced they were jumping on SpaceX to the moon. Then, to Justin: "You're missing the Fourth?"

"Oh, I'm sorry, Mrs. Lombardo," Kate said, immediately

recognizing the tension. She glanced between Justin and his mother. "It was all my idea. I just thought since we're here basically all summer, it would be a good time to slip away for a bit."

Carmen took a stab at her salad. Justin picked up his own fork, trying to think of what he could say to get dinner back on track. He was at a loss.

He didn't know if Kate had genuine disregard for his opinion about the Fourth, or if there'd been a miscommunication between them. One thing he did know: if he'd officially agreed to go to Boston, he would have made sure he'd been the one to tell his mother. And not in the middle of dinner. It was a sensitive situation. He didn't want his mother to think he'd made the decision to miss it lightly.

His phone rang. He reflexively began to send it to voicemail. Then he saw the incoming number: Shelby.

"Excuse me for a minute," he said and pushed his chair from the table. He walked towards the host stand close to the street. "Hello?"

"Sorry to bother you," Shelby said. "But there's a turtle stranded here on Herring Cove."

He asked her to describe it to him. It sounded like a Kemp's ridley, one of the most endandered species of sea turtle.

"I'll be right there."

Thirty

Shelby put her phone away and hoped she didn't look as uncomfortable as she felt. She'd done the right thing making the call, but it interrupted the romantic vibe.

"Sorry about that," she said.

"No need to apologize," he said. "Amazing you know just who to call."

She blushed, feeling bad for not disclosing that she knew exactly who to call because it was her ex-boyfriend. It seemed a little presumptuous to offer up that kind of information—as if Anders cared.

"Do you mind waiting until help arrives? I just want to make sure no one comes by first and messes with it," Shelby said to Anders.

"Not at all. Do you think it's injured?"

She eyed the helpless animal. Sometimes the seals, or sea turtles, or dolphins were ill or injured, and sometimes it was just the tricky geography of the coast. The Cape was shaped like a hook encircling Cape Cod Bay, which made navigating back to open ocean challenging.

Minutes later, Doug MacDougal appeared on the dunes carrying a large duffel bag and a banana box. "Hey there, Shelby!" He gave her a wave and began roping off the perimeter.

She turned to Anders. "You met him at your book reading. His girlfriend owns the bookstore."

"Such a small world out here."

Justin appeared right behind Doug with a first aid kit. *Very small world.*

"We can go now," she said quickly.

"Well, we can't leave *now*. This is the interesting part," Anders said. "Who was it who wrote, 'In the eyes of an animal, we find a reflection of our souls'?"

She didn't know. But she *did* know that it was Carrie Bradshaw from *Sex and the City* who said, "Sometimes we need to leave our exes where they belong—in the past."

Justin took the lead on giving the turtle a cursory examination.

"Good eye," he called out to her.

"Oh, yeah. Well, thanks for coming to help."

"It's my job," he said, looking at Anders.

"Oh—Justin, this is Anders Fleming."

"We met at the book reading," Justin said evenly, glancing up from his crouched position.

"That's right," Anders said, a look on his face like he was putting pieces together. "You were there with Kate from Hendrik's Books."

Justin nodded. "Thanks again for the call," he said to Shelby, punctuating the conversation by turning his back to them. He conferred with Doug before they slowly and carefully lifted the stunned animal.

"Let's go," she said, touching Anders's arm. He put his arm around her. They walked back towards their beach blankets. She felt the heat coming off his body, and her own stirrings of attraction. "I think I've had enough of the great outdoors for the night," she said, looking up at him.

He stopped walking and turned to face her. His intelligent

gray eyes had just the faintest crow's-feet in the corners. "I hate to see our evening end so soon."

She reached for his hand. "Who said anything about ending the evening?"

"I've always wondered about this house," Shelby said when they reached the landmark East End Victorian where he was living for the summer. She'd passed by it many times.

"Fine Arts Work Center arranged it for me. It's quite lovely," he said.

The kitchen was small but welcoming, with granite counters, blue-gray backsplash tiles, and a white vertical-board island where he opened a bottle of New Zealand sauvignon blanc and a California pinot noir.

"A friend brought over the red last night so I can't vouch for it," he said. "We have the white for backup."

He handed her a glass of the red. "I'm sure it's fine," she said.

"I have to admit, the first time I visited Northern California I expected everyone to be practically guzzling wine," he said, pouring her a glass.

"But they weren't?"

"No. Everyone seemed far more interested in cannabis." He waved his hand dismissively.

"Not a weed enthusiast?" she said.

"Over a sublime cabernet franc? No. And if we must debate that, I need to fortify myself first. Cheers."

She laughed. "I suspect that's a debate I'd sorely lose."

It felt easy to be around Anders. Partly, it was because he was a writer and so they already had a shorthand. But more than that, he seemed so comfortable in his own skin, so sure of himself. Not just sure of himself, but sure of his place in the world. Shelby could tell he wasn't the type of man to be threatened by an ambitious woman.

"Shall we venture out to the veranda?" he said.

He led the way, carrying the bottles of wine while she took care of their glasses.

It was almost dark out, just a thin ribbon of light on the horizon. The back porch overlooked a small yard bordered by a hedge of white hydrangeas. They sat on a wicker sectional and he moved a bunch of throw pillows out of the way.

"So," he said, crossing his legs and looking at her intently. "We haven't talked much about our respective works in progress. Is that by design?"

"Not at all," she said. Though maybe it was a little, on her end. She wouldn't trade writing beach books for anything, but she was sure he'd never read one and probably wouldn't find her novel compelling. "What are you writing?"

He nodded, sipped from his glass, then set it down on a wrought iron side table.

"A challenging project. My editor is pushing me to aim for a younger readership."

"Really? Why?"

He lit a cigarette. "We must keep with the times or risk becoming mummified, creatively speaking. And financially speaking. The sad truth is that awards don't necessarily translate to sales."

"Well, if they don't, what does?"

He held up his phone and rolled his eyes. "Videos of people dancing around their living rooms talking about books, apparently." He put the phone down on the table next to his wine. He leaned closer to her. "I apologize. Let's not be boring, talking shop on a gorgeous summer night."

A breeze rustled through the tree branches, bringing with it the smell of jasmine from a nearby garden. A small animal rustled in the hedges, and the air felt electric, the way it did before a storm. Maybe being near Anders just made her senses seem heightened.

"No," she said softly. "Let's not be boring."

He took the wineglass from her hands. She felt a flutter in her stomach. Seconds ticked by, or maybe minutes. Time did that funny thing where it seemed to stop or at least, bend.

And then he kissed her.

Thirty-One

There was no such thing as a typical day in the office at the Center for Coastal Studies. It was one of the things Justin liked best about his job. That morning, he headed to the Wellfleet office to map out the data for red tide contamination over the past decade. The lethargic sea turtle they rescued last night seemed like a classic case of red tide poisoning, but they still couldn't say for sure.

He'd done triage on the animal, found some swelling in its joints, and now she was on antibiotics and resting comfortably while they waited for test results. They named her Ladyslipper, after a type of shell that they'd accidentally scooped up along with her. After the office, he'd stop by the marine animal rehab facility to check on her.

Doug said he'd give him a lift, and Justin planned to meet him at his apartment before eight. But he only made it halfway down his street when he spotted his mother making a beeline for his house. She was dressed in her kitchen uniform: New Balance walking sneakers, black capri pants, and a red-and-white Lombardo's T-shirt.

He stopped walking.

"Ma, what're you doing here? Is something wrong?"

"You tell me," she said, out of breath by the time she reached him. "Why aren't you answering your phone?"

He patted his pocket. It was right there.

"I didn't know you called."

"You ran off last night and then I never heard from you again."

He couldn't argue with that. When he got Shelby's call, he dropped his credit card on the table and apologized for having to leave. Kate stood to leave with him. But Carmen waved her back into her seat.

"Stay. Eat. Just because Justin has to run, there's no reason the rest of us can't eat."

Kate had given him a trapped look, but he just kissed her on the cheek and whispered, "I owe you one."

He never followed up with his parents. He had, however, immediately called Kate when he drove back from Wellfleet. She'd been understanding about the work emergency. But he could tell now from the look on his mother's face she wouldn't let him off quite so easily.

"We had a stranded sea turtle. Sorry about that. But I can't talk now. I'm meeting Doug to drive out to Wellfleet."

His mother frowned. "You could have told me about the Fourth of July ahead of time. I felt a little blindsided. Your father, too."

Justin sighed. It was too much to hope that she'd let that slide.

"I'm sorry, Ma. I should have told you."

"After you left, I made sure Kate understood it was a family tradition to be together on the Fourth, thinking she might change her mind. But she didn't seem to get the hint."

"Well, you're the one who always told me relationships are about compromise."

Her eyes narrowed. "And how is she compromising for you?"

There was really no talking to his mother when she was in a

mood. She was annoyed with him; she was judging Kate. But he loved her and he knew she meant well and so he texted Doug he'd be five minutes late.

"Mom," he said, walking closer and putting an arm around her. "Kate's out here all summer so we can spend time together. Trying out a new location for Hendrik's *is* a compromise. A big one."

Carmen waved a finger at him. "So is that why you denied Shelby beach access? To give Kate's store an advantage?"

Justin stepped back. Where did that come from? "No, Mom. It was an impartial decision. I vetoed the beach access because it's not what's best for the larger community."

"You want to talk about community? We've been friends with the Millers your entire life. Land's End Books has been part of this town for eighty years. I love you, but you're on the wrong side of this one. And I'm very disappointed if Pam and Annie's business suffers because of your unresolved feelings for Shelby."

"I don't have feelings for Shelby." He ran his hand through his hair. "Mom, I have work to do. Again, apologies for running off last night. And I don't want to sound harsh, but I'm a grown man with my own life."

Carmen reached out and patted his cheek. "And like it or not, no matter how old you are, I'm always going to have something to say about it."

She turned and walked in the other direction. He shook his head, and watched her go.

Shelby leaned on the bookshop counter with a yawn. She wasn't just exhausted; she was guilt ridden over not writing before work. It was the price she paid for spending the night with Anders. If it weren't for her deadline, it would be worth every minute of exhaustion. But she needed to be more disciplined. She had time for exactly two things: working at the store and writing her book. That was what the summer was all about, and it was important to remember that.

Mia walked in, dragging a box that had been delivered to the front stoop.

"This is our Ann Brashares order," she said. "The movie theater is playing a revival of *Sisterhood of the Traveling Pants*, and Colleen planned a whole table."

Pam and Annie were always creative with their display tables, like the "blind date with a book" displays on Valentine's Day or putting historical fiction front and center if a new period drama was streaming. She was happy to see Colleen continuing the tradition.

"Fantastic. By the way, did you read that ARC I gave you from HarperCollins? Was it great?"

"I didn't read it yet," Mia said.

"Oh, okay. Well, if you don't have time, feel free to just bring it back to the shop. I'll take a look." She didn't want to overburden Mia, and besides, there was something else she wanted to ask her to read.

The idea came to her that morning in the shower. She was writing her new book so fast she didn't have perspective on whether or not the story was working. She thought about asking one of her friends from the city to read what she had so far, but she was embarrassed to show them something so rough. Maybe hitting the *New York Times* bestseller list should have made her more confident, but it had the opposite effect. She imagined showing the draft to someone, that person telling her it was awful and wondering how, really, she'd ever had a bestseller in the first place. But she'd feel less anxious about showing the manuscript to someone who wasn't in her incestuous little publishing orbit. And she thought of Mia.

She thought, also, she could ask Anders to read the manuscript. Although, he might not be comfortable doing so after their night together. She valued his opinion enough not to take any notes too personally. But she understood, too, that it was a complicated dynamic. They'd discussed the idea of early reads.

Anders admitted he only felt comfortable letting interns or "underlings" read his rough drafts.

"Underlings?" she'd said. "What does that mean?"

"Just readers or writers who aren't peers. Does that make me terribly insecure?" he'd said. The comment surprised her. If Anders Fleming, with all his bestsellers and accolades didn't feel confident in the first-draft stage, how could she expect to?

"Not at all," Shelby said.

"I'll tell you something: the only time you should worry about your first draft is when you *don't* think it's absolute rubbish." That made her smile. She decided to write it on a Post-it and stick it on her laptop.

Still, her first choice would be to give the manuscript to Mia.

"Mia, feel free to say no, but I was wondering if you might have time to take a look at the first draft of my manuscript so far."

"Me?" She stopped unloading the book delivery.

"Well, yes. I know you read everything, and I trust your opinion. I'm only halfway done, but I'm just too close to it to tell if it's working. And it would be so helpful to get some perspective before I get much further."

Mia appeared daunted by the request. It was like Shelby had asked her to scale the Pilgrim's Monument.

"But if you're too busy, I completely understand," she said quickly. "It was just a thought."

Shelby had meant it when she said feel free to say no, but deep down she felt a little offended. When she'd been in high school, she would have been thrilled to read a work in progress by an author. Even in college, she would have dropped everything. She couldn't help but wonder if it was personal.

It reminded her that the only one who wanted her in town was Colleen. Everyone else was merely tolerating her. It hurt, but then, she'd brought it on herself. It seemed like things were going better, it appeared on the surface like good things were happening—that maybe in some small ways she was redeeming herself. But that was wishful thinking.

It was fine, really. She'd fulfill her promise to Colleen, finish her novel, and then she'd be able to get back to her real life.

"Okay," Mia said. "I'll read your book."

"Really?" Shelby said, relieved. "Oh, that's great, Mia. I really appreciate it."

Mia smiled weakly. She thought about what Carmen asked of her, and realized maybe Mia *did* need someone to talk to. That something was bothering her. Or maybe Mia just didn't want to go to college. Lots of people didn't, and they found their path. She was surprised that Carmen and Bert, having raised their children in an unconventional place, would have such a conventional view of education. But then, they were very hard-working people, and she knew from Justin how they'd instilled the value of doing the right thing even when it was hard. Maybe they thought Mia's attitude towards college came from fear. And maybe they were right.

"Is everything okay? In life, I mean?" Shelby said.

"Sure," Mia said. "Why?"

"Oh, I don't know. I just remember heading into senior year was stressful. College applications, all that."

"Yeah, well, I don't want to go to college. So I'm not stressed about it."

Shelby nodded. "Got it. So what do you think you want to do?"

"Exactly what I'm doing now." She cocked her head to the side, as if finding it difficult to understand the question.

"Right," Shelby said. "You know, I worked here every summer during college. And then the summer before grad school. You can do both."

"I don't want to do both." She pulled her headphones over her ears.

Okay. She wouldn't push the issue. It was time to quit while she was ahead.

Thirty-Two

Hunter sat across from Anders in his bright, airy kitchen. He leafed through his manuscript, reading the pages she'd annotated, glancing up every now and then to comment. Hunter felt nervous, as if he were evaluating her work instead of the other way around.

"This is very thorough, Hunter. I appreciate it. You're a skilled editor."

She beamed. "Thank you. Well, it's easy with such brilliant material to work with."

It was true. Reading Anders's new manuscript made the Seaport Press slush pile all the more discouraging. She was never going to find a career-changing novel in Duke's submissions. They weren't all bad; they were just…small. Niche. Nothing jumped out as a novel that would make a splash in the marketplace. Her idea of finding a diamond in the rough and shining it up to make a name for herself seemed more and more like a fantasy. Seaport would never be anything more than a placeholder for her. She could justify taking a summer to work at a small Cape press, but the narrative would grow stale by the fall.

She had to either find the proverbial needle-in-the-haystack manuscript, or she needed a Plan B. And soon.

"I'm wondering," he said, "does the Katarina character read authentic to you? Since you're roughly the same age…the same generation."

"Absolutely," she said.

"Specifically, how so?" he said.

She sat back in her seat, thinking. "The way she relates to technology? And her views on sex. The whole 'situationship' thing."

He nodded. "I want to dig a little deeper here, if you'll indulge me. Let's say, for the sake of narrative argument, that you *were* Katrina. Would you still want Claud even after realizing the 'situationship'—as it were—was purely transactional?"

Hunter maybe wasn't the best person to ask about this.

"What's wrong with purely transactional sex?"

Clearly, it wasn't the response Anders had been expecting. He looked at her in surprise and shifted in his seat.

"What about the power imbalance?" he said.

Hunter tilted her head to one side. "I'd say power is in the eye of the beholder."

"That's beauty," Anders said. "*Beauty* is in the eye of the beholder."

She leaned forward. "Personally? I think their scenes together are hot."

Their eyes met, she felt a jolt, and with it all her stress evaporated: the disappointing manuscripts. The fruitless job search. Shelby. She couldn't control any of that. But men? Men, she knew. And in that moment, she was in "the zone"—an ignited spark between herself and someone she wanted. The zone was the one place she never failed and that never failed her.

She reached for the iced tea he'd served her, and took a long sip. "I'm sorry. If you're looking for an authenticity reader, I have to admit that when it comes to sex, my attitudes might be more casual than the average person."

Anders messed with his manuscript, shuffling the pages into a neater pile, and nodded. When he looked up at her, his expression was unreadable. "Well, Hunter, thank you for your feedback. It's been very…illuminating."

"Anytime," she said, reaching for her phone. She stood up, taking her time pushing the chair back in place. "Well, see you in class. I can find my way out." She took her time making her way across the kitchen. And felt him watching her every step of the way.

Justin's parents instilled in him the importance of doing the right thing even when it was hard. *Especially* when it was hard. And so he stopped by Land's End after work.

His mother's accusation that he was biased against the store nagged at him. He took his committee jobs seriously, and his primary responsibility was to act in the best interest of the town. When it came to the issue of beach access for Land's End, he was afraid maybe he'd failed to do that.

He was relieved to find the store busy. It validated his belief that a town filled with art-lovers could support two bookshops—as it did the many art galleries and wide variety of live shows. Hendrik's was additive, not detrimental. There was always room for people who wanted to contribute to the town. How else could any of them endure their hometown swelling to ten times its population every summer?

He spotted Shelby standing on a ladder to retrieve a book from the top of a shelf. Standing below, holding on to the ladder to keep it steady, was Elise, the owner of the tea shop across the street.

"Sorry to make you risk your neck," Elise said. "Maybe you need to move Margaret Atwood out of alphabetical order. She's too iconic to be out of reach. Give her an honorary spot on a lower shelf."

"I like the way you think," she said with a laugh.

He smiled at seeing her smile.

She climbed down, spotted him, and raised her eyebrows in surprise. He hung back while she rang up Elise's purchases. When the front counter was clear of customers, he walked over. She finished punching something into the desktop, took off her computer glasses, and rubbed her eyes. Her hair was up in a messy ponytail, and she looked extremely pretty.

"Scouting the competition?" she said.

"Very funny."

"I'm only joking. Well, mostly joking."

A few customers walked in behind him. She called out they should let her know if they needed any help.

"I'm not sure what you're looking for, but I still recommend *The Overstory*. If you haven't read it," she said. She'd been talking about that book since they first got together, refusing to believe he didn't enjoy fiction. And after a while, witnessing her habit of reading in bed every night, he thought maybe he was missing out. "Okay, what's one novel I should read?" he'd asked. And she'd named, without hesitation, the Richard Powers novel.

"I still haven't," he admitted.

She walked from behind the counter to a shelf marked Pulitzer Prize Winners. She pulled a copy and brought it to him.

He took the book from her and shifted his feet uncomfortably. "I'm not here for a book recommendation," he said.

"Oh?" Her green-gold eyes were wary. Or maybe it was just the way the sun was hitting them. "So why are you here?"

"To apologize."

She looked at him warily, as if waiting for the punchline.

A customer carried over an armful of books, and Shelby rang her up, slipping a bookmark into the novels and packing them into a recyclable Land's End paper bag. When she was gone, Shelby said, "What do you have to apologize for? I was under the impression I was the bad person."

He sighed. "I never said you were a bad person, Shelby. I was hurt. How would you have felt if things had been reversed?"

Her face softened. "I would have been hurt. So, that's what I mean. You have nothing to apologize for. Unless it's about the bookstore, in which case you should apologize to Colleen. She's really stressed about Hendrik's. It's the last thing she needs right now."

Yes, he'd gotten that message loud and clear from Doug.

"That's what I wanted to talk to you about. I was maybe shortsighted when I shot down your petition to use the beach for book events."

"Really?" she said, looking directly into his eyes. He hated to admit it, but the past few years had only made her more beautiful. Her face had become defined, losing the last remnants of adolescent roundness. A lot of time had passed. It was time to move forward.

"Yes. So if you're still interested in it, I'll talk to the committee."

She gave him a big smile. "This will make Colleen really happy, Justin. Thanks."

"No problem," he said. "Ah, but I'm not going to need this." He put *The Overstory* on the counter.

"Consider it a gift," she said. "On the house. A token of bookseller gratitude."

He smiled. "I can't guarantee I'll read it."

Her face turned serious. "There are never any guarantees, Justin. We're all just doing the best we can."

She was right. So maybe instead of resenting her or trying to pretend she didn't exist, he should try something else. Something that made a lot more sense considering how intertwined everything and everyone was in Ptown.

"This is probably something I should have said two weeks ago. And I hope it's not too late: I'd like us to be friends."

She smiled with a new warmth in her eyes, and her gaze felt as strong as a physical touch.

"I'd like that, too."

In that instant, he knew that he'd said the absolute right thing. And he also knew that it would be impossible for him.

Thirty-Three

Shelby looked up from her laptop, realizing it was dark and she hadn't even noticed the sun setting. When the world around her disappeared, that was when Shelby knew she was writing productively. And after a quick email exchange, Claudia signed off on the idea of two competing Provincetown bookstores with romantic tension between the protagonist and the newcomer. She suggested the title *Bookshop Beach*. Shelby felt back in business.

> Seagulls lined up on the wooden planks and thick twine dividing the shrub-filled sand and the bookshop. Emily stood on the beach, wondering why her competitor agreed to share the space. She wanted to take the gesture at face value, but it was difficult to trust Jackson Lowe. It was even more difficult, after the news from her doctor, to trust herself. She didn't know how she was going to get through the summer...

Colleen knocked on the apartment door. She'd been expecting her; she wanted to tell her the news about the beach space in person. And Colleen wanted to get out of her place for an hour or two.

"Hey. Come on in," she said, opening the door for Colleen.

She was dressed in baggy jeans and one of Doug's Center for Coastal Studies T-shirts. Her hair seemed to have grown inches in just a few days. Her eyes looked slightly puffy.

"I would've been here sooner, but Doug was late. He wanted to have dinner together. Anyway, thanks for agreeing to meet up here instead of my place."

"No problem. Your hair looks really long."

Colleen nodded. "It's growing like weeds. I think it's a pregnancy thing."

Shelby suggested they go down to the beach. They'd missed the sunset, but there was a bright crescent moon and her phone told her it was a breezy seventy-five degrees. She packed a tote with towels and water and cookies from Connie's Bakery. Outside, she heard the Miley Cyrus song "Party in the USA" playing at a nearby restaurant's outdoor seating.

"I should do more things at night," Colleen said, kicking back on the oversize towel, resting on her elbows. "Maybe I wouldn't feel like the summer was passing me by."

"If it's any consolation," Shelby said, arranging herself a few inches away, "I'm not going out much, either."

Colleen seemed dubious. "Really? That's not what I've heard."

"What do you mean?" Oh—of course! Doug mentioned seeing her on the beach with Anders.

"Okay, I went out last night. But it wasn't a big deal."

Colleen shook her head. "I can't believe I had to pry it out of you."

"I hardly call that a 'pry.' I would have told you. I've just been busy. And more focused on the store than my personal life."

"Do you have any idea how bored I am? It's your job, as my friend, to keep me posted about things like this. At least one of us has a life this summer! So what's going on?"

Shelby felt herself flush. "I'm not sure. Something, I think. But who knows. Anyway, that's not what I wanted to talk about. I have good news about the bookshop: Justin changed his mind about Land's End using this space for events."

"Really?" Colleen said, sitting up straighter.

Shelby nodded. "He still has to get it past the committee or whatever, but I get the sense it's a done deal."

"What changed his mind?" Colleen said.

Shelby shrugged.

"Maybe he wants to impress you."

Shelby rolled her eyes. "Absolutely not. And it doesn't matter why; it's great for the store."

"Great for the store, and good timing. With my parents coming to town for the baby shower I feel like I need something to make them bullish on the store. They're certain Hendrik's Books is a sign we've stayed too long at the party."

"I don't know why they feel that way." Shelby scooped up sand with her nails and rubbed it between her fingers nervously. She closed out the "drawer" every day, and the store seemed to be doing okay, as far as she could tell.

"I don't know. Maybe it's not even rational. But I'm getting a lot of 'We told you so's.'"

Shelby frowned. She was surprised to hear that. "What about Anders's book event? Were they happy about that?" They'd sold out of the inventory they ordered for his reading, and the *Cape Cod Times* covered it. Shelby emailed a link to Annie and Pam.

"I think their attitude is, we need those numbers once or twice a week, not once a month. And yeah, partly it's my fault for not being more aggressive scheduling events. But the tourist traffic had always been enough—more than enough. It's like, everything's changing and at the worst possible time." She put her hand on her belly and lay flat on her back, looking up at the stars. Shelby followed her gaze. The constellations were like old friends she hadn't seen since she moved to Manhattan. She turned to Colleen, propped up on her side, resting on one elbow.

"The summer just started," she said. "Let's look at July Fourth as the real starting mark. The past few weeks have only been a warm-up."

Colleen nodded, but didn't seem convinced. "I'm sorry to put this all on you. I know you have your own work. It's just… I don't know what I'd do without you." A foghorn sounded in the distance.

"You don't have to think about that," Shelby said, reaching out and squeezing her shoulder. "I'm not going anywhere."

At least, not yet.

Thirty-Four

Carmen heard sobbing down the hall. She'd been headed to her bedroom to fold laundry, but instead did an about-face and walked to Mia's.

The door was closed, and Carmen knocked. When there was no response, she turned the knob and walked in to find Mia sitting on her bed with printed pages spread out in front of her.

"What's wrong?" Carmen asked, her stomach in knots. Her mind flooded with various scenarios of what could possibly have her daughter ending the day in tears. Boy problems? Argument with a friend? Had she gotten into trouble at the bookstore?

"Nothing," Mia said, hugging her knees to her chest and wiping her nose with the edge of her T-shirt.

"Let me get you a tissue," Carmen said, leaving the room just long enough to retrieve a box of Kleenex from the linen closet. After handing it to Mia, she folded her arms across her chest. "Obviously, something is wrong."

"I just…finished reading Shelby's new book. It's sad."

"Oh!" Carmen said, relieved. "Okay. Got it. All right hon— love you."

She kissed the top of her head and left, closing the door behind her.

Only later, after she'd folded the laundry, did she remember what Shelby said the other day at the bookstore: *I always write happy endings.*

Kate's father was in town to check in on the bookstore.

Martin Hendrik was medium height, with wide-set blue eyes, thick gray hair, and a quiet confidence. The only signifier of his wealth and success was the expensive diver's watch on his wrist. He had the relaxed demeanor of someone who worked hard, but had nothing left to prove. Justin liked him.

Since her father followed a strictly paleo diet, Kate suggested they eat at Fishtail Restaurant instead of at Lombardo's. Justin actually preferred it that way; after his mother's little office visit, he didn't want her to feel like he was being passive-aggressive and foisting his new relationship onto her.

"I have to thank you for luring my daughter out here for the summer," Martin said over an icy tray of Wellfleet oysters. He had a deep, booming voice. "A Hendrik's Books seaside outpost is a great idea. Lots of untapped potential here."

Justin nodded, even though he had the opposite view of the development of Ptown. Decades ago, it was untapped potential. Now it was overrun.

"That's an interesting perspective," Justin said. "I feel like things are closing in on us in some ways."

"Justin's very involved in the town," Kate said, placing a hand on his forearm. "I've gone with him to some committee meetings and it's interesting. It does feel like a bit of an inflection point."

"Growing pains are normal," Martin said. "It's a sign of progress. My father started with one Hendrik store in Dover, and we ended up with ten fanning out all over the state. Now eleven, counting Katie's little venture here. And now, with so much brand equity, my son Karl is branching out into hospitality."

Kate nodded. "I told Justin about the resort."

Her older brother, Karl, had opened a boutique hotel in Chatham, a wealthy beach town on the southeast tip of the Cape.

"You'll meet Karl on the Fourth. Glad you'll be joining us," Martin said.

"Looking forward to it," Justin said.

After dinner, they walked fifteen minutes down a bustling Commercial Street to Hendrik's to show Martin the space. The store was closed because Kate still hadn't found reliable part-time help.

"Katie, you can't close the bookstore so early in a walking town like this," Martin said, appraising the space with his hands on his hips.

"The housing crunch here trickles down to staffing issues," Justin said. "If people can't afford to live here, they can't work here."

Martin seemed unconvinced. He ran his hand along the shelving and straightened a display table. "You should have said something, Katie. I can transfer someone from another location..."

Kate shook her head. "It's fine, Daddy. I've got it under control."

"If you don't have part-time help, how are you going to come home over Fourth of July?" Martin said.

"I'm closing it for the weekend," she said.

"Closing over the busy holiday weekend? Sweetheart, that's just bad business. I won't hear of it."

Kate looked at Justin, but he didn't know what she wanted him to say. He basically agreed with Martin, but she would think he was just siding with her father because he wanted to stay in Provincetown for the holiday. Which he did.

"Katie, you stay here and mind the shop. And next summer,

you'll plan ahead to have more help. Summer retail business means sacrifice. Am I right, Justin?" he said.

"I can't argue with you on that," he said. Kate gave him an annoyed look. But Justin could tell that while she would debate *him* over where to spend the Fourth, she would not debate her father. He didn't hold that against her. It was hard to disappoint parents. He was a grown man and still he felt bad missing his parents' anniversary party. But now it seemed the Boston trip was off.

When he told his mother the good news, he'd make sure to make it seem like the change in plan had been Kate's idea.

Thirty-Five

Fourth of July weekend dawned bright and hot. Shelby stood on Hunter's deck, looking out at the beach below. The baby shower theme colors, cobalt blue and peach, really popped against the sand and sea. Six round tables were set with fresh sunflower centerpieces and icy carafes of pink lemonade. The plates, glasses, and striped table runners were coral, blue, and white, with two decorative white starfish resting atop each folded cloth napkin.

Shelby passed the deck's sangria bar, dropping her gift off on the designated table covered with gifts wrapped in pastel-colored paper. The centerpiece was white, eco-friendly helium balloons tied to glass baby bottles filled with jelly beans. On the beach below, two dozen or so guests milled around. The Harry Styles song "Watermelon Sugar" played over the outdoor sound system. The salt air met Shelby like a kiss, a moment of pure summer that took her breath away.

"Shelby!" Pam Miller called out, rushing across the deck to give her a hug. It was typical Pam exuberance, just as it was exactly like Annie to smile quietly and trail after her.

Pam was in her fifties, tall and lean. She wore her gray hair boyishly short, and always seemed to be dressed in a white button-down, faded jeans, and Converse. Her familiar scent, a cinnamon-sugar mix, made Shelby feel like a college kid again.

"Look at you—a bestselling author. And we can say we 'knew you when.'"

"I tell everyone who will listen about my summers at Land's End," Shelby said. It was true; she mentioned Land's End whenever she spoke about her path to becoming a novelist.

"You've done us proud," Annie said, pushing up on her toes to kiss Shelby's cheek. She had a round face framed by shoulder-length blond curls and wore a pale purple T-shirt, cargo shorts, and Birkenstocks. "And thank you so much for helping with the store. And all of this!" She waved a cocktail napkin decorated with a pink-and-blue anchor in the center and above it, the words *Babies on Board*.

From the beach below, Colleen caught her eye. They shared a smile.

"Excuse me for one minute. I just want to say hi to Colleen."

Shelby took the wooden stairs down to the sand and followed the tarp path leading to where tables had been set out. Colleen was already seated at a table with a centerpiece of coral balloons anchored by a balloon weight wrapped in turquoise foil.

She noticed Colleen's T-shirt and laughed.

"I didn't think you'd be wearing it *today*." Shelby bent down to give her a hug. When she'd stopped by to visit a few nights ago, she gave Colleen a T-shirt that said on the front, Sorry, I Just Can't…and on the back, I'm Busy Growing Two Tiny Humans.

"Oh, I'm wearing it *every* day," Colleen said, leaning into her hug. "Thank you for putting all this together. You and Hunter. I love you guys."

Hunter stood near the neighboring table, talking to a young local, Jaci Barros, whose family owned the boatyard. Shelby waved, but Hunter either didn't notice or pretended not to notice.

Shelby hadn't seen her since the night of Anders's book reading. Aside from their initial shower planning meeting at the house, they'd only communicated by text or DM. Since Shelby was hunkered down writing every night, she didn't even have the chance to run into her after work. She wondered, for the first time, if Hunter was upset with her again for some reason.

"It's just like the old days," Colleen said, following Shelby's gaze. The expression on her face was hopeful. "The three of us. Here on the beach."

"Yeah, for sure," Shelby said.

She felt people hovering nearby, waiting to say hi to Colleen. It made it easy for her to slip away, to get Hunter's attention and pull her aside.

"Can we talk for a sec?" Shelby said. Hunter tried to shake her off, but Shelby wouldn't take no for an answer. Shelby turned towards the sun, watching the way it seemed to bounce off the ocean. The water was dotted with boats, and a test firework sounded off somewhere. Shelby almost forgot it was the Fourth of July; the town's festive vibe felt like an extension of the baby shower.

They walked towards the water.

"What is it?" Hunter said impatiently, glancing back at the party.

"I just wanted to say I'm glad we did this together. And it makes Colleen really happy to see us friends again."

Hunter barked out a strange laugh. "Is that what we are?"

Shelby stopped walking. "I thought so."

"Just like nothing ever happened. How convenient for you."

Was she serious? "Is this about my book? Because I thought we were past that."

Hunter stopped walking and turned to her. "It's not about the book. The book just confirmed it. You're not capable of being anyone's friend. Or girlfriend, apparently. I'm not sure how Colleen convinced you to come out here this summer, but I'm sure you'll let her down somehow, too."

Shelby was confused.

"Hunter," she said quietly. "What's this really about?"

Hunter opened her mouth to speak, then stopped. Shelby glanced back at the other guests, hoping no one would interrupt them. She wasn't going back to the party until Hunter spilled it.

"Just tell me," Shelby said.

"Fine," Hunter said, crossing her arms. "Do you remember that last summer we went sailing with my parents?"

The question was so out of context, it took Shelby a second to think about it. "We did that a few times."

"Right. But the day when we did edibles and kept hanging out belowdecks and they didn't know why we were freaked out by the wind?"

Shelby smiled. She did remember that day. They'd accidentally gotten way too high. It hadn't been funny at the time, but it was now that she thought back on it. Still—what did that have to do with anything?

"That morning, before the boat, I told you there was a guy I liked," Hunter said. "But that I wasn't ready to talk about it yet." Hunter's face turned red and she toyed with the small gold hoop near the top of her ear the way she did when she was upset.

Shelby had no recollection of the conversation.

"He was someone I'd been thinking about for a while. Someone I thought I had, I don't know, some sort of connection with that might turn into something more. I was, like, sure of it."

"I'm sorry, Hunter. I don't remember you telling me about him."

"That's because I never did. Not specifically. Because a few nights later, you showed up at the Canteen with him."

Shelby tilted her head to one side. It took her a beat to be sure she was understanding her.

"You don't mean… Justin?"

"I do mean Justin. The night we went to dinner after his talk at Town Hall, I felt like we connected. And for some reason, I just couldn't get my mind off him all year. I thought, I don't know, that something might happen that summer."

Shelby's jaw dropped. Hunter had just described exactly the way she herself had felt after that first night with the Lombardos. And she didn't wonder why Hunter never mentioned it; Shelby hadn't, either. It was too ephemeral. It felt, well, silly. And they were not silly girls.

"When he picked you, I could live with it. I was happy for you. I thought, okay maybe it's true love or something, and how could I compete with that? Who was I to even try? But then you just dumped him. Like it was *nothing*. And it seemed like…such a waste."

Shelby pressed her fingers to her temples. "I'm trying to process this. Are you saying this was all about Justin? Not the book?" She lowered her hands, incredulous.

"It all ties together. I saw how you ended things with Justin, and I thought, wow, she turned it off just like that." She snapped her fingers. "But I guess we all make choices."

"That's not true," Shelby said. "I didn't… Nothing turned off." In fact, breaking up with Justin had been one of the hardest things she'd ever done. But she knew it came down to a case of "right guy, wrong time." She'd learned, moving around so much as a child, that goodbye was a part of life. Understanding this, acting accordingly, wasn't a character flaw. It was her strength.

"I felt bad for him," Hunter said. "I couldn't imagine losing you as a friend. And I thought, well, she'd never do that to me. But when you moved to New York, you kinda did."

"Hunter, that's not fair. Our lives changed. You got busy, too."

"True. And I didn't blame you. You had other things on your mind, new friends. So did I. And maybe you forgot about me a little. I had no problem with that. But you didn't forget about me at all, did you? In fact, you remembered so much, *you felt the need to write it into a book.*"

Shelby stared at her. Hunter looked away, her attention caught by something beyond them. Shelby turned to see Pam walking over.

"Ladies, I've been looking all over for you," Pam said. "Doug's about to make a toast before he leaves."

"Lead the way," Hunter said, brushing past her.

Stunned by the turn things had taken, all Shelby could do was follow along.

Doug stood on the deck, Colleen by his side. He raised a champagne flute filled with orange juice. Shelby's heart was pounding like she'd just run a six-minute mile.

"They say timing is everything in life," Doug said. "We've all heard that. But what I never realized was how much of that timing is out of our control. This summer is nothing like Colleen and I had planned. And it's better than anything we ever imagined."

"Actually, I imagined getting out of bed a lot more," Colleen said, and everyone laughed.

"It's true: you have the harder part of this bargain. And as soon as I can share the load, I'm there! But if it makes you feel better, after the babies arrive, I'll stay off my feet for a few months just to even things out."

People laughed again. "Seriously, though, to the love of my life, mother of my children, and current champion of our latest Scrabble tournament—Colleen."

Shelby raised her glass. "To Colleen," she echoed, part of the chorus around her.

Doug bent down to kiss Colleen, and she was radiant. Shelby thought about what he'd just said—that timing was everything in life. He was absolutely right.

The deck felt hot and crowded. She needed space. She needed

to think. And with everyone busy pouring champagne and hovering around Colleen, it was easy for her to slip away unnoticed, back inside the apartment.

Shelby took refuge in the guest bathroom and locked the door. It was decorated with paper hand towels that matched the cocktail napkins outside, and a conch shell filled with small soaps wrapped in patterned paper. She stood in front of the sink and ran the water, avoiding her reflection in the mirror. Instead, she watched the water hit the steel drain stopper, a shallow pool forming. When she realized she was being wasteful, she turned off the faucet.

All this time. All this time, Hunter had feelings for Justin? Well, maybe not for him—not really. But feelings *about* him, certainly. Shelby tried to remember that last summer together. Not a single moment came to mind that suggested she should have somehow known Hunter had been interested in him. If she had, would it have changed anything? Maybe. She might not have risked a friendship for a guy. Shelby had been deeply attracted to Justin, but at the same time, she'd known on some level that any summer relationship would have its limits. As Doug said, timing was everything. That summer, her priority had been her writing career. It still was.

Shelby faced herself in the mirror. Then she walked back to the party.

Thirty-Six

By evening, Shelby was able to put her personal—and her past—firmly in the background. She had a book event to host: Claudia's new author was in town.

"This space looks even better than I imagined," Mia said.

They stood next to one another on the beach behind Land's End. Shelby agreed with her. They'd taken their decorating cues from Duke's successful backyard event for Anders. They borrowed folding chairs from the Lombardos, and set plush beach blankets alongside the aisles for potential overflow. They strung red, white, and blue twinkling lights on the stairs behind the shop and arranged the signing table between the store and the audience. A refreshment table was set with bottles of wine, water, and a covered cheese and fruit tray.

"Having this space makes a big difference," Mia said. "My brother really delivered." The tone of her voice was incredulous.

"Does that surprise you?" Shelby said. It didn't surprise her. Justin didn't say something if he didn't mean it. She'd known this early in their relationship. That was why when he'd said he could never live anywhere but Ptown, she believed him. As she'd meant it when she said she would be moving to New York City.

How could Hunter judge her so harshly?

Well, she wasn't going to make things worse by being hard on herself. She had a lot going on, and she was managing to keep all the balls in the air, including running Land's End and staying on track to meet her book deadline.

"Mia, no pressure, but have you read any of my manuscript? I'd love to hear your thoughts."

Mia's rubbed the back of her neck. "It's getting hot out here. I'm going inside."

Shelby tensed, certain now that Mia had read it and didn't like it. She followed her back into the store. They both walked to the front counter, where Mia made herself busy checking the hold shelf.

"It's okay if you don't like it," Shelby said. "I want to hear what's not working so I can improve it. I didn't give it to you for you to tell me how great it is, or anything like that."

Mia shook her head, her dark curls falling into her face. Still, Shelby could see the flush that was creeping up her neck to her cheeks.

"I haven't read it," she said.

Shelby gave a wave. "Okay, don't worry about it. Really. We're all busy."

"I want to read it. But I can't," Mia said.

"Oh. You mean… I don't understand."

"I can't read."

"Very funny. You've read more books than I have this summer."

"I've *listened* to more books. Audiobooks."

Shelby froze. The headphones. The constant headphones.

"I love stories," Mia said quickly. "I like talking to readers. I like matching people with the right book. But…"

Shelby pressed her fingers to her temples. "Wait. You shelve books. You log inventory. What do you mean, you can't read?"

Mia tugged on a lock of her hair. "I can read individual words.

Names. A sentence. But I can't read paragraphs, hold it in my mind, and then add another paragraph to it. I can't process a narrative in written form."

Shelby leaned against the counter.

"Do your parents know?" She thought of Carmen's visit a few weeks ago. She thought about Mia's attitude towards school. It all made sense.

"When I was younger it was obvious there were delays or whatever. My mother got so upset, and the tutors didn't help, and so to make everyone happy I started pretending the extra help worked—just to get them to stop worrying about it. I thought it would get better, but it didn't."

Shelby reached out and hugged her, feeling terrible.

"You could talk to your brother," Shelby said, feeling Mia's slender small frame tremble. "He's good at finding solutions. That scientific mind, you know."

"No!" she said, pulling away. "And you have to swear you won't tell him."

Shelby hesitated. "I'm not sure I can do that."

"Why? You're not together anymore. And we're friends. So why would you choose him over me? Please, swear," she said, getting worked up again.

Shelby couldn't bring herself to make such a promise. Her mind raced, retracing the time she'd spent with Mia in the shop. She realized she might have created false memories of Mia reading books when she had, in fact, never seen her hold an actual open book.

Before she could say anything, Ezra Randall walked in with their guest author for the evening.

The reading began late. So many people showed up that Shelby had to bring out more chairs. The one person who couldn't make it was Colleen; she was exhausted after the shower. She texted Shelby, No worries: I couldn't imagine a better reason to be tired and miss the reading—I loved it. Thank u!!!!

Shelby sat in the front row between Pam and Annie. She saved a seat for Anders, and he made it just before the reading started. Dressed in a lightweight seersucker blazer and a pale blue button-down, he looked every bit the distinguished, award-winning novelist.

Anders leaned in and kissed her. "Since your part-timer is here, and the store owners, maybe you'll be able to slip away a little early?"

Anders's friends from London, married literary critics Mimi and George Oaks, were in town for the week and hosting a big party. When Anders invited her, she said, "I didn't think British people celebrate the Fourth of July. Considering…"

"Oh, it's not a Fourth of July party," he said. "It's sort of a… salon. For us expats here for the summer—and the Americans who tolerate us." He'd winked.

It had sounded like fun at the time. But now she wished she hadn't committed. She wanted to find a minute alone with Mia. She still couldn't process what she'd just told her, and wished they hadn't been interrupted. Terrible timing.

"I don't know how soon I'll be able to leave," she said, looking around at the growing crowd. "I think this might go awhile. We could just stay here, then grab something to eat on our way to the fireworks?"

He smiled appreciatively, as if she'd said something clever. Then his expression straightened, and he said, "Oh…you're serious."

"Well…yeah," she said. Anders glanced behind them, probably plotting his escape, she thought. "Look, I don't want to keep you here if your friends are expecting you. Why don't you go to the party, then meet me at the pier later for fireworks?"

He was visibly relieved. "Brilliant." And she thought, how

easy it was to have a relationship with a man who was secure enough in his own life to allow her to have her own.

They faced the bay, and the sunlight played on the water like a painting. The author, holding a copy of her book in front of her, looked like someone staged in a stock photo. It made her wish Anders had been to one of her own events, and she realized it wasn't too late: she could invite him to go with her to Boston.

Pam leaned in close and whispered, "We've had our doubts about the store, what with Colleen on bed rest and all. But you've really come through, Shelby." She squeezed her arm.

She exhaled. She thought about what Doug had said earlier that day, about timing and life and things not always going according to plan. When *Secrets of Summer* had published two months ago, she never imagined where the summer would lead. And that day at lunch with Claudia, she'd wondered if she'd ever get to the finish line with the new novel. And now she'd almost finished a draft. In fact, she hoped to be done before she went to her next book event. That way, she and Claudia could meet in person to discuss the manuscript.

Thinking of Claudia, Shelby snapped a photo of the author reading from her opening, then turned around to get one of the packed audience. Texting it to Claudia, she had an idea to send it to one more person—someone at least partly responsible for the successful event.

She typed up a text, then erased it. She started again: Thanks for your help with the beach. Annie and Pam are really happy. She attached the photo, and before she could change her mind, sent it to Justin.

Thirty-Seven

Hunter heard about the literary critics' Fourth of July party from two other students in Anders's class. They gossiped about it, whispering about who would be there—mentioning half a dozen writers Hunter would love to meet. She decided she'd go. In her experience, Ptown had a fairly open-door policy when it came to most holiday parties. She was willing to bet that was the case for this one.

Hunter stood in front of her mother's walk-in closet. She felt like she'd exhausted her own wardrobe already. Surrounded by racks of her mother's clothes, Hunter missed her parents for the first time in a while. She spoke to them once a week or so, but only in a superficial way. They didn't ask about her job or her life because they assumed she was fine. As long as there was money in the bank, what could be wrong? It seemed to be true for them. But Hunter always felt something nagging at her. Something missing.

She found a Dolce & Gabbana embroidered silk corset top that would look amazing with jeans. She pulled off her T-shirt, dropped it to the floor, and slipped the straps over her shoulders. Reaching around to zip it up, she assessed it in the full-length mirror.

Her phone buzzed. She walked over to where she'd left it on her parents' bed. It was a text from the agency guy, the one she'd hooked up with after Shelby's reading at the Red Inn. Hunter smiled—so random. She'd actually thought about him just a few days ago. But tonight, she was big game hunting: Anders Fleming would be at the party.

She ignored the text.

Justin's phone pinged. He hoped it was Kate saying she was on her way. She'd insisted on keeping the store open late that night in a way that seemed almost spiteful. He just wasn't sure who the spite was directed towards—himself or her father.

After Martin shamed her into staying in Provincetown to take care of business instead of spending July Fourth in Boston, Kate didn't bring up the holiday again. When Justin reminded her of his parents' dinner party at the restaurant, she said she was working late.

"I'm not going to stay in Ptown for the store, and then not work at the store," she'd said, as if it were the most obvious thing in the world. Maybe it was. It had just surprised him. But they made plans to meet up for dinner and go to the fireworks. So really, there was plenty of time left in the night to celebrate.

But the text wasn't from Kate. Shelby sent a photo of a packed book event on the beach.

He'd done the right thing. And he was glad his mother had nudged him. It wasn't any of her business, but that had never stopped her before and—as she herself admitted—probably never would. Some things didn't change, and that was a beautiful thing. Wasn't his entire job, in some ways, about fighting change? As his father always said, "There's a difference between change and progress."

He peered down the table at his smiling parents; a three-decade wedding anniversary was a small miracle. How did two people ever make it work for so long?

The music piped outside was what his parents referred to as "yacht rock." Sappy songs from when they'd been kids from bands with names like Air Supply and Chicago. Votives flickered on the tabletops around them, and Mia had strung paper lanterns, along with a banner reading Happy Anniversary!

"Where *is* Mia?" one of his aunts asked his mother.

"Working at the bookshop," Carmen said proudly. Justin knew that even though his parents had given Mia a hard time about the restaurant, he suspected his mother secretly saw Mia's interest in the bookstore as a good sign. It took the sting out of all her complaints about college. How could someone who loved books that much not want to continue their education?

After dinner, his mother brought out a triple-layer chocolate cake topped with chocolate ganache. She'd been baking the cake every Fourth of July since her wedding day.

"Remember you and your sister used to fight over who got to eat the icing flowers?" His mother leaned over with the cake knife and sliced a piece with a fat, fluffy bloom of icing on top. "Speaking of your sister—I'm bringing her a piece."

"Bringing it to her…where?"

"The bookstore," she said. "It's bad luck if she doesn't have a bite."

His mother always laughed at his grandmother—her own mother—for such superstitions. Carmen didn't see that the older she got, the more often she said the same sort of irrational things as if they were scientific fact.

"Mom, it's not bad luck. And there's a reading there tonight—a party. That's why Mia's not here in the first place. You can't just bring over a random piece of cake."

He wondered how many glasses of wine she'd had. His father had kept them coming, all the best reds. Justin might have had one too many himself.

"It's not a *random* piece of cake," Carmen said. "It's our anniversary cake. Besides, I want to see Annie and Pam. You should come say hello, too."

Justin started to say no, but then he realized he had another hour or two before Kate closed the shop and was able to meet up with him. He looked at the photo Shelby sent him again.

Why not?

Thirty-Eight

Hunter, feeling out of place, wandered around the party. The house was a cozy, gray-shingled cottage, but it didn't feel like a Ptown crowd, and it certainly wasn't welcoming. The hostess, dressed in all black, chain-smoked on the back deck while inside, people huddled in tight little groups.

She walked around the living room in one final loop before conceding the party was a total fail. She'd made a mistake not answering Ezra Randall's text. Just as she was reconsidering her strategy for the night, she crossed paths with Anders.

"Hunter! What a surprise." He was dressed in a casual blazer and dark pants, holding an amber-colored drink in one hand and a cigarette in the other. When he kissed her cheek, the scent of Scotch and smoke made her want to pull him into the bedroom right then and there. "I'm headed to the bar. Come."

After claiming two glasses of wine, they found a quiet corner.

"This doesn't feel like a bookish crowd," Hunter said.

"Well, Mimi's from Berlin," he said, as if that explained it. Which, maybe it did. Hunter really had to get out of Massachusetts more often. She surveyed the room, recognizing a few notable authors but deciding most of the people just looked like she *should* know who they were. Anders took her on a loop and generously introduced her to people whose names she knew from title pages and bylines and screen credits, until she finally noticed a familiar face.

"That's Kate Hendrik," Hunter said, relieved to finally be able to point someone out to *him*. "She owns the new bookshop in town."

He nodded and swept his hand out in front of them as if to say, *Lead the way.*

"Oh—you mean…introduce you?" Hunter had only spoken to Kate a few times, once at the Bollard at the start of the summer when she'd been with Justin, and then the night of Anders's book reading. She looked elegant, dressed in a white linen dress and black ballet flats, her straight hair tucked behind one ear. "Okay. Sure."

They approached Kate and it was clear she immediately recognized Anders, but not Hunter, which was embarrassing since Hunter was supposedly making the introduction.

"Anders Fleming," Kate said, extending her hand. "I've been looking forward to meeting you."

"The pleasure is all mine," he said.

"I was at your book reading a few weeks ago but didn't get a chance to say hello."

Probably because Shelby whisked him away to dinner, Hunter thought. She wondered if Anders and Shelby had spent more time together, but doubted it. Colleen said Shelby was hunkered down like a hermit writing a new book.

"I heard you're teaching a semester in Boston this fall," Kate said.

"That's right," Anders said, smiling. "And speaking of Boston, I remember visiting the original Hendrik's on my first book tour. It was a highlight of my year."

Hunter cleared her throat, and interjected with "Good to

see you again, Kate." Kate turned, her eyes flickering with recognition but clearly not placing her. "I'm friends with Justin," she added.

At the mention of his name, Kate consulted the slim Cartier watch on her wrist. It was yellow gold on a black snakeskin band. "I actually need to excuse myself. I stopped by to say hello to Mimi, but I'm meeting Justin at the fireworks. And I'm late as it is. Hunter, nice to see you again. And Anders—we'd love to have you come into the shop and sign some books."

"Anytime," he said, smiling.

Hunter was not sorry to see her go. The big bay windows displayed the sun beginning to set over the ocean.

"I'll be right back," Anders said before slipping away in the crowd. Hunter hugged her arms in front of herself, feeling suddenly alone and out of place and thinking maybe she should just go to the fireworks. But then Anders reappeared, holding two flutes and a bottle of champagne.

"Shall we venture down to the beach? I could use some fresh air."

Shelby poured herself a cup of red sangria and watched Mia opening copies of the book to the title page, making sure the signing line moved efficiently. What was she going to do? Telling Carmen Mia's secret would be a betrayal of Mia's confidence. But Carmen already knew something was wrong. In a way, she'd made a promise to Carmen first—that if she learned what might be bothering Mia, she'd let her know. Well, tonight's little bombshell more than qualified.

"Now *this* is what I call a great use of beach space."

She turned around. Justin was unusually dressed up, wearing a powder blue oxford shirt and khaki pants. Carmen was close behind, carrying a plate covered with aluminum foil and making a beeline for Mia. "My mother felt compelled to bring Mia a piece of anniversary cake. There was no reasoning with her," he said with a shake of his head.

That was right: it was his parents' anniversary. That summer they'd been together, they'd included her in the big dinner party in the restaurant's outdoor space. There'd been two long tables covered with white cloth. She had a vivid memory of how, by the end of the night, they were splattered with red wine stains. She'd contributed to the mess after knocking over her own glass. The Lombardos didn't bat an eye and simply offered her a refill. When the first firework cracked in the sky above, Justin squeezed her hand under the table.

She felt a lump in her throat.

"Well, I'm glad you're here to see for yourself," she managed to say.

"Me, too," he said, giving her a smile. She thought about Hunter's recrimination earlier that day. If even part of what she'd said were true, then she owed Justin an apology.

"Justin, this might sound out of the blue. But I've been thinking and I just wanted to say, I'm sorry about the way I handled things three years ago. I think I was just so focused on what was ahead of me, I didn't give enough respect to…what we had."

His smile faded and his dark eyes registered something she couldn't decipher. He seemed almost angry for a second, but it was so fleeting she might have imagined it. Or misread it.

"It was a long time ago, Shelby," he said, looking into her eyes.

"Oh, I know. I'm not suggesting that it's on your radar or anything. I just felt…it needed to be said." She smiled to lighten the mood, to show it wasn't a big deal.

"I'm with Kate now, and it's good," he said.

"Of course. And I'm happy for you." See, all the drama was a product of Hunter's imagination. Justin wasn't thinking about the past.

And neither was she.

Thirty-Nine

The beach behind the party house was pebbly and framed with untamed shrubs. Hunter wished they had a blanket or something to keep the sand off her favorite Mother jeans.

The sunset was a vivid mural of pink and gold. Beside her, Anders uncorked their second bottle of champagne. From their spot on the sand, they were near enough to the party that they could still faintly hear the music, and every once in a while another guest or two would pass by and they'd say hello. But the people always moved on, leaving Hunter and Anders alone.

"What are you thinking?" he said, his words sliding together in a way that suggested they should maybe slow down on the champagne.

"I'm not sure I should tell you," she said, smiling.

"Why not? We're friends, right? Please…speak freely." He gestured expansively with both hands.

"I was just thinking that it's not fair. You're a brilliant writer *and* extremely hot."

He didn't respond, and for a few seconds she thought she'd weirded him out. But then he leaned forward and kissed her.

She'd never hooked up with someone ten years older, and she'd never been with anyone famous.

Anders pulled back. "I'm sorry," he said, a little breathless.

"Don't be," she said. She leaned in and kissed him, and he put his hand gently on the back of her neck before stopping again. "What's wrong?"

"We're still on the beach, you know."

Hunter was confused. "Yeah, of course I know."

He laughed. "Well, okay. I must be getting old because I prefer this sort of thing to be a bit more discreet."

"So let's go to your place," Hunter said.

He hesitated. "You're in my class."

She smiled. "I've been meaning to drop it."

He nodded. "I'm sorry to hear that."

"Are you?"

"No," he said, kissing her again before standing up and holding out his hand. "Not at all."

The book party showed no signs of disbanding until Pam and Annie said their goodbyes. Then everyone realized it was getting dark and headed to MacMillan Pier as one big group.

The air smelled sweet, like cotton candy and salt and beer. Or maybe it was Shelby's clothes. The street was electric, full of people young and old decked out in Independence Day red, white, and blue. Some had painted faces, some wore costumes, and everyone streamed towards the dock.

When they reached the pier, it was so crowded that the group had to break apart. Shelby ended up with Mia, Duke, and Justin. They all chatted comfortably until Mia left to meet up with her friends. Then Max found Duke and they wandered off.

When it was just the two of them left, Justin checked his phone. She did the same, wondering what was taking Anders so long.

"Is Kate around this weekend?" she said.

"Yeah. She's supposed to meet me," he said. "I'm actually surprised she's not here yet." He looked around.

"I'm sure she'll be here soon," she said, realizing immediately it was an absurd thing for her to say. How could she possibly be sure of that?

A spot opened on the nearest bench, and Justin moved quickly to claim it, waving her over. "Plenty of space," he said, gesturing to the few inches on the edge of the bench. She hesitated for a second, but then didn't want it to seem like she was uncomfortable sitting next to him.

But when their thighs touched, Shelby felt the contact ripple through her body. She inched away just shy of slipping off the bench. She sent a text to Anders to check in.

He messaged her back: I don't think I can get away from the party. Networking, all that. Enjoy your eve and let's connect tomorrow.

"Great turnout tonight," Justin said. "At Land's End, I mean."

She looked up. "Yes," she said. "It was." She glanced over at him. A lock of hair fell across his forehead from the breeze, and she had the urge to reach out and brush it back. He caught her gaze, and stared back.

"Found you!"

Shelby turned around to find Kate Hendrik a few feet behind her. She jumped up, forcing a smile on her face. Justin walked over to Kate, hugged her, and the two of them kissed with a deep intimacy that made Shelby uncomfortable.

Kate smoothed the hair from his forehead.

"Well, happy Fourth!" Shelby said with a cheer that felt grotesque. She walked away towards a dense part of the crowd, wanting to get lost. A firework burst into the sky, and she stopped to look up at the giant stars forming in blues and purples and gold. And then another—a smattering of red hearts. They peaked, then dissolved, disappearing from the sky like they were never there.

Forty

After a sleepless night, Shelby realized she should have just left Land's End with Anders when he suggested it. Then she would have avoided that weird moment at the pier when she felt something for Justin.

But in the light of day, she knew the longing she'd experienced was just old habit—emotional muscle memory. And it made sense; she'd never given herself time to grieve the relationship. She'd left and never looked back. How could she have expected to see him for the first summer since then and feel nothing? It was unrealistic.

She checked her phone for any word from Anders, but nothing. Maybe that was what it was with an older man: fewer texts, more phone calls. Less interest in fireworks, more interest in cocktail parties. She should have been a grownup last night instead of acting like a nostalgic baby. So, she did what a mature, grown-up person did and got herself dressed, picked up two take-out cups of coffee, and walked over to Anders's house. She knew as soon as she saw him, all thoughts of last night would disappear.

★ ★ ★

Hunter woke up next to Anders with one thought: that she'd had sex with one of the great literary voices of her generation. Well, of his generation.

The bedroom was awash in greens of every imaginable hue, a perfectly balanced yet imaginative palette. One of the things she loved about the town was that the interiors of even modest-looking homes often had an astonishing visual touch. She felt like she was on a film set. It was one of those perfect moments she wished she could post, but doubted Anders would appreciate that.

The doorbell rang. Anders sat up slowly, running his hand through his hair and looking around as if he wasn't quite sure where he was.

"It's bloody early for a visitor, wouldn't you say?"

Hunter assumed it was a rhetorical question. He reached for his phone on the nightstand.

"Shit!" he said.

Hunter rolled towards him. "What is it?"

"Don't mean to be rude—sincerely apologize. But you need to leave. I'm going to answer that door, bring my guest out back to the patio, and then you slip out the front."

Hmm. This was sketchy—to say the least. Was there a girl-friend in the picture?

Hunter didn't mind. If she wanted to lounge around in bed all morning with someone, she'd find herself a boyfriend. Still, she had to admit she was a little curious about the mystery lady.

Maybe after she left, she could sneak around back for a little peek.

It took a few rings of the doorbell, but when Anders finally opened the door it was with a big smile and a kiss. She didn't realize she'd woken him until she followed him in and noted that his white T-shirt and rumpled khaki pants had clearly just been pulled on.

"I'm so sorry," she said sheepishly. "I wanted to surprise you." Mission accomplished, clearly. She walked inside and he took the coffees from her.

"And I'm so glad you did. Come, let's sit out back on the veranda."

In the kitchen, before they reached the back door, he said, "You go out and relax. I'll bring out some croissants."

He ushered her to the porch before she could offer to help.

Settling onto the couch in the same spot where she'd sat the other night, she inhaled deeply, glad she'd had the sense to stop by. Any uncomfortable feelings she had last night were already fading, no more significant than the fireworks show. A burst of color, a loud boom, but not real. Not real at all.

The hydrangeas to her left between Anders's yard and his neighbor's rustled loudly. She turned to look.

"Thanks for your patience." Anders appeared, holding a tray of pastries and having changed into a fresh shirt, linen pants, and boat shoes. He hadn't taken the time to shave his morning stubble, and she was glad. The contrast between his proper clothes and a weariness in his eyes that suggested an evening of debauchery was kind of sexy.

"Late night?" she said.

"Let's just say you were quite brilliant to skip the party. Not worth the loss of sleep."

"Well, you didn't miss anything at the fireworks," she said.

"Excellent. Let's agree to not miss anything together next time."

He kissed her, and she felt worlds better than she had an hour earlier.

"I wanted to ask you something," she said. "I'm going to Boston in two weeks to speak at the Arts Club. Would you like to come?"

He reached for her hand. "As your date? I wouldn't miss it," he said.

Shelby leaned closer to him. Everything was better already.

Forty-One

Hunter's sun hat blew off her head and into her parents' oval pool. She put down the manuscript she was reading and ran after it, using the long net to pull it back out.

She'd finally found a compelling novel in Duke's slush pile, and she was too damn distracted to focus. Oh, how she wished she hadn't sneaked around to Anders's neighbor's yard to spy on his early-morning visitor. Whoever said "Ignorance is bliss" knew what they were talking about: Anders was hooking up with *Shelby*? At first, Hunter indulged in a bit of denial: Shelby had simply shown up to discuss something bookshop related. Or a writing issue. But by the time she reached home, Hunter accepted that there was only one plausible explanation: Shelby and Anders were involved.

How could Hunter not know that? *Easily*, she told herself. It was easy not to know.

She'd been too busy keeping her distance from her old friend. And now look what she'd done.

She felt a little queasy. And it wasn't because she wanted Anders for herself. Hunter was fine with "one and done." But she'd gotten so comfortable being angry with Shelby, standing on her moral high ground about the book, that she didn't see herself making a huge stumble. Whatever Shelby had done to offend her, it was arguably not as bad as what Hunter had done last night. Shelby probably wouldn't believe her that it had been an accident—that she hadn't known about the two of them.

Forget about it, she told herself. There was nothing to do about it now. She'd pretend it never happened. Put that one in the vault and move on.

She settled back in the shaded lounge chair and tried to pick up where she left off with the manuscript. It was a domestic thriller with an unreliable narrator, and she couldn't stop turning the pages. Halfway through, she'd already read enough to know she was going to discuss it with Duke. She wanted to contact the writer and offer to publish her at Seaport Press. It was the first time since she started the job that she'd felt that way about a novel.

Her phone buzzed with an incoming text: Any chance you're free for dinner? My last night here...

It was Ezra. The agency assistant. She had to give the guy points for persistence. Shaking her head, she turned to the next page of the manuscript. And then, the relentless intruding thought: *It's bloody early for a visitor, wouldn't you say...*

She had to do something to forget about last night. Hunter put down the manuscript, reached for her phone, and texted back that she was, in fact, free for dinner.

Ezra Randall was exactly the distraction she needed.

Carmen was surrounded by her family on the sailboat, yet somehow felt alone. Justin and Kate stood together on the bow, and Carmen tried to reconcile it with last night.

Maybe no one else noticed, but she could tell he had his eyes on Shelby the whole time they were at Land's End. And when the party moved to the fireworks, he'd fallen to the back of the group in step with her. That was when Carmen lost sight of him, until hours later when she and Bert ran into Justin and Kate at Spiritus Pizza.

"Pull towards me," Bert called out to Mia. She watched Mia help trim the sails to adjust to the sudden wind. With her curls tousled, no makeup on her face, and the flush in her cheeks, Mia seemed closer to twelve than seventeen. Maybe part of the reason why Carmen was so anxious about her disinterest in college was deep down, she didn't want her to leave. She wondered if, in some way, Mia picked up on that. Internalized it. It was Carmen's job to push her a little—to reassure Mia that college was a natural life progression and should be embraced.

The wind lifted Carmen's sun hat, and she flipped her arms up to hold on to it. The thermos by her feet toppled over.

"Is the weather turning?" she called out.

"A storm system changed direction," Justin said, looking at his phone. "I just got an alert from work." He turned to Kate. "If you're going to Boston, you should go tonight instead of tomorrow."

Bert said something to Mia, but a gust made it hard to hear. She stepped down from the controls and walked to the back of the boat towards Carmen.

"Dad said to go belowdecks," Mia said.

Carmen didn't like the sudden turn in the weather, but she didn't mind having Mia in a spot where she couldn't run away from a conversation.

Last night, Carmen witnessed the contrast between "bookstore Mia" and "home Mia." She'd barely recognized the enthusiastic, confident young woman sitting next to the author, handing her books turned to the right page for signing. Writing down names on Post-its so the author knew how to personalize the copies. Refilling the pitchers of sangria, handing out napkins, folding and unfolding chairs. Taking direction from Shelby, but also showing initiative. Why couldn't she apply herself like that to school?

Carmen filed in behind Mia, taking the steps down to the

cabin. While Bert never involved himself much in their home decor, he'd painstakingly refurbished the interior of the boat, replacing the original paneling with fresh teak, updating the sleeper sofa cushions with modern, marine-grade upholstery that could endure exposure to the elements, and adding brass portholes. Carmen's minor contributions included nautical-themed needle-point pillows handsewn by Annie Miller, and a framed compass rose mosaic.

She turned on the overhead LED lights and opened the fridge in the small galley for a thermos of iced coffee. "You did a great job last night," Carmen said, taking a sip and passing it to Mia.

"Thanks," Mia said, fiddling with the cap.

"I know you love it. And you're good at it. And someday, you can work at a bookstore full-time or own your own bookstore—whatever you want. But you're seventeen years old, and the priority right now is college applications. You need to do something proactive—test prep, decide on your essay topic, start a list of where you're applying."

"There's time for that even if I wanted to go to college, which I don't."

"Well, you *are* going to college. And if you don't start making some effort in that direction, we're going to have to reconsider the hours you're working at the bookstore."

Mia jumped up. "You can't tell me when I can and can't work."

Carmen shook her head. "If you were being responsible about your future, I wouldn't have to." She saw Mia shutting down, the glazed look in her brown eyes, like she was looking at her but not seeing her. It was so infuriating, she wanted to shake her. Mia walked away and took the stairs back up to the deck. Carmen resisted the urge to run after her. It wasn't safe for things to escalate on the boat, in that wind. But enough was enough.

If she had to take away the bookstore job to make her understand how serious she was about college, she'd do it.

Forty-Two

Hunter hadn't been back to the Red Inn since the night of Shelby's book event at the beginning of the summer, and she'd preferred not to think about that. Making her even more uncomfortable was that it was unquestionably a "date" place. Right on the water, with a view of the Long Point lighthouse, it was one of the most romantic spots in town—especially at sunset.

When Ezra invited her out, Hunter had been thinking more along the lines of lobster rolls or tacos.

The restaurant host led them through the dining room to the deck. The barroom was full and lively, with sounds of corks popping and live jazz music. Now that she was there, she was glad she'd made an effort getting dressed. She'd thought carefully about what to wear, aiming for a look that said "friends with benefits"—though she was mostly interested in the benefits. She decided on black skinny jeans, a lace tank, and her silver Tiffany padlock pendant necklace. The look in his eyes when he picked her up had been worth the extra thought. He was hotter than she remembered.

When they reached their table, Ezra said, "This is the first place I saw you."

She looked at him in surprise. It was true, and also a remarkably romantic thing to say.

"Don't tell me that's why you picked this place."

"Actually, I'm staying at the hotel here. I've been wanting to try the restaurant, but it seemed like kind of a sad place to eat alone."

It was expensive to stay at the Red Inn. She wondered if his company paid for the room. No one could afford that place on an assistant's salary. She didn't care if he had family money, except that it neutralized the complicated feelings she had about her own.

After the server brought a bottle of wine, Ezra said, "I was hoping you'd be at the Land's End book reading."

"No offense, but there were a lot more interesting things to do on the Fourth of July."

He frowned. "As an editor, I wouldn't admit that on your next job interview."

She laughed. "Fair enough."

His sexy dark eyes locked on to hers. She was so glad she'd accepted his invitation.

"How's the job search going, by the way?" he said.

She shrugged. "Slow. There aren't that many positions in Boston, which is where I'm looking."

"Are you sure you want to be an editor and not an agent?"

She looked at him quizzically. "Yeah. I mean, I think so. I never thought about being an agent. I've been in editorial for three years."

He nodded. "Just asking because there are agencies all over the place, but the major publishers are still primarily in New York."

"I've been applying for remote positions," she said. But maybe that was holding her back. She hadn't gotten called for a single interview. But if she switched to the agency side instead of the publishing side, three years paying her dues as an editorial assistant would be a waste—not in terms of experience, but in terms of her place in the office pecking order. It would be starting over.

"Well, one bit of advice: don't work for Claudia Linden."

"Oh?" Interesting. It was the last place she'd want to send her résumé. She couldn't imagine anything more demeaning than working as an assistant for Shelby's agent. Still, she was surprised by his hot take. "Well, she's good at what she does. Great at it."

He nodded. "She is. But she could probably have the same level of success without being a nightmare of a person."

Hunter tried to remember if Shelby ever said anything negative about her, certain she hadn't. Maybe her abrasiveness was only something Claudia revealed to her staff, or the editors she negotiated with. She imagined writers wanted an agent who was a little scary. Really, if she managed her career right, in twenty years, her assistant would be saying the same thing about her. "Do you know anyone in Boston?"

He seemed to consider the question. "I'll think about it. But why not New York?"

She shrugged. "Boston's in my blood, I guess."

"But the idea of you moving to New York gives me much more incentive to start asking around." He smiled coyly. There was a small gap between his front teeth that she found sexy and her eyes lingered on his mouth.

"Ezra," she said. "That is very sweet. But I told you, I don't do relationships."

"That's right. You did mention that. So…what then? Just friends?"

She tilted her head. She meant just sex.

"Um, sure?" Was he testing her? His attitude was confusing. Most guys were perfectly fine with keeping things purely physical.

Ezra refilled her glass of wine and then his own. The waiter appeared with their appetizer of panko-crusted shrimp. After he slipped away, Ezra leaned forward and said, "Can you keep a secret?"

"I can." She held her seafood fork and offered him a flirtatious look, head cocked, chin down, peeking out from underneath her lashes.

"You can't say anything to Shelby," he said.

"Oh?" Well, after what happened last night, what was one more secret? "Okay. Sure. I'm a vault."

"I have a job offer from a different agency. I'm giving notice as soon as I get back to New York."

"What agency?"

"Paragon."

Paragon Literary Group was a thirty-year-old literary agency run out of a brownstone at Sixty-third and Lexington. It was legendary.

"I can check if there are any other openings when I get there," he offered.

"That's really generous," she said. He was starting to make her wish she was the type of woman who wanted a relationship. She knew there were a million of them out there who'd give a limb to have Ezra Randall's undivided attention.

So when he walked her home, kissed her on the cheek, and said, "Well, friend, I'll let you know if I hear of any jobs in the city. And at the very least, I'll hit you up if I'm ever in Boston," she was surprised by how much she hoped he meant it.

Forty-Three

Monday was slow at the bookshop. Outside, rain fell in dense needles, and the sky turned dark. Land's End hadn't seen a customer in hours. Mia paced in front of the windows, headphones on. And Shelby, standing at the counter with her laptop, typed the words *The End*—her favorite in the English language. At least, today they were.

She'd finished her first draft of *Bookshop Beach*.

Closing her laptop, she exhaled. Writing a novel was usually a marathon; this one had been a sprint. And it was challenging to write about Emily's illness without losing the upbeat tone of the book, but she felt that storyline was balanced out by the frenemies-to-lovers plot. And in the end, everyone got their happy ending: Emily's health stabilized and she had her bookshop. Jackson lost his shop but got something more important: the first genuine relationship of his life. Shelby felt, in many ways, it was a better book than her debut; Emily was a more sympathetic heroine, and the love story was more dramatic than the friendship arc in *Secrets of Summer*.

She wondered if she should reread the whole thing before

sending it to Claudia, and decided not to. She was sure Claudia would have notes, as she had for *Secrets of Summer*, and Shelby would comb through the manuscript again when she got it back from her. There was no reason to stall. She sent the email with a little tremor in her gut. The feeling, like the last time she'd handed in a book, was exhilarating and terrifying. And it felt like a weight had been lifted from her shoulders.

She looked up to see Mia sorting through the window display. Shelby was waiting for the right time to bring up her reading problem, feeling a lot of responsibility to get it right. With the store so dead and near closing time, it was as good a time as any.

"How's it going over there?" she called out. Mia didn't hear her. Shelby walked out from behind the counter and waved to get her attention. Mia pulled off her headphones. "Hey. You can go home. I'm going to close early." A clap of thunder made her jump.

"Home is the last place I want to be," Mia said, pulling the hood of her sweatshirt over her head.

"Okay," Shelby said, taking a breath. "Well, since we're here, I've been thinking a lot about what you told me—about the reading. I really appreciate that you confided in me. And if keeping it just between us was the best thing for you, I'd have no problem doing it. But I know it's not the right thing to do."

Mia's eyes widened. "You can't say anything. You promised!"

"Okay, okay, I won't," Shelby said, trying to walk it back a little. "But *you* should. Talk to your mother. Or even your brother. They can help you, and at the very least, they'll understand why you're avoiding college applications."

Mia shook her head. "You're wrong. They won't understand." Her eyes filled with tears. Shelby moved closer and put her arm around her.

"Sometimes, it's hard to have perspective when it's your own parents. But I know Carmen. All she wants is for you to be okay."

She was clearly unconvinced. "No—all she wants is for me to go to college. It's bad enough that I'm letting her down. I don't want her to freak out about the reading on top of it."

"I think you're underestimating her," Shelby said gently.

Mia shook her head vehemently, crossed her arms, shrank away from her. Shelby wanted to stop pushing, but knew she had to be the adult in the room.

"You can't hide this forever, Mia. It's going to catch up with you. It *has* caught up with you."

Mia pulled on the drawstrings of her hood. "No. It hasn't. I've been working here all summer and you never would have known if I hadn't told you. Just forget I said anything."

"I can't, Mia. One summer in a bookstore doesn't mean you have the tools you need to get through the rest of your life. That's why I need to tell you this. Whether you want to hear it or not." Her phone sounded with a shrill alarm. She glanced down: there was a flood alert.

"Saved by the bell," Mia said dully. The rain pelted the windows so hard it sounded like ice. They could no longer see across the street to the restaurant.

"I'm going to check that the back door is closed tight," she said, heading to the rear of the store. Before she reached it, her feet were soaked. "What the hell?"

Water was pouring inside like a scene out of *Titanic*.

"Mia!" she called out.

The books in the storage room were no doubt a lost cause. But they could start moving books off of low shelves and onto tabletops.

"This is bad," Mia said, standing behind her, but avoiding water line.

"Let's go—the hardcover shelves first." They rushed to the front of the store and started pulling books into their arms.

"We need help," Mia said. "I'll call Justin."

"No!" Shelby said sharply. "I mean, we've got this."

But Mia was right—they needed extra hands. She could call Doug, but she didn't want to leave Colleen alone in the storm. She was sure he wouldn't want to, either. Maybe Hunter? They hadn't spoken since their argument at the baby shower. Duke? Anders. She'd call Anders.

He didn't pick up the phone. She didn't bother sending a text. It was fine—she and Mia would manage.

Something loud crashed to the sidewalk outside the store.

"We *don't* have this," Mia said, pulling out her phone. "I'm calling my brother."

Justin adjusted his windshield wipers and plugged his phone into the charger. He pulled a flashlight from the glove compartment, and then texted his father to see if he needed help securing the restaurant.

He'd been tracking the storm since Sunday morning. It was going to be a southeaster, unlike recent storms that had pushed from the north to the west and built up around the breakwater. This one was going to hit different. How different—and how hard—they just didn't know. Last December, a storm had flooded dozens of basements and Bradford Street with three feet of water. It was the price of living at the water's edge. And for decades and decades, the trade-off for living among such natural beauty was well worth the risk of a storm every now and then. But the increase in storms, and the dramatic severity of storms, was changing the risk-reward calculation.

He thought about the havoc this storm was wreaking on the marshes, the tidal flats, the estuaries. It was going to be a long week.

He made his way down Route 6, traffic at a crawl. The rain picked up, reducing visibility. The headlights only seemed to make things worse.

His phone rang with a call from Mia.

"You okay?" he said.

"I'm fine, but Land's End is flooding. We need help saving some of these books."

His wipers flipped uselessly. He tried turning his headlights off, then on again. A text came in from his father: they wanted Mia to meet them at the restaurant, but she wasn't picking up her phone.

"Okay listen, Dad's trying to reach you. Go the restaurant right now, and I'll be at Land's End to help Shelby in a few minutes."

Mia protested, but he said if she didn't listen to their parents then he wasn't going to go to Land's End. Thankfully, she didn't call his bluff.

She agreed to go to the restaurant. He headed for the book-shop.

Forty-Four

Shelby considered texting Justin not to come, that she had it under control. It was utterly irrational, but she didn't want to deal with the awkwardness of being around him. She didn't know why she'd had confused feelings the night at the fireworks, and she didn't want to risk experiencing them again. But before she could contact him, Colleen called.

"Please tell me the shop is fine," Colleen said, her voice catching in her throat. Shelby looked around at the water pooling on the floor, the books piled onto every elevated surface.

"Don't stress," Shelby said. "I've got it under control."

She owed it to Colleen to do her best to save the store. She needed Justin's help.

When he arrived, a burst of thick, humid air and more water washed in with him. He was soaked, his blue all-weather jacket and a baseball cap useless against the torrent of water. His dark eyes were shining, and she could tell he was adrenalized. It gave her a renewed surge of energy and determination.

"Thanks so much for coming," she said.

"No problem. So what's the game plan?" he said, looking around.

"I'm just trying to get the books from the windows and the lower shelves to the tables."

He walked a loop around the store. When he finished, he asked, "Would you say the water level is rising since you first got here or holding steady?"

She looked down at her submerged ankles. "About the same. Do you think we'll lose electricity?" she asked.

"No way to tell." He turned his attention to the new-fiction section left of the entrance and ran his hand along the shelving. "But I have some bad news for you. There's water leaking from this wall, so it's not just the bottom shelves we have to worry about."

Justin walked another loop around the store while she pulled novels from the compromised wall. They were already wet. She felt a surge of frustration, and felt like a failure, like somehow this was her fault. The thought of telling Colleen how bad it was made her move more quickly, piling the damp books on top of dry ones, knowing that she was making things worse but afraid to stand still, unwilling to accept defeat.

With a crack of thunder, the lights flickered off and then on again. Outside, something heavy crashed up against the door, pushed there by water.

"Shelby," Justin said, appearing next to her. "It's not safe in here. We have to go."

She hesitated. "Maybe we can just—"

He shook his head impatiently. "You have to know when to cut your losses."

Of course. Hadn't she always? Letting go. Moving on. It was her specialty. Still, she hesitated. Seconds ticked by and the moment felt increasingly surreal, like the world outside the front door had disappeared and it was just the two of them. Dreamlike. Justin took a step towards her. The air felt charged, and the humidity and stress left her short of breath. Or maybe she was holding her breath. He put his hands on her shoulders, looking her in the eyes.

"Come on. Let's go."

Every cell in her body defied logic and instead urged her to stay. And she realized it wasn't about the books, or the store. It was about him.

The lights flickered again, then died.

That was it. They were out of time.

Forty-Five

Shelby woke up in Hunter's sun-filled guest room.

Last night, realizing she couldn't stay in the apartment above the store, she'd reluctantly called Hunter. Her only alternative was to sleep at Colleen's, and she didn't want to face the conversations about the storm damage. She needed some rest, a full reset, before she dealt with that dose of hard reality.

Hunter had been surprisingly welcoming. Before Shelby could even tell her the full story Hunter insisted she stay over. Buildings east of Commercial had been spared the worst of the storm.

When she was settled in the guest room, Hunter joined her for a chat, curling up in the walnut armchair and wrapping herself in a chenille blanket.

"I'm sure the Millers have insurance," Hunter said, seeing how worked up she was about the whole thing and trying to make her feel better. While there was nothing she could say to convince Shelby the storm wasn't a total disaster, she appreciated the effort.

Maybe their contentious conversation at the baby shower—as painful as it had been at the time—helped clear the air. Maybe

Hunter had just needed to get some things off her chest. It was impossible to know for sure. But something had changed. Something for the better.

"I put the coffee on," Hunter said, standing in the bedroom doorway on her way to work.

Shelby sat up in the queen-size platform bed. The guest room was all neutrals, with white walls dotted with framed black-and-white photos of seascapes. On the nightstand beside her, a moss green ceramic bowl from Simon Pearce was filled with white and gray stones from the beach. And from the window, there was a view of the Atlantic. She only wished she felt as tranquil as her surroundings looked.

"Thanks again for letting me crash here," Shelby said. "I'm sure I can go back to the apartment tonight." Outside, the sky was clear and blue. It was almost enough to make Shelby feel better about the situation: the shop would dry out. The books could be replaced. Her feelings for Justin would pass.

"No rush," Hunter said cheerily. She had a thick manuscript tucked in one arm and a stuffed tote over her shoulder. Shelby wished she could have confided in her last night about Justin, her uncomfortable, inconvenient desire, but she knew it was a sensitive topic. No matter how healed their friendship seemed to be, she'd never bring up Justin again.

When she left, Shelby turned on her phone and saw a bunch of missed calls: three from Pam Miller, and one from Colleen. Pam left a voicemail about engineers headed to the shop, and damage estimates, and a bunch of other things. She called her right back.

"Shelby," Pam said. "Colleen told me you did a good job getting to the store quickly, so thank you. Are you in the apartment?"

"No." She'd only spent a few minutes packing up her laptop and a change of clothes by the light of her phone. "It lost power. I slept at Hunter's."

"Okay. Engineers are heading over in an hour or two. You should probably go pack all your things. It could be a while before you can stay there."

Shelby looked around the room, running her hand through her hair. She hadn't anticipated that. "Of course. What else can I do?"

There was a pause.

"You've done what you can. And we appreciate it. Colleen does, too. But we've made the difficult decision not to reopen."

Shelby felt her stomach drop. "You mean…for the summer?"

There was a pause. "No," Pam said. "We're selling Land's End Books. It's time."

Shelby closed her eyes for a minute. "Pam, are you sure? I can help. Maybe there's a temporary space—"

"Annie and I have discussed all the options, and we feel this is the right decision."

"What about Colleen?" Shelby said.

Another pause. "She's taking it hard. But she'll be okay. She's got bigger things to think about right now."

When Shelby got off the call, she immediately dialed Colleen. It went straight to voicemail.

So that was it. She'd come to help with the bookstore, and it was a failure. Not her fault, but a failure all the same. Now what? She didn't have any reason to stay in town. Her book was written. Colleen, as Pam said, had bigger things to worry about. Really, that only left Anders. She'd take the trip with him to Boston, and then figure it out from there. She had mixed feelings, but mostly a sense of relief. She'd shown up for one friend, and mended things with two others. What more could she ask of one summer?

There was just one piece of business left. And she couldn't leave without taking care of it.

Hunter was anxious to get Duke's thoughts on the domestic thriller. She'd emailed him a copy and they were set to talk about it at the morning editorial meeting. But when she showed up at the office, Duke wasn't in a work frame of mind.

"I heard about the damage to Land's End," Duke said, dressed up in a pink-and-blue pin-striped button-down and navy linen pants. His face was sunburned, probably from a weekend out on the water. His blue eyes were especially bright and vivid. "Have you spoken to Shelby or Colleen?"

"Shelby stayed at my place last night," she said, unpacking her laptop on her desk. She set her creased copy of the manuscript pages beside it.

It felt good opening her home to Shelby. Of course, it didn't change the fact that she'd slept with Anders Fleming. But maybe that wasn't an issue after all; Shelby didn't mention him once. "I haven't spoken to Colleen, but I'm sure it will be fine. This house flooded once, right?"

He shook his head. "No, not a flood. Leaky roof."

Same difference. And she didn't want to waste time on weather-damage small talk.

"Did you get a chance to read the novel?" she said. She was eager to call the author of the thriller before someone else did.

He nodded, picked up the manuscript from his desk, and said, "Let's discuss."

They moved to the armchairs near the bookshelves where they had their editorial meetings. Hunter knew it was going to be good news. If he hadn't liked it, he would have just put it back on her desk with a Post-it note reading Pass.

She opened her laptop so she could take notes on his feedback. Duke had very good editorial instincts and, if she was being honest with herself, he reminded her she still had a lot to learn.

"You're right," he said. "It's very good. She's talented."

Hunter beamed with excitement. Okay—now they were getting somewhere! "I'm so glad you agree."

"But we can't publish her." He removed his reading glasses and rubbed his eyes.

"Why not? I mean, if she gets an offer from a major publisher and wants to go with them, fine. But there are lots of examples of great writers who made their debut with a small press. Donna Tartt published with the *Mississippi Review*."

He stretched out his legs. "I know. And stories like that were in the back of my mind when I started this little venture—"

"Great. So I'll reach out to her."

"No," he said.

"Duke, what's the problem? I'll do all the work. Let me take the lead on this. Just go for the ride. You can trust me."

Duke sighed and straightened up. "It's not about you. Or this book. It's bigger than that. I've been doing a lot of thinking. And soul-searching. I suppose I have for a while now. At any rate, I've come to the difficult decision to shut down the press."

Hunter leaned forward. "Excuse me?"

"I know, I know. It sounds like it's coming out of nowhere. But since spending so much time with Max, seeing how things work behind the scenes at Malaprop, I've realized a few things," he said. "One of them is that I'm never going to get the distribution I need."

"Don't say that."

"No, it's true. And it doesn't matter so much to me—I do it because I love it. But ultimately, it might not be fair to my authors."

"And what did Max say about this?" she said.

"He tried to talk me out of it." Duke crossed his arms.

Hunter stood up. She hadn't realized how seriously she took the summer job until that moment, learning it had an expiration date.

She shook her head. "This is a mistake," she said.

Duke smiled at her in a way that was almost paternal. "It's okay, Hunter. I'll be fine. And I know you never intended to stay on past the summer."

She bit her lip. Had it been that obvious? Had she seemed un-grateful? "I appreciated the job here. I liked it a lot."

"Let me rephrase that: I never thought you *should* stay here past the summer."

Hunter didn't know what to say. She had the urge to cling to her desk and ask for more time.

"Go on," Duke said. "Get out there. You found a great manu-script. That hasn't changed just because Seaport Press is closing."

He was right. But it did change her options for what she could do about it. She wasn't ready to go out on her own.

She almost wished she hadn't found it in the first place.

Forty-Six

Justin was on the beach shortly after sunrise. He'd gotten a call from his boss; in the wake of the storm, the Office of Emergency Management needed help assessing water quality and damage to the seagrass beds.

It was an early morning after a late night. He'd barely been able to get to sleep after trying to help Shelby at Land's End. He felt a connection between them, and it was unnerving. Hours later, alone in his bedroom, he wondered if she'd felt it, too.

Now, in the light of a new day, he wanted to stop thinking about her. And from what he could see of the driftwood- and seaweed-littered beach, he just might be busy enough to stop.

He waded into the bay and collected water samples to check for any contaminants that might have washed into the water and for any HABS—harmful algae blooms—that might threaten marine life. When he finished, he packed up his filled test tubes and drove his truck west for another sample area. By then, last night was all but forgotten.

Until his phone rang with a call from Shelby.

He considered sending it to voicemail, but made the split-second decision to just act normally. "Hey," he said, looking out at the jetty. It was over a mile, a distance spanned only by walking across slippery boulders. But at the other end, spectacular views and empty beaches rewarded adventurers who made the trek. Today, no one was attempting to traverse the uneven rocks. It was always that way after a storm; after a show of force, water temporarily lost some of its recreational appeal.

"Thanks again for your help," she said.

"No problem."

There was a pause. Then she said, "Can I talk to you in person for a few minutes? I'll meet you wherever."

The right answer—the rational answer—was to tell her no, he was working. But he was curious about what she might want to say. He hoped it was a second chance at the conversation she'd started on the Fourth of July, when she'd apologized to him. When she acknowledged what they'd once had. He hadn't been ready to have the conversation that night. Now, he felt differently. Maybe talking to her, really talking to her after all this time, might be exactly what he needed for closure.

"I'm at the West End breakwater," Justin said. She told him she'd be right over.

It was a fitting place for them to talk. During their summer together, he learned that she'd never walked the full length of the jetty. So he checked the tidal charts (every year, visitors made the mistake of crossing the breakwater only to find a high tide when they wanted to walk back) and picked a day to take her for the adventure. Along the way, she'd delighted at spotting quahogs, and even a starfish between two of the rocks. Terns flew overhead with fish dangling from their beaks. When they reached Wood End lighthouse on the other end of the breakwater, they found a secluded spot and, looking at the pure delight on her flushed face, he impulsively said, "I love you, Shelby." She told him she loved him, too. Three weeks later, she ended it.

He kept a lookout for her and spotted her walking from the

street towards the water, dressed in a gray Ptown sweatshirt and faded jeans, her long hair blowing in the breeze. He walked towards her and they met on the edge of Pilgrim's Landing Park.

"Hey," he said. "I don't have much time…"

"Of course—I get it. I wouldn't bother you if it wasn't important. It's about Mia."

She wanted to talk about his sister? He was confused. And disappointed. And in some ways, relieved. The connection between them last night had been in his imagination. Where it should remain.

Shelby faced him, framing her eyes with one hand against the sun even though she was wearing shades. He gestured towards one of the park benches, and they found partial shade. She sat and he remained standing.

"I know why she's pushing so hard against college," Shelby said.

"Oh?"

"Yeah. She told me that she can't read."

Justin pulled off his sunglasses. He sat down. "Can't read what?"

Shelby took a breath. "She can't read long passages and put the information together. She said she always struggled with reading, and at one point your parents knew and they were trying to address it with the school. Nothing worked but Mia pretended it did. She wanted the pressure off of herself and found coping mechanisms and…now she's at a point of no return, I guess. Or at least, that's how she feels."

"Jesus," he said, leaning back on the bench. "She told you all this?"

"Yeah," she said. "On the Fourth of July. But I didn't want to betray her confidence. I tried to convince her to talk to you or your mother. But she refuses, and I don't feel comfortable telling Carmen myself. It feels, somehow, like less of a betrayal to tell you. Maybe you can talk to Mia about it?"

He tipped his head back and closed his eyes. This explained so much. Still, it wasn't going to be easy to break the news to his parents. He straightened up.

"I don't know what to say except…thanks for telling me."

"You'll take it from here?" she said.

"Of course."

Shelby nodded. "Also, I tried calling Mia and can't reach her; Land's End isn't reopening. The Millers are going to sell."

He shook his head. He was sorry for the town, and he was certain his sister would take the news hard. Mia. What had she been thinking keeping the reading problem to herself?

"I'm sorry to hear that," he said. "This is a lot to take in."

She stood. "I know. I'm sorry to drop this on you today, but I'm heading back to New York soon."

He nodded, trying not to think about what he'd thought—hoped—she'd come to him to talk about. There was no point, now.

Once again, she was leaving.

He held out his hand. "It was good having you around again. Take care, Shelby."

Forty-Seven

Shelby organized her clothes in piles around Hunter's guest room, wondering how she seemed to have so much more than she thought she'd packed for the summer.

Picking up her belongings from Colleen's place made the sudden turn of events more real. The entire time, she felt a sinking feeling in her gut. She wasn't sure what was making her the most upset. To put things in perspective, she called Anders. But he sounded distant on the phone. When she told him she was staying at her friend Hunter's because of the storm damage, he didn't invite her to his place instead. It wasn't that she *wanted* to stay at his place. But if the situation had been reversed, she would have at least offered.

Although, now that she thought about it, maybe he was insulted she hadn't gone straight to his place during the storm. She briefly considered it, but didn't feel comfortable enough yet to show up like that. Maybe that had been a mistake.

"Are we still on for Boston next week?" she said. Before she went back to New York, she had her book reading at the Boston Arts Club.

"Wouldn't miss it. In fact, I reserved us a suite at the Four Seasons."

So maybe she was imagining things. Maybe she was projecting. *She* was the one spending too much time with her ex-boyfriend. She was the one who'd felt a disconcerting little pang when she said goodbye to Justin that afternoon. Anders hadn't done anything wrong.

And then there was Colleen; she hadn't answered any of her calls all day. Shelby stopped by Doug's apartment before meeting up with Justin, but no one answered the door. Colleen was no doubt devastated by her parents' decision. Shelby wanted to talk to her about it, but maybe it was best to give her some time. What could she really say, anyway? There was no silver lining to this.

She heard the back door slam shut. Hunter was home from work. She needed to talk to her.

"Hey," Shelby said, walking down the stairs.

"Hey." Hunter headed straight for one of the living rooms and sank onto a blue velvet Jonathan Adler lounge chair. Shelby followed, sitting on the nearby champagne-colored settee with pointed brass legs. The "second" living room was the least beachy room in the entire house. Maybe Hunter wasn't feeling the summer vibes today. She opened her tote bag and pulled out a thick manuscript, setting it on a coffee table.

"So, I have a book event in Boston in a few days," Shelby said. "I'd rather not go back to New York just to turn around again. Is it okay if I stay here until then?"

"Sure," Hunter said absently. She stared at the floor.

"Everything okay at work?"

"No," Hunter said, rubbing her left eye and smudging her already smudged smoky liner. "I read the most amazing novel over the weekend. I asked Duke to check it out and he agreed it's great. So I was like, let's try to publish it."

Shelby nodded. "Okay. That sounds good."

Hunter pulled a vape from her bag and took a hit. She shook her head on the exhale.

"Nope. He's shutting down Seaport Press. Game over."

Shutting down? Seaport was Duke's passion project. She'd never once heard him talk about *slowing* down, never mind *shutting* down.

"That's hard to believe. Did he give you a reason?"

Hunter sank back against the chair. "Distribution issues. I mean, I know the press operates on a small scale but isn't that part of the charm?"

Shelby sighed. "I don't know. Clearly, he doesn't think so. At least, not anymore. But Hunter, you're going to find a new job. And there are countless other manuscripts out there waiting to be discovered."

"Easy for you to say." Hunter leaned forward, elbows on her knees. "What if you lost your publisher, and I told you, well— there are plenty of other publishers out there."

Point taken. "I'm sorry. I get it. I do."

Hunter toyed with the gold hoop in her right ear. "I'm rethinking my whole career strategy. I've been talking to Ezra. Your agency guy."

Shelby leaned forward. "Ezra Randall? How do you know him?"

"We met the night of your book launch," Hunter said, as if it were obvious.

Shelby tried to remember seeing them together, but she was certain she hadn't.

"At the Red Inn?"

"Well, technically yes. But he was also at the Bollard after."

She smiled. She couldn't believe it. But also, it made perfect sense: Hunter was Ezra's mystery woman. "Why didn't you ever mention it?"

"There was nothing to mention until now. So, we were talking and he had the crazy-slash-genius idea that I should become an agent."

"Okay, give me a minute here." She was still processing the fact that Hunter and Ezra had somehow been together and she'd had no idea. "Wait, so how often do you see him?"

Hunter shook her head. "I'm not seeing him. It was a one-time thing and now we're friends. The point is, he gave me the idea to look for an agency position. I'd be able to cast a wider net for a new job. What do you think?"

Shelby considered it. Hunter could make a good agent. She was an astute reader, a fast reader, a decisive reader. She knew the market, she had contacts, and she had three years' editorial experience. She was a workaholic—always had been. She had strong opinions and would be a fierce advocate for any project she believed in.

Her phone rang. It was Colleen.

"Sorry, I have to take this," Shelby said. "I've been trying to reach Colleen all day." She picked up the call and heard sobs on the other end. Of course. The loss of the store was devastating.

"Hi, Colleen. I'm so sorry. I know it's a loss. I feel terrible—"

"It's not the store," Colleen said. At least, that was what Shelby thought she said. And then, the barely intelligible words "Boston" and "risk."

Heart racing, she snapped at Hunter to get her attention and put the call on speaker.

"Colleen, slow down. I can't understand what you're saying," Shelby said. Hunter took the phone from her.

"Is Doug there? Put him on."

Shelby jumped up. "Let's just go." She took her phone back and told Colleen, "We'll be right over."

Carmen sat in the back office of Lombardo's in stunned silence for a good five minutes after Justin left. She then walked upstairs to the kitchen, shrugging off the sous chef's questions about their parmesan vendor. There was only one member of the staff she wanted to see and that was her daughter.

She'd done the right thing talking to Shelby that day in the bookshop. If it weren't for Shelby telling them the truth, how much longer would they have been in the dark about Mia's problem? She just wished Shelby had come to her directly with the information so she could have given her an enormous hug. She was sure Justin hadn't expressed enough gratitude.

Mia couldn't read.

Carmen wasn't just upset about the news itself. She was upset because she felt responsible: she too had struggled with reading. She'd been a terrible student. Maybe it was why she was so impressed with Shelby's work—her strength was Carmen's greatest weakness. And maybe, just maybe, it was also why she hadn't wanted to admit all along that Mia had a persistent reading problem: because it was her fault.

The dining room was packed. Mia circled one of the smaller stations near the front windows, delivering a salad course. Carmen waved, but she pretended not to see her. She walked closer so Mia couldn't ignore her.

"I need to talk to you for a minute," Carmen said.

"I have the big section," she said. "One is a six-top. And a customer at table four wants something with no tomato sauce, pasta, or seafood, but they don't just want a salad. So, later, Ma—okay?"

Carmen took her by the elbow. "Forget about the tables. Come with me."

They walked to the front of the house, where Carmen directed the hostess to send another server to pick up Mia's section.

"Why all the drama?" Mia said, following her out the door.

They walked a block up the street and crossed over to the beach side of Commercial where there were picnic tables and benches. Carmen faced the bay and told Mia to sit directly across from her.

"You're freaking me out," Mia said. "What's going on?"

Carmen took a breath. "I know about your reading."

Mia averted her eyes. "What are you talking about?"

"Stop it," Carmen said sharply, then took a beat to soften her tone. "Shelby told Justin. And I'm glad she did. Why didn't you let us know? We can—"

"Shelby?" Mia crossed her arms "Wow. Justin was right."

"Right about what?"

Mia shook her head. "I should have quit the bookstore the minute Shelby showed up. I never should have trusted her."

"This isn't about Shelby's trustworthiness," Carmen said. "It's about *you* having a problem and your father and I wanting to help you fix it. But we can't do that if we don't know what's going on. So I'm grateful Shelby said something about it, and I think one day you will be, too."

"Don't hold your breath." Mia turned to walk away and Carmen reached out the gently take her arm.

"Trust me."

Her daughter looked back at her with furious, tear-filled eyes. "I'm not going to college," she said.

"Fine. I don't care about that. I care about you. I want you to be happy. And I don't think you will be until you work on this. Can you give me a chance to help you?"

Mia stood rigid. Carmen gingerly stepped forward, and Mia let her put her arms around her. Neither said another word.

Forty-Eight

Doug waited for Shelby and Hunter outside the apartment door. He had dark circles under his eyes and fidgeted with his phone.

"Thanks for coming by," he said, accepting their hugs. "I want to update you guys before we go in because she just calmed down and I don't want to get her upset all over again."

"Just let us see her," Hunter said impatiently. Shelby touched her arm: *Relax*.

"What's going on?" she said.

Doug took a breath. "She's having a lot of bleeding. The placenta previa is getting worse so she's being hospitalized tomorrow."

"Are the babies okay?"

He nodded. "The delivery will be a scheduled C-section, but the doctor is waiting as long as possible."

Shelby wrapped her arms around her waist, hugging herself. Doug looked scared. She didn't blame him.

"Are Annie and Pam headed back?" Hunter said.

"They're meeting us in Boston."

Hunter pulled her keychain from her bag and unhooked a

key, handing it to Doug. "You can stay at my apartment for as long as you need."

"That's very generous, Hunter."

"I want to see her." Now Shelby was the one who was impatient. Doug said since they were there, he was going to run out and do some last-minute errands.

Inside, they found Colleen in bed watching *Booksmart*, her favorite movie, on her laptop resting beside her. Her face and eyes were puffy and red. After Shelby and Hunter took turns hugging her, Colleen turned to adjust the whirring fan on her nightstand.

"It's so hot in here," she said. Shelby and Hunter shared a glance. It wasn't the least bit warm in the room.

"Doug told us the game plan," Shelby said.

Colleen closed her laptop. "I guess now I really have no basis for arguing with my parents about selling the store."

"Don't worry about that right now," Shelby said.

Colleen had a faraway look in her eyes. "I thought this time in my life would be all about Land's End. Being a bookseller." She turned to Shelby. "I'm not ready to be a mother. I'm not a housewife. I'm not even a wife!"

"Colleen, Doug would marry you tomorrow," Hunter said.

She looked at her. "Do you know he never proposed? He never asked *if* I would marry him, he just asked me *when* I wanted to get married."

Shelby understood the distinction she was making, but she also thought maybe Colleen wasn't thinking clearly. She didn't blame her.

"Well, things happened sort of fast," Hunter said. "His heart's in the right place."

"I guess you think my parents' hearts are in the right place, too—closing Land's End, subleasing the space, getting rid of the inventory. Cutting our losses. Maybe I *should* just be cutting my losses. Maybe I have the wrong attitude."

Shelby sat gingerly on the edge of the bed and took Colleen's hand.

"We know you're upset," Shelby said. "And the timing is bad. But isn't this what you would have wanted ultimately? To be with Doug? To have a family?"

"Yes. But the store, too," she said. "I always imagined both. I appreciate you guys coming over. But I'm tired. And I don't want to talk about this anymore."

Shelby and Hunter kissed her goodbye and left the bedroom, closing the door behind them. They waited in the living room for Doug to get back before they left.

They sat on the couch, and Hunter pulled one of the needlepoint pillows on her lap, tracing the sunflower design with her finger. "I wish there was something we could do."

"There is," Shelby said. "And we're doing it: we're her best friends."

MacMillan Pier was crowded with people waiting for the incoming ferry. Justin was certain none of them was as happy as he was to see the line of passengers disembark. The past few days had been confusing, and having Kate back in town would put things in perspective.

"Hi!" Kate called out, dropping her overnight bag to the ground so she could hug him. Her navy linen dress was freshly pressed, and her sharp bob was tucked neatly behind her ears.

"Welcome back," he said, pulling her into his arms. He handed her a small bouquet of Gerbera daisies.

"These are lovely. I should go away more often," she said, kissing him.

"Please don't," he said.

They picked up dinner from the Canteen, which was only serving takeout because of the flood damage, then walked to his house. The early evening was temperate and breezy. They settled on his front deck with their lobster rolls, a bottle of white wine, and a chilled six-pack of beer. Kate talked about the past forty-eight hours with her family, and while he tried to follow what she was saying he was distracted, thinking about his own.

His parents took the news about Mia as well as could be expected. He sensed his mother was, in a way, relieved. Her gut had told her something was wrong, and now she had confirmation. She could stop wondering and start fixing.

"I've been in meeting after meeting," Kate said. "My father and brother have all these expansion plans and now they're looping me in. It's like, branching out here with Hendrik's is making them take me more seriously."

"They *should* take you seriously."

He smiled, and she leaned over and kissed him. "I have to go back tomorrow for a few more planning sessions, but I promised I'd be here tonight so…here I am."

"I would have understood if you didn't want to go back and forth," Justin said. She shook her head.

"It's easy. And Justin, thanks again for checking on the store after the storm." She'd been lucky: shops on that side of Commercial had been spared. "I feel bad about Land's End getting hit so hard."

He nodded. "It's a blow."

"But on the bright side, with Land's End closed, locals will be a lot more welcoming to Hendrik's."

He put down his bottle of beer. "Maybe. But I'm not ready to view the loss of our eighty-year-old bookstore as a positive," he said sharply.

Kate's brows knit together. "I understand," she said, her tone softer. "Change is hard. But we have to move forward."

He offered a smile. The flood wasn't her fault. The Millers' decision to close wasn't her fault. And she was right: it was time to look to the future, not the past. Over the past forty-eight hours, he'd lost sight of that.

It was a mistake he wouldn't make again.

Forty-Nine

The morning of Shelby's Boston Arts Club luncheon, all she could think about was Colleen, a few short miles away in her hospital room. *That's where I should be right now*, Shelby thought. Instead, she stood in the marble bathroom of the Four Seasons Hotel, zipping up the back of her pale pink cotton dress and fighting off guilt. Shelby pulled her hair into a high ponytail and applied Lisa Eldridge lipstick in Velvet Ribbon. That was all the beauty prep she had the patience for.

But the reality was, even if she planned to visit Colleen that morning, she wouldn't be able to. Pam and Annie said she didn't want visitors. So Shelby might as well focus on her job, and today, that meant being an author and promoting her book.

She walked out into the living room of the spacious suite, where Anders sat on the couch wearing a dove-gray blazer and tie. Behind him, sunlight poured in through windows that overlooked Boston Common and the gold-domed State House. He let out a low whistle.

"Look at you, all dressed up. My girlfriend is a beauty," he said.

Shelby looked at him in surprise. She hadn't known what he thought of their relationship. She was still figuring it out herself.

"I didn't realize you have a girlfriend," she teased.

He stood and walked over to her, cupping her chin in his hand before kissing her. "I'd like to think I do."

She waited to feel the rush of happiness the comment should have triggered, but mostly she felt confused. Soon, she was headed back to New York—back to her real life. Anders's immediate future would be Boston for his teaching gig at Harvard. She hadn't let herself think that what she had with Anders would last beyond the summer. And now wasn't the time to start.

"We should get going," she said. Claudia was meeting her at the arts club. Shelby was anxiously anticipating her thoughts on her *Bookshop Beach* manuscript.

The Boston Arts Club was housed in a Victorian mansion dating back to the gilded age, originally owned by Mayor Frederick Octavius Prince. Shelby and Anders learned this from their guide, club trustee Margaret Pierce-Able. She was in her seventies, with a white bob and a Chanel suit and a pillbox hat.

With a little less than a half hour before the reading and luncheon, Margaret led them on a tour through a portrait gallery honoring past club honorees like Toni Morrison, Margaret Atwood, and John Updike. They walked through an elegant dining room with a stained-glass domed ceiling on the way to the event space. She could tell Anders was impressed.

The room was full, the air conditioner cranked up high. Shelby greeted a few people she recognized, looking around for Claudia. She didn't see her until she stood in front of the room to speak, and Claudia slipped into the back row.

Shelby spoke a little too fast at first, but soon fell into a comfortable rhythm. It felt good to do that part of her job again. She thought of the portrait gallery, of all the writers and artists who'd stood in that very room. And for the first time since Hunter's outburst the night of her Land's End reading, she felt at peace with her writing again. She'd made a mistake, but she'd learned from it.

She sensed Anders's adoring gaze, and she returned it.

The luncheon following the reading was in a room straight from the set of *The Gilded Age*, with carved wooden arches, stained-glass windows, and velvet-cushioned settees. The elegant vibe made Shelby feel like she should be wearing white opera-length gloves, or at least some pearls. Anders was seated at her table, and everyone seemed just as eager, if not more so, to talk to him. She didn't mind; she was proud to have him as her date.

Between the salad and the main course, she whispered to him she wanted to get some air and together they ducked into a wood-paneled corridor. They walked through a hallway decorated with antique sideboards and gilt-framed paintings. There wasn't any place to sit but on the top step of a wide marble staircase.

"You're a star," he said, kissing her.

"Me? We barely reached our table before Margaret hit you up to give a lecture here in the fall," she said.

"Ah, maybe. But it's your day."

"There you are," Claudia said from behind them. Shelby jumped up.

She was dressed in a white blazer and vintage Chloé pants with a horse print. "I've been looking all over for you! You were fabulous, as always." Claudia gave her an air kiss. Shelby introduced her to Anders, who said they'd met sometime ago at the London Book Fair. Of course they had. Claudia knew everyone. "And I finished reading *Bookshop Beach* last night. I absolutely love it."

Shelby pressed her hand to her chest. "I'm so glad you feel that way. And thanks for your patience."

"My pleasure. Now let's get things moving. Send the manuscript to your editor." She leaned over to give her an air kiss. "Congrats. I've got to run—catching a flight to Nantucket.

Let's talk next week." Claudia blew her another kiss and walked down the stairs.

No notes from Claudia? Shelby considered that an accomplishment in itself. She'd revised *Secrets of Summer* twice before Claudia submitted it to publishers.

Anders turned to her. "You finished your novel?"

"I did," she said. She felt a little sheepish for not telling him. But she hadn't wanted him to think she was angling for him to read it.

"Why didn't you mention it?"

"Oh… I don't know." She knew she was skittish because of the way Noah had reacted to her success. But it was probably time to stop thinking that way. She'd found someone who was an equal partner, someone who wouldn't hold her back. Not because of geography, not out of insecurity. Not for any reason.

She had, though, shared the final manuscript with one person aside from Claudia, and that was Colleen. She was sure the novel wouldn't be nearly as good if Colleen hadn't asked her to come back for the summer. "No pressure to read it," she'd told her. "I just want you to have it."

Walking back to the luncheon table, Anders said, "I was just thinking: Why not stay with me an extra night or two? Unless there's a reason you have to rush back to Manhattan."

She didn't have to rush back. All she had to do was email her editor her manuscript and wait for notes. Then, next Tuesday, she had her friend's book launch at Union Hall—at the same place where Shelby had celebrated the publication day of *Secrets of Summer*. Shelby RSVP'd that she'd be there once she decided to leave Provincetown. But now, she didn't know what to think about rushing back to New York. Why not spend a little more time with Anders before their relationship turned long-distance? They were at a turning point; either they could write it off as a great summer romance, or work towards something that could be truly lasting.

"Sure," she said, "I'd love to."

Fifty

Colleen seemed comfortable in the hospital room. Maybe more comfortable than she'd been at home all summer. The restlessness was gone. Hunter told her she looked more peaceful.

"I do feel better mentally," Colleen said, her hands resting on her large belly. "It was hard being in Provincetown because I constantly felt like I was missing something—the store. Or spending more time with you and Shelby—everything, really. But here…'everything' is the babies. And so I feel less conflicted." She raised her hand to shield her eyes from the sun reflecting off the window.

Hunter walked over to lower the shade. With her back to Colleen, she closed her eyes for a few seconds. *Just say it.*

Spending so much time with Shelby was getting to her. If she didn't confess to someone about Anders Fleming soon, she was going to get depressed from holding it all inside. She could already feel the dark cloud setting in emotionally. And who else could she tell but Colleen?

Colleen reached for the e-reader next to her bed, and Hunter walked over to retrieve it for her. She stood by Colleen's shoulder, a metal rail between them.

"Thanks. Shelby sent me her new book."

Hunter bit the inside of her lip. She'd planned on waiting until later in the conversation to talk about Shelby, but it seemed impossible to avoid it now.

"Sit," Colleen said. "You're making me nervous with your hovering. Pull up that chair."

Hunter obliged, dragging the bulky wooden chair forward a few inches. The simple task left her feeling weak. "I actually wanted to talk to you about Shelby. But I don't want you to think that I'm visiting you for this reason or anything."

"Okaaay," Colleen said, frowning. "I would never think that about you. What's up?"

Maybe this was a bad idea. Selfish of her. All she was going to do was put Colleen in the middle. Of course she shouldn't tell her.

"Oh, nothing," Hunter said, looking around. "So how's the food in this place?"

"Hunter," Colleen said, sitting up straighter. "There's enough going on that's out of control and leaving me wondering. Don't tease me. Spill it."

Hunter bit her lip. "Has Shelby mentioned anything to you about Anders Fleming?"

"That there's something going on there? Yeah, of course," Colleen said, looking confused. "Why?"

"Well, she never told me. And I accidentally slept with him."

Colleen leaned forward, her eyes wide. "How do you 'accidentally' sleep with someone?"

"The sex part wasn't the accident. I just didn't know about Shelby."

Colleen pressed her hand into her forehead, squeezing her temples with her thumb and forefinger. "When?"

"Fourth of July."

"What the hell, Hunter!"

"I know! I know. But what can I do about it now?"

"You have to tell her." Colleen's blue eyes were uncharacteristically hard. So much for her being distracted by her pregnancy.

"I was thinking more along the lines of: what she doesn't know won't hurt her."

"Wouldn't *you* want to know?"

"No, I wouldn't," Hunter said. "And maybe they're both seeing other people. Maybe it's not serious."

"You're not 'other people,' Hunter. You're her friend. And really, I'd think you'd know better. You got so mad at her about what she wrote in her book. But you know what? I don't think you were mad about what she wrote in the book. I think you were mad about her moving to New York and leaving you behind. And becoming an author before you became an editor. And the only reason you were surprised about the character when the book published was because you were too envious to read the early copy I gave you."

Hunter's jaw dropped. She didn't know what to say. It felt like she'd taken a punch.

"I'm sorry," Colleen added, "but it's the way I see it."

Colleen was right. Hunter would have to confess to Shelby. All she could hope was that Shelby would believe the truth: that she would never have slept with Anders if she'd known. She was just thankful she'd already forgiven Shelby for the book.

It was hard to ask forgiveness if you couldn't give it yourself.

Fifty-One

In the morning, Shelby went to the hospital right after a quick room-service breakfast with Anders. She found Doug standing outside Colleen's room looking pensive. He was dressed in a polo shirt and khaki pants and was pale despite his tan. She wondered if he was sleeping at the hospital or going back and forth between there and Hunter's apartment.

"Hey, Doug," she said gently. She was half-hidden behind the towering fruit basket she'd picked up at a gift shop near her hotel. It was filled with pears and pineapple, Colleen's favorites.

"Shelby?"

Why did he look so surprised? Hadn't Pam and Annie given them the green light for visitation?

"How's she doing?" Shelby shifted the basket and reached forward to give him a hug, but he pulled away from her. She stepped back. "Is this a bad time?"

Before he could answer, Colleen called out, "I want to talk to her!"

Doug put a hand on her shoulder. "Please don't let her get worked up. I'm going for coffee. It'll give you time to talk."

Confused, Shelby inched into the room. It was sunny and bright and more cheerful than she expected. "Hey," she said, setting the fruit basket on the windowsill. "How're you feeling? You look good." Her hair was loose and lustrous, and she seemed flush with new energy. Shelby walked around to the side of the bed to hug her, but Colleen shrank away. What was going on?

"I read your book," Colleen said. The expression on her face made Shelby's stomach drop.

"Okay," she said, sitting in the nearest chair.

"You took the hardest summer of my life and turned it into story material," Colleen said.

Shelby was taken aback. "Colleen, the book isn't about you! It's about a bookstore, but there are a lot of bookstores. And the heroine isn't pregnant. If anything, she's more like me. I wrote *my* experience this summer. The love interest—"

"Bullshit, Shelby! The main character might lose her family bookstore because of her health issues. It might as well be titled *Colleen Miller Loses a Bookstore*."

"Colleen, absolutely not! I would never—"

"The new bookstore in town…the flood. All of it! You know, I was the one who defended you to Hunter. Now I see she was right. She was right all along."

Shelby's eyes filled with tears. *This couldn't be happening.* "I thought you'd like the bookshop setting. It's homage. It comes from my deep feelings for my summers working at Land's End. And my heroine saves her bookstore in the end. She triumphs."

"But in real life, 'she' doesn't," Colleen said.

"Colleen, if there was anything I can do to help convince your parents not to sell, I'll do it. I could stay longer and—"

"It's too late. Kate Hendrik made an offer on the bookstore."

"What?" Shelby said.

Colleen shifted and seemed to wince slightly. "Yes. So, you finished your novel without knowing the ending of the story. My story."

Shelby tried to imagine the wooden Land's End sign replaced with one that read Hendrik's.

Her phone rang with a call from Hunter. She sent it to voice-mail.

"Just go," Colleen said dully.

Shelby was too stunned to move. Her phone vibrated with a text. Are you still in Boston? I need to talk to you. ASAP. She ignored it, turning back to Colleen, who'd moved onto her side, facing away from her with pillows supporting her enormous belly.

"Shelby, I think you should leave," Doug said from the doorway.

She didn't want to go, but she wouldn't argue with him. She stood awkwardly and walked to the door. Maybe that was why Hunter was trying to reach her: she wanted to warn her. Or admonish her.

"And take that with you," Colleen said. Shelby turned around, and Doug handed her the gift basket.

Fifty-Two

Shelby closed herself in the hotel room and turned off her phone. She was deeply shaken. She never imagined Colleen would have a problem with her novel. She'd written the novel as a love letter—to Provincetown, and to the bookshop. She certainly didn't intend for her best friend to get hurt. After what happened with Hunter and *Secrets of Summer*, she'd been extra careful to avoid any personal, real-life details. Now it was happening all over again.

The front desk called up. "Ms. Fleming? You have a visitor in the lobby."

"Uh…okay. I'll be right down." *Ms. Fleming.* She shook her head.

It could only be Hunter. She'd ignored her texts and calls.

The Four Seasons lobby was a dramatic space, with a black-and-white-tiled entry court, brass lanterns, and a front desk in embellished leather backed by an impressionist mural. Hunter paced in front of reception. She was dressed in a black denim skirt and black tank top, her hair pulled back in a clip. Her red lipstick was smudged.

"Why aren't you answering your phone?" she said.

"Because I don't want to talk. Obviously. What's so important?"

Hunter looked around. "Is there anyplace more private?"

"My room?"

"No," Hunter said quickly. "Maybe a…lounge?"

The concierge directed them to a bar called the Library. It had bookshelf-lined walls and cognac-colored velvet armchairs. Shelby sank into one, feeling exhausted.

"I know why you're here," Shelby said.

"You do?" said Hunter, eyes widening.

Shelby nodded. "I just spoke to Colleen. I swear I didn't mean to encroach on her life, or her story. I felt like if anything, I was writing about *my* summer."

Hunter looked confused. "I don't know what you're talking about. But Shelby, I need to say this before I lose my determination to do the right thing." Her kohl-rimmed eyes were pained. "I totally messed up, and I hope you can forgive me."

A pretty female server dressed in white with an auburn bob stopped by to take their order. Shelby asked for an iced tea and Hunter ordered a shot of tequila. When she was gone, Shelby said, "Messed up how?"

"I didn't know you were seeing Anders Fleming."

Shelby shrugged. What did that have to do with anything? "I'm sure I mentioned it at some point." The conversation between men at a nearby table grew louder, and she glanced over.

"Yeah, I know *now*," Hunter said. "But I didn't know on the Fourth of July. And I ran into him at a party that night. And went home with him."

"You…went home with him?" What was she talking about? Maybe she should have ordered food. The stress about Colleen was making her head fuzzy. "I don't understand."

"In my defense, I was a little drunk and he was definitely wasted. It was nothing. It was…"

Shelby pressed her hand to her forehead. She felt dizzy, and bent over her knees for a second. *Hunter and Anders?* She replayed the night...the texts and phone calls going back and forth. The visit to his house the next morning. Had Hunter been there?

Shelby stood slowly and walked out of the lounge. Hunter followed, but she ignored her, heading straight for the elevator. When it arrived with a ping, Shelby stepped inside and held out her hand to keep Hunter away.

"Don't. Just...go."

She'd pack her things before Anders got back from his meeting. She would reach New York by nightfall. And this time, she wouldn't look back.

Justin wanted to get out of town for a few hours. He rarely felt that way, but he was so disappointed by the news from the town council, he didn't know what else to do. They'd lost their chance at the wharf building. An offer came in from some corporation. There was no way the Community Trust could match it.

"What's the corporation plan to do with the building?" Justin asked.

Gene Hobart had turned red in the face. "A resort, I believe."

It was infuriating. Good intentions be damned, everything was always about money.

At least Kate was happy by the surprise. When she showed up at her apartment, she threw her arms around him. He clung to her, wanting to ground himself in her scent, her voice. Her optimistic certainty that everything always worked out for the best.

Kate lived in the beautiful Back Bay neighborhood, and they moved outside to sit on her apartment's wraparound terrace. The sky was clear, but heat and the noise of car traffic rose from the street below. Kate poured him a glass of wine.

"We had a setback today with the wharf building," he said. "A corporation swooped in and bought it out from under the Community Trust."

"I'm sorry," she said very matter-of-factly. "But maybe it will be something good for the town?"

The calm demeanor that he usually loved was suddenly maddening.

"I know what's best for the town," he snapped. She looked surprised. "I'm sorry. But we need more housing for workers, not hotel rooms for tourists."

She nodded. "Okay. But didn't you once tell me that some ecosystems need to work things out on their own?"

"Sure. In nature. But towns aren't organic. They're based on economics, and a social pact."

"Yes. Which makes them imperfect. As any social pact is."

She was right. Anything created by humans, experienced by humans—was subject to setbacks and problems. Towns. Institutions. Relationships.

Kate moved her chair closer to his. "Maybe this will make you feel a little better: I'm buying Land's End."

Justin put his drink on the round side table. "You are?"

"Yes," she said, sitting on the edge of her chair, her knees together and hands clasped on top of them. "We're buying the inventory, taking over the lease, and the location will be our Hendrik's Cape Cod outpost."

She reached for his hand. "I'm sorry I've been so torn all summer. I wanted to be in Ptown for you, but I still had one foot in the Boston store. I don't like doing anything by half measure. And now, I won't be."

He leaned forward and kissed her. She was right. Sometimes, change was good. And there was no sense doing anything by half measure.

He'd ask her to move in with him.

Fifty-Three

After a week back in New York City, Shelby still hadn't adjusted. She felt as much a visitor in her own town as she'd felt all summer on the Cape. She was back in her "real" life, but her head and her heart were with Colleen. She thought about her pregnancy and her babies every day. The only updates she got were from social media.

"Are you Shelby Archer?" the woman asked, shouting over the loud music. "I adored *Secrets of Summer.*"

Shelby was back at Union Hall. She'd considered skipping her friend Eve's party, but thought she'd feel worse just sitting alone in her apartment.

"Thank you," she said to the woman, who introduced herself as "Wendy from Woodstock." Wendy had long gray hair and wore a spangly caftan. She ran a famous writing retreat in upstate New York. In fact, Eve had mentioned to her at the beginning of the summer the night she'd been debating whether or not to go to Provincetown. Maybe Shelby should have headed upstate instead.

She still couldn't believe the way things had gone down with

Anders. After her conversation with Hunter that day at the Four Seasons, she had tried to leave before he returned, but she had the misfortune of running into him on her way out. Their messy conversation played out on the sidewalk in front of the hotel.

"Did you really think I wouldn't find out about Hunter?" she said to him.

"That's what this is all about? Hunter is inconsequential to me."

"You and I were *together*, Anders!"

"As far as I'm concerned, up until two nights ago in New York, you and I never discussed our relationship in terms of long-term plans. We've only just met. I assumed I was free to go about my life, as you have been free to go about yours. Like choosing to spend quite a bit of time with your ex-boyfriend."

She had to admit, that comment took her by surprise. She'd never have guessed he noticed. But he couldn't get away with conflating the two things.

"I didn't *sleep* with my ex-boyfriend. You did sleep with my friend. There's a big difference."

The fact that she even had to go through the absurdity of explaining it to him made her realize the conversation was futile. Better to cut her losses and get away from him.

Her feelings about Hunter were more complicated. Hunter's night with Anders had been an honest mistake. Hunter was just being, well, herself. In fiction, a character's actions needed to stay consistent with who they were. Why should it be any different in real life? Plus, Hunter admitted it. By telling her the truth, she saved Shelby from getting in any deeper with Anders. It didn't change the hurt, and it didn't mean she wanted to see her or talk to her. But on some level, she did forgive her.

Wendy from Woodstock looked at her expectantly, and Shelby realized she'd lost the thread of their conversation.

"I'm sorry. Where were we?" Shelby asked.

"I wanted to know if you'd be interested in teaching at my

writing retreat this fall. You'd only have one class a day and the rest of the time is yours to write your own books. It's free room and board, and a great community of novelists."

It was an appealing offer. Teaching would give her days structure, and she liked the idea of writing her next book in a place with no baggage. She missed the writing community she'd had at graduate school, and wondered if that was why she'd struggled to write her follow-up novel.

"I'd love to," Shelby said. They exchanged information, and Wendy said she'd be in touch soon.

Feeling a little more optimistic, Shelby decided to get her first cocktail of the evening. She walked over to the bar and recognized the bartender—also a writer. She knew she had to count her blessings; she was making a living doing what she loved. If Claudia Linden hadn't believed in her, maybe she'd be behind the bar that night instead of in front of it.

Before she could get the bartender's attention, she felt someone close behind her and she turned around.

"Noah," she said. He looked different. The facial scruff was trimmed and his hair was shorter. He'd traded in his usual jeans and a T-shirt for slacks and a sports jacket. She realized, seeing him for the first time since the beginning of the summer, that she'd barely thought about him. The last time they'd stood in that room together felt very long ago.

"Hey, stranger," he said. "You look great."

She let him kiss her on the cheek.

"So do you."

"I'm really glad to run into you. I've owed you an apology."

She waved her hand, signaling him not to give it a second thought.

"No, really," he said. "I acted badly. I was stressed out about my manuscript submissions, and I admit, I was jealous of your success. But I have an agent now, and it put things in perspective, and I realize I acted like an idiot."

"Noah, we don't have to get into it."

He smiled. "I know we don't have to. But I miss you. I was going to text you a few weeks ago, but I heard you were on the Cape for the summer. Are you back for good now?"

Noah's expression was so hopeful, she almost felt sorry for him. She knew how it felt to realize you'd blown it with someone you actually wanted in your life. It was the pain she'd experienced all summer. Now, standing in the middle of the crowded party, she realized every single person she wanted in her life was three hundred miles away. So what was she doing there?

"No," she said. "I'm not back for good. Not at all."

Carmen believed the adage that a parent could only be as happy as their most unhappy child. It explained why she'd felt such a weight on her shoulders all summer, and why she felt such relief now: a doctor in Boston had diagnosed Mia with a treatable type of orthographic processing disorder.

She invited the kids to come to the house for Tuesday night dinner, even though it was the time of summer when they typically abandoned the weekly gathering. It was peak party time for tourists while locals ran on fumes.

"So, I hear you'll be spending some time in Boston," Justin said to his sister.

They were in the process of finding her a reading specialist. Ideally, they'd get an appointment with someone based near the Boston Seaport, so Mia would be taking the ferry back and forth a few times a week. In the fall, when the ferry stopped operating, Carmen would drive her.

"I like it," Mia said. "If I ever do go to college, I want to go there." She glanced at Carmen.

"That's a wonderful goal," Carmen said.

Bert veered off topic, venting his frustration with the town council. She really didn't want to waste the dinner on local politics.

"Justin, what's going on with you? Work is okay?" she said.

"Actually, I have news," he said.

"Oh?" She could tell by his smile that it was something exciting.

"I'm going to ask Kate to move in with me."

Carmen set down her fork. "Isn't that rushing things?"

He shot her a look that made it clear her input wasn't welcome.

"Mom, give it up," Mia said. "We all know you're Team Shelby, but it's time to let it go."

Carmen turned to her. "And it's time for you to let go of your anger at her. She did the right thing in telling us about your reading. One day, you'll be thanking her. Tell her, Justin."

He pushed his chair away from the table and stood. "I came here to talk to you about Kate. Not Shelby. If you want to thank her, *you* thank her." He walked his plate into the kitchen, called out a perfunctory thanks for dinner, and left.

Carmen shook her head. Fine. She *would* thank her.

And then she would try, as Mia so bluntly suggested, to let it go.

Fifty-Four

Shelby called Claudia and asked for a meeting. She didn't want to go to lunch. This was a conversation she wanted to have at the office.

The agency occupied two floors of a six-story building in Flatiron. It had high ceilings and an open floor plan, with lots of glass and brushed steel and exposed pipes. Lucite chairs added pops of bright color. Claudia had one of the few offices with a door.

A new assistant showed her to Claudia's office, asking her if she wanted coffee or sparkling water.

"Nothing, thanks, I'm good," Shelby said.

Claudia, dressed in a white pantsuit and lots of gold jewelry, rounded her desk, air-kissed Shelby on both cheeks, then took her seat. Shelby sat on the red leather couch facing the desk. Large windows overlooked Fifth Avenue.

"So, what's on your mind, lady?" Claudia said cheerily, checking her phone. She looked up. "I told you I spoke to your editor a few days ago, right? She launched *Bookshop Beach* last week, and Team Shelby Archer is very excited."

Launching the book meant that her editor had presented it to the publicity department and sales force and officially positioned it for next summer. Shelby tugged the rubber band out of her ponytail and wrapped it around her middle finger, tighter and tighter until it hurt.

"I'm having an...issue with the book," Shelby said.

"Problem with the notes? Just do the ones you agree with and leave the rest. The same as last time."

"It's not the notes. It's bigger than that. I don't think it's the right book for me to publish."

It didn't matter if Shelby believed she'd violated Colleen's privacy in writing the book; Colleen did. So, she had two choices: she could move forward with *Bookshop Beach* and lose her best friend, or she could try to repair her friendships and lose the book. The more she thought about it, the more obvious the right choice seemed. She'd write something else. Sure, she'd lose the chance to have a follow-up to *Secrets of Summer* publish next summer. But it was a small price to pay for saving her friendship with Colleen.

Claudia tilted her head to one side. She unscrewed the cap of her sparkling water.

"Shelby, the book is good. What's giving you cold feet?"

"I just don't want to publish it. I changed my mind."

"You changed your mind," Claudia said, sitting up straighter. The expression in her hazel eyes changed from concern to something noticeably cooler. "Where is this coming from?"

"It's just the way I feel. But I'll get started right away on something else." Authors had pulled books before. Books much further along the publishing process than her own. It wasn't even listed online yet. Yes, it was on the publisher's calendar. But things moved all the time. She just needed Claudia's support. Claudia would smooth things over.

"Shelby," she said slowly, choosing her words with obvious

care. "This is your job—not a hobby. You were paid a lot of money for that book."

"I'll give it back," Shelby said quickly. If that was the biggest issue, she had no problem taking the financial hit. She'd make it back on the next one, and she'd get by on royalties from *Secrets of Summer.*

"And what about your editor's time investment? And mine? Can you give that back as well?"

Shelby hadn't thought of it that way.

"No, but—"

"I'm sorry," Claudia said coldly. "Let me back up: Do you need to postpone this book for mental health reasons?"

"No," Shelby said, shaking her head. "It's nothing like that. I just don't want to publish the book—ever."

Claudia nodded. "I see." She clasped her hands in front of her on the desk and leaned forward. "In my capacity as your agent, I strongly advise against doing this."

Shelby was confused. She thought as her agent, she was supposed to help her navigate the situation.

"I understand. But I can't publish a book I don't feel good about. I know what it's like now to have a book out in the world, to promote it and live with it and get all the feedback— wanted and unwanted. I realize a book isn't just a book. It's a link between myself and everyone who reads it and if that link is not right—"

"I suggest you give this careful thought. Because if you pull this book, I can no longer represent you."

Shelby looked at her in surprise.

"Do you have any questions?" Claudia said.

She didn't. Except the one only she could answer: Was she really going to do this?

Claudia summoned the assistant to show Shelby out.

Fifty-Five

"Surprise," Hunter said, breezing into Colleen's hospital room with an armload of art supplies. "You can't make it to Carnival, so I'm bringing Carnival to you."

It was Colleen's favorite week of the summer, and she'd been especially excited about the Wizard of Oz theme. Hunter had the idea for them to spend the day together making decorations.

Colleen nodded absently. She'd been the one to introduce Hunter and Shelby to the tradition of painting banners for Commercial Street. Carnival began in the late 1970s, and there seemed to be an unspoken ethos that making decorations and costumes by hand was superior to the modern day click-and-buy method that left everything looking the same. Even people who typically weren't crafty still turned out inventive, beautiful signs and decorations just for this one time of year.

The shades were pulled down, and Hunter reached over to let the light in.

"Don't," Colleen said.

Hunter stopped trying to brighten the room and instead turned her attention to getting the supplies set up. She wheeled a table from the corner and set out the paint and brushes and canvas and reams of paper from Michael's and Ace Hardware. "I had to go to three different places to find green paint. The town is already in Emerald City mode."

Colleen used the remote to turn off the wall-mounted television.

"I'm tired," she said.

Hunter stopped unpacking the art supplies and moved to sit on the edge of Colleen's bed.

"Are you okay?" Hunter said, moving closer.

"Fine," she said, reaching back to press on the small of her back. Hunter leaned over to rub it for her. "But I found out one more thing about the bookstore now that Hendrik's is taking over: it's only going to be open in the summer. So we'll have a bookstore, but not a year-round bookstore. For the first time since 1943." Colleen lifted her heavy curtain of blond hair and asked Hunter to hand her a clip from the bedside table.

"You can't get stressed out," Hunter said. "Doug said so, your doctor said so. Your health and the babies' health are more important than a bookstore."

"Easy for you to say."

Hunter stood so she could pull Colleen's hair back for her. "That's not fair."

"I'm sorry. I'm just frustrated. The store… Shelby's book… Being stuck here." She lifted a hand then dropped it into her lap.

"It's going to be okay," Hunter said.

Colleen had called her freaking out about Shelby's book. She seemed to be as upset about it as she was about Land's End going up for sale. Then Colleen emailed a copy of the new book and insisted she read it. Reluctantly, she did, and concluded that Colleen was overreacting. But then, who was she to say? Colleen had thought *she* was overreacting to *Secrets of Summer*. Hunter suspected there was some wisdom to be found in the irony, but she couldn't figure out what that might be.

"I don't think Shelby's book is as personal as you think it is," Hunter said for at least the third time. "And I know how that sounds coming from me. But really, what's going on, Colleen? This can't all be about the bookstore. Or the novel."

Colleen nodded, a blank expression on her face. A tear trickled from her eyes.

"This was not my plan," she said.

"The pregnancy? I know it's been hard. But pretty soon you'll have the babies and it will all be worth it. It's what you wanted eventually, right? You always wanted to be a mom. And you love Doug."

"That's not the point," Colleen said with irritation. "Imagine not having the energy to do *anything*, let alone the things you love. You can't even read, never mind edit. You can't even walk around. Do you know what it's like to feel like you no longer *exist*?"

"No," Hunter said, "I don't. But you do exist. You more than exist—you're going to be someone's mother. I think you'll feel so differently once the babies are born. You're going to be so happy."

Colleen pulled the covers up higher and turned away from her. "It doesn't work like that. Real life isn't a Shelby Archer novel."

Fifty-Six

Justin made dinner reservations, but Kate was running late at the bookstore. Evidently, she was learning what every vendor in town figured out sooner or later: summer hours of operation tended to be viewed more as suggestions than regulations.

He recognized a few of the people browsing the Hendrik's shelves as being Land's End customers, locals like Walter Tegan, a balding former linguistics professor who always dressed in a white polo shirt, denim shorts, and suspenders.

"I'm looking for a book," Walter said to Kate. "The cover is green."

When Kate didn't find that to be enough information to go on, he became irritated.

"Colleen would know what I mean," Walter said.

"I'm sure Kate will be able to help you if can think of what the book's about, or maybe one word of the title?" Justin suggested.

Walter shook his head and walked out.

Kate frowned. "Not exactly a satisfied customer."

"Can't win 'em all," he said, leaning over the counter to kiss her. "I'll wait for you outside."

After Kate managed to close shop, she told him that her last few customers were tourists, and that she could always tell the difference between locals and visitors because the visitors didn't ask what happened to Land's End.

"They seem to almost resent me," she said. "But I didn't put Land's End out of business. It was the flood. It's a strange customer dynamic I've never experienced before."

"It will improve in time. People will just be happy to have a bookshop. I can't imagine this town without one."

"And now they'll have two."

Justin was confused. "You're keeping your current location and the Land's End space?"

Kate flushed, tucking a lock of hair behind her ears. It was a habit of hers, and it always slipped right back to hang straight along her cheek. He usually found the familiar gesture endearing. "Let's talk over dinner," she said, seeming almost flustered.

"I'd rather talk now." He stopped walking. "What's going on?"

She tucked a lock of hair behind one ear and avoided his eyes. "My brother, Karl, is opening a hotel here. I'm planning to have a boutique bookshop in the lobby catering to his clientele—beach books, some nonfiction about Provincetown, postcards—that sort of thing."

Justin was confused. He didn't presume to know everything that was happening in town, but after all his town council meetings, how could he have missed the news of a new hotel development? Unless...

"Don't tell me your brother bought the wharf building," he said slowly.

"No," she said. "My father did."

"Your father?" He thought back to their lunch with Martin Hendrik at Fishtail. What was it he'd said about Ptown? *Untapped potential.* Justin still remembered the comment because it was the opposite of the way he viewed Ptown. "So, your father bought the building you knew we were trying to turn into affordable housing? Did you ever think to mention that to me? Or better yet—tell him to back off?"

"You're making this personal," she said.

"You made this personal when you stood by as your father took it out from under us, and you made it even more personal by not telling me after the fact. How could you lie to me?"

"I didn't lie to you. I just didn't talk about my family's business plans. Just because we're together doesn't give you a right to that information."

He couldn't believe she could say that with a straight face. "When I told you, the other night in Boston, that we lost our bid for the building, you looked me right in the eye with some platitude about how it might be something good for the town."

"It's hard for visitors to find places to stay, too. A new hotel's not *bad* for the town."

"Who's going to serve food and sell clothes and coffee to all the tourists filling yet another hotel?"

She shrugged, and he understood she didn't care. It wasn't her problem. And he realized her decision to turn Land's End into Hendrik's, to stay in town, had nothing to do with investing in their future together. It had purely been a business decision—and possibly not even her own.

"I'm going to pass on dinner," he said.

She appraised him coolly. "I understand."

No, she didn't. And clearly, she never did.

Backyard Movie Night was a fundraiser for the Province-town Film Society. Two dozen people gathered on the lawn of the historic Mary Heaton Vorse house to watch the early-'90s film *The Prince of Tides*. Hunter bought tickets at the beginning of the summer and planned to go with Colleen and Doug. Instead, she brought Duke and Max.

The air was herbal and salty, a scent that brought Hunter

back to her earliest memories of the Cape. All around her, people chatted and unpacked picnic baskets and a contented hum filled the air. Hunter could barely sit still. All she could think about was Shelby, and the look on her face when she'd confessed about Anders.

"I wish I'd been here back in the day," Duke said. "This house used to be the center of *it all*. Any night of the week, you might find yourself rubbing elbows with Eugene O'Neill or Sinclair Lewis…"

Hunter wasn't following him; she was lost in her own thoughts. When she wasn't ruminating over Shelby, she was thinking about a call she received from Ezra that morning: Paragon had a job opening for an assistant. He gave her the contact information for the HR person she needed to email. "But jump on it," he'd said. "The gig isn't even posted yet."

"It's very cool of you to think of me," she'd said. "But I told you I'm only looking for jobs in Boston."

"This is *Paragon*," he said. She knew he was right. Still, twenty-four hours later, she hadn't emailed her résumé. Hunter felt like a poser wearing her vintage Blondie T-shirt. She had no right to wear images of rock rebels when she herself played life so safe.

"You really should read the novel after you see the movie tonight," Duke said. "There's no one like Pat Conroy."

Hunter, as a rule, did prefer to read the book before seeing the movie. But the author they were talking about had never been on her radar.

A deeply tanned guy around her age wearing a shark-patterned golf shirt handed out snack trays of artisanal crackers, apple wedges, Stilton, and mini-wine bottles. The sun started to set, but it wasn't dark enough yet to begin the film. She was impatient for the distraction from the Paragon dilemma.

Why was she so intimidated by New York City? She knew plenty of people from school who'd ended up there and were successful. Just look at Shelby. The thing was, all her life in Boston, whatever room she was in, people assumed she was only there because she was a Dillworth. If she moved to New York and failed, she'd be proving them right.

"You guys?" she said, interrupting their debate over whether Pat Conroy's best novel was *The Great Santini* or *The Lords of Discipline*. She told them about the Paragon job opening, and they were quick to weigh in.

"It would be madness not to apply," Duke said. Max agreed, and said he'd be happy to be a reference for her. They made it sound so simple. Maybe it was.

Mia Lombardo wandered over from where she'd been sitting with her parents. Hunter hadn't seen her since the flood shuttered Land's End.

"How's Colleen?" she said. "I messaged her, but I haven't heard back. And I really miss the store. But I haven't told her that. Obviously."

Hunter's phone rang. She'd meant to silence it, but was glad she hadn't when Shelby's name appeared on the screen. They hadn't been in touch at all since the conversation at the Four Seasons. Hunter shuddered to think about it.

"Hey," Hunter said, pressing the phone closer to her ear.

"Do you have a minute?" Shelby said. She sounded casual. Almost as if Hunter hadn't slept with her boyfriend. Or maybe that was just wishful thinking.

"Sure! Yes. Of course. It's just a little loud here—"

"Did Colleen tell you she's upset with me? About the book?"

"Yeah. But for the record, I don't agree with her. And I know how that sounds coming from me of all people—"

"I'm not trying to convince you I'm right or that Colleen's wrong. I just want to fix this."

Hunter liked the sound of that. A lot. "I am *so* glad to hear that. Is there something I can do to—"

"Can I stay at your place tonight? I just got off the ferry."

"You're here now?" Hunter thought it would be a long time before she saw Shelby again. "Sure. Of course. I'll meet you at the house to let you in. Give me ten minutes."

She ended the call. Duke, Max, and Mia looked at her expectantly.

"That was Shelby," she said. "She's back in town. I have to go. Sorry."

"You're missing the movie?" Max said.

Hunter pulled her bag over her shoulder and brushed a few strands of grass off of her pants. "I'll read the book. I'm sure it's better, anyway."

Fifty-Seven

Shelby walked straight from the ferry to the shuttered Land's End storefront in a sort of pilgrimage. But if she expected to find answers in the shadows of the darkened building, she knew in that moment it wouldn't be that simple.

Shelby hadn't known what to do with herself after leaving Claudia's office. She'd set the meeting certain she was pulling the book. But while she was willing to lose her pub date and the book, she hadn't expected she'd lose her agent, too.

Wandering around New York, wringing her hands, wasn't going to help. Impulsively, she bought a train ticket to Boston and ferry tickets to Ptown.

As promised, Hunter was waiting for her at the house. They sat out back, on Adirondack chairs with a chilled bottle of vodka and two shot glasses on a small table between them. The air smelled particularly pungent. Shelby knew from Justin this indicated a possible mass of seaweed washed ashore, or possibly an algae bloom. But she didn't want to think about Justin. Justin was another thing to feel bad about.

"I know you don't want to talk about it," Hunter began. "But

I have to say again I'm so sorry about the thing with Anders. I wish I could undo it."

Hunter's pretty face was tense, her eyes cast downward. "I've moved on," she said. "Really."

Shelby offered a small smile. "I'm not here to get into all that. I just want to make things right again. With all three of us. But Colleen won't take any of my calls or answer my messages."

"It might take her some time to get over her feelings about the book," Hunter said. "I don't think there's anything you can say that will change that."

Animals rustled in the shrubs below the deck, their motion turning on the automatic light sensors.

"I know there's nothing I can *say*. But there's something I can do. I can cancel the book."

Hunter, filling her shot glass, put the bottle down and turned to her. "Are you serious? That's an option?"

"My agent will drop me. But I can do it."

Hunter knocked back the shot and poured one for her. "You sure about this?"

"No. I'm not sure. But I can't publish and promote a book that cost me a best friend. And the whole point of the book was to celebrate Land's End, and now it's gone so it seems… It's just not right anymore. I can't live with it." She accepted the shot glass and swallowed half the vodka, feeling the burn and realizing she didn't want it after all. She set the glass down.

"And you haven't told Colleen?"

Shelby shook her head. "I'm trying to. She won't take my calls, and in the meantime, she's sitting there all upset about a book that isn't going to publish. I need to get through to her."

Hunter nodded, but looked uncertain.

"What is it?" Shelby said.

"I mean, logically she should forgive you if you sacrifice your novel. But there aren't any guarantees."

"I know," Shelby said. She couldn't control how Colleen reacted. She could only do what she felt was right. "But it's a moot point right now. She won't take a call from me. And this isn't something I want to text."

Hunter nodded and picked up the phone resting beside her. "I'll call."

"You'll tell her for me?"

Hunter shook her head. "No. It has to come from you. But I'll get her on FaceTime."

Shelby considered it for a few seconds, then nodded. Hunter made the call, alone in the frame.

"Hey," Hunter said. "You got a minute? I'm here with Shelby. She has something to say that you need to hear."

Before Colleen could respond, Hunter passed her the phone. Shelby took a breath, then faced Colleen through the screen.

"I really don't have the energy for this," Colleen said. Her blond hair was up in a ponytail and her face was puffy. "Put Hunter back on."

Shelby hesitated. She didn't want to stress her out, but the only way to alleviate her worry was to push forward with the conversation. "Okay. But one thing first: I'm not publishing the novel."

Colleen frowned. "What do you mean?"

"I told my agent I'm scrapping the book. You're more important to me."

"Wait. Are you serious?"

Shelby felt a weight lift, as if she'd been holding her breath for the past week and just now exhaled. "I just hope you'll forgive me and forget about all this and enjoy being a new mom." Beside her, Hunter reached out and touched her shoulder.

After a second or two of silence, Colleen said, "That means a lot to me, Shelby."

Shelby felt a lump in her chest. She didn't know if it was relief, or the intensity of the call, or lingering terror at what she was doing to her career.

All she could do was hand the phone back to Hunter.

★ ★ ★

Hunter lay in bed wide-awake. The click and hum of nocturnal insects in the tall beach grass outside her bedroom window was usually enough to lull her to sleep. Well, that and a few drinks. But she was wide-awake hours after saying good night to Shelby.

There was no reason for her mind to be racing so much. Colleen was happy that Shelby was pulling her book. And Shelby seemed to be in a forgiving mood herself; maybe they'd be able to move past the Anders Fleming fiasco after all.

Now all she had to do was figure out her job situation. It shouldn't be that hard, especially compared to what Shelby just did with her own career. Hunter had to give her credit for a very gutsy move.

She hated to admit it, but seeing Shelby's sacrifice she realized that personally, she made her own major life decisions out of fear. Fear of people using her for her parents' money. Fear of never accomplishing anything on her own because so much had been handed to her. Fear of failure. Fear of relationships.

But she'd never been afraid of her friendships with Shelby and Colleen. That was why the character in *Secrets of Summer* had stung so much. She felt exposed by one of the few people she trusted. But now, seeing how Colleen reacted to the new novel, she realized she'd actually been most upset with herself. Shelby's character had reflected herself back at her, and she didn't like what she'd seen.

At close to midnight, she gave up on sleep and padded down the hall to Shelby's room. She opened the door slowly.

"Shelby?" she called out softly. The window shade wasn't entirely drawn and moonlight cast a wide beam across the hardwood floor.

"Mmmm," Shelby said.

"Are you awake?"

She heard sheets rustling around and could see in the shadows that Shelby sat up.

"Sort of."

Hunter climbed into the king-size bed next to her. After being college roommates for four years, the right to wake each other up in the middle of the night was baked into their relationship. The room was cooler than her own. She shivered under the whir of the overhead fan, and folded the edge of the comforter so it covered her bare legs.

"I have a job interview on Monday," she said.

"Where?"

"Paragon agency. I'm not sure about it. I don't think I belong in New York."

Shelby shifted position, lying back down. "I don't belong anywhere. Sometimes you just have to go where you need to go."

Hunter considered this. Shelby was quiet, and Hunter thought maybe she'd fallen back to sleep. But then Shelby said, "You'll do great. You can stay at my apartment if you don't want to go back and forth."

"Really?" Hunter said. "Okay, thanks. And you can stay here. We can house-swap. Just like in a movie." The idea of it made her feel buoyant, like her job interview was less of a solitary venture. Shelby would be waiting for her when she got back. They could analyze it and gossip about the people she'd meet. Even if she didn't get the job, she'd have a story to share.

She felt less afraid already.

"Shelby, I missed you these past few years."

"I missed you, too."

She lay down next to her, knowing she'd finally be able to sleep.

Fifty-Eight

Shelby woke up to her phone ringing. It was almost ten-thirty in the morning, not an unreasonable time for someone to call. But Shelby slept restlessly. Yes, she'd solved one problem by canceling her book—the most important one. Colleen was grateful and seemed ready to move on. But now she'd created another one: her career was uncertain.

Hunter, sprawled out next to her, groaned and put a pillow over her head. It took Shelby a beat to remember what she was doing in her room and their late-night conversation. She answered her phone.

"I didn't wake you, did I?" Carmen Lombardo said, her voice energetic and upbeat.

"No, not at all," Shelby said, sitting up. Hunter grunted with annoyance.

"A little birdie told me you're back in town. And I just can't let you leave this time without thanking you in person for your help with Mia."

"You don't have to thank me," Shelby said. But she agreed to stop by for coffee. How could she not? She just hoped Mia would be there—that she'd forgiven her for telling her secret. And yes, deep down she hoped Justin would be there, too. Even if he wasn't, it would feel like he was there. The Lombardo house, was, after all, his childhood home. Going there, saying good-bye to Carmen, was probably a fitting place to end her summer in Provincetown. And maybe then she could finally move on. For real this time.

The Lombardo house hadn't changed a bit since the last time she was there. The kitchen had the same farmhouse sink, the same cherry table, and the same framed mosaics from Mia's middle school art classes.

Carmen, wearing a floral T-shirt and jeans, greeted her with a hug, ushered her to the eat-in table, and brought over two mugs of coffee.

"After Justin told us about Mia, we were completely consumed with finding specialists and getting her help. When the dust settled, I realized I hadn't had the chance to thank you. And you were gone by then. I should have called."

"Oh, no worries," Shelby said. "I'm glad I was able to find out what was happening. How's she doing?"

Carmen smiled. "Good. I feel like I have my daughter back."

Shelby glanced at the swinging door that led to the dining room and the rest of the house.

"Is she home? I'd love to see her. She wasn't very happy with me when we last spoke."

"Oh, hon, she's with friends." Carmen frowned.

"I feel bad. She thinks I betrayed her secret. I guess I did."

Carmen shook her head. "You would have been betraying her by *not* telling us. Someday, when you have children of your own, you'll understand that."

Children of her own. It was hard to imagine ever making the right choices that would lead to having someone in her life with whom she wanted to have a baby. She could barely keep her friendships from blowing up.

"You're probably right," Shelby said. Carmen started to say something, then stopped. Shelby had the odd feeling that Carmen knew *her* secret, the unspoken shadow that followed her all summer: she might have made a mistake in breaking up with Justin. But it would remain unspoken; letting that out in the open would be more terrifying than telling Claudia she was canceling her book.

"How long are you staying?" Carmen said after a silence.

"Just a few days." Shelby drained her coffee. She should get going.

"But you'll come back next summer?"

"I really don't know." Shelby hadn't thought that far ahead, but realized in that moment that no, she wouldn't be back. She needed to move on—emotionally. Creatively, she'd find another muse, follow a different path to a story far outside her own life. And she'd do it not just to avoid hurting her friends, but because if she wanted to keep growing as a writer, she had to leave her comfort zone. If the Woodstock teaching job came through, it might be exactly the change she needed.

"Well, for what it's worth, I hope you do," Carmen said.

The back door opened, startling them both. Justin walked in.

"Oh!" he said, stopping short in surprise. "Am I interrupting something?"

"Not at all," Carmen said with a wave, as if the two of them having coffee together in the kitchen was routine.

He looked at Shelby, and she offered a small smile. Her heart picked up an extra beat. He was dressed in a faded T-shirt and blue board shorts. He dropped his keys and phone on the counter and leaned against it facing them.

"Is Dad around?" he said.

Shelby stood. "I should get going…"

"Don't rush off," Carmen said. "And no, your father's at the restaurant. What's going on?"

"Nothing's going on," he said unconvincingly.

"Well, you're here instead of at work."

Justin paced a few steps, then joined them at the table. She could smell the salt on his skin and feel the heat radiating from his body. It took effort for her not to lean closer to him.

"I found out who bought the wharf building," he said.

Shelby wasn't sure what he was talking about but could tell that it wasn't good. "What's the wharf building?"

"It's a property on MacMillan Pier that the town trust hoped to buy to turn into affordable housing for workers. So we can fix the staffing shortages that has everyone scrambling this summer. But someone outbid us."

"Who?" Carmen said.

"The Hendriks." He said it almost like it was a question, like he didn't quite believe it. Shelby didn't understand. Wasn't Hendrik's buying Land's End?

"That doesn't make sense," said Shelby. "They're supposed to be buying Land's End."

"They bought both. Kate's brother is opening a hotel on the water."

Carmen let out a low whistle. "She hid this from you?"

Justin shot her a look. "No. She *told* me. That's how I know."

"Well, she told you now. After it's a done deal."

"Ma, please. This isn't helpful." He stood up. "I'll catch Dad at the restaurant."

It seemed unfair that someone from Boston could just sweep in and buy their way into town, when someone like Colleen who'd lived there her entire life couldn't sustain a family business.

"So, instead of affordable housing we get a hotel. That seems about right with the way things have been headed." Carmen stood, her chair legs rumbling against the floor. "You're on a dozen committees, but none of them can fix the fundamental problem, and that's the human weakness for selling things to the highest bidder."

"I'm not trying to change human nature," Justin said. "I just hoped that this time, the highest bidder could be one of us."

Shelby turned to Justin. "What happens now to the money the Community Trust raised to buy the wharf building?"

"I haven't even gotten that far," Justin said. "Why?"

She took a beat, an idea forming. "Could you...use it to make a counteroffer on the bookstore?"

Justin leaned back in his chair. She saw his eyes narrow behind his glasses. "What do you mean?"

"I'm not sure," Shelby said, her thoughts becoming more clear. "I guess I'm thinking, the trust buys the bookstore and Colleen can run it. Does that make any sense?"

He nodded slowly. "It does. It actually does."

"We'd have to talk to the Millers, of course."

Carmen clapped her hands together, beaming. "Well, isn't this a great idea."

Justin held up one hand. "Let's not get ahead of ourselves. The sale to the Hendriks might be signed and done. Even if it's not, the trust would have to approve the purchase. Certain criteria have to be met."

"What criteria?" Carmen said, with an emphasis on the word *what*. As if it were an absurd suggestion.

"The business has to be deemed essential to town, and it has to be run by a local," Justin said.

"I'll set up a call for you with Colleen and her parents," Shelby said. Maybe good news like this would help further mend their rift. Their phone call last night had been a start, but Colleen was still distant. Still not herself.

"You should be on the call, too," Justin said. "The Millers trust your judgment about Land's End. I think it will be reassuring for them to see that you're here and involved."

"Sure. No problem," she said.

She was in no rush to leave.

Fifty-Nine

Turned out, New York and Boston weren't all that different. At least, that was Hunter's feeling walking out of the Paragon office. She wasn't intimidated by the city, but she did feel conflicted about the job.

It was a good opportunity. She knew that. And she was qualified for it. The three years she'd spent in editorial prepared her well, and the more she talked to the man who would be her boss, the more she felt she'd get an offer. Raj Mason, in his early forties with several bestsellers and one Pulitzer Prize winner on his roster, seemed impressed by her academic transcript and the books she'd worked on at Malaprop.

"Do you have any questions?" he said finally.

She did. One that meant a lot to her: "If I find a manuscript that I think I can sell, can I represent it myself?"

His smile indicated the question was sweet but naive.

"It will be a couple of years before you're promoted to junior agent. Until then, you'll be reading queries and editing manuscripts and answering phones, but you won't be making any submissions to editors. But by the time that you do, you'll be extremely prepared and capable of competing aggressively. That much I can promise you."

A couple of years. She'd be twenty-seven at least. Pushing thirty by the time she had her own clients. She knew that wasn't out of the ordinary, and there was no reason why she should jump the line. But there was the nagging sense that she was losing precious time.

She'd promised Ezra she'd call after the interview to let him know how it went, and she did.

"I'm sure you killed," he said. He invited her to meet him and some friends at a bar on Canal Street.

The place had an unassuming facade that made the high energy and hip crowd inside surprising. It had tin ceilings, hanging fans, candles on mismatched tables, and a long wooden bar. Ezra and his friends filled a table near the back.

"Glad you made it!" he said, waving her over. He stood and kissed her on the cheek, introducing her to his friends. The women were dressed in hoodies and cargo pants and wore their hair in messy ponytails, like they'd just rolled out of bed but in the sexiest possible way. Hunter had changed after her interview, but now felt like she was trying too hard in her tight black jeans, Radiohead T-shirt, choker necklace, and heavy eye makeup.

He slid over so she could sit next to him. Someone poured her a glass of red wine. She downed it.

They all worked in publishing and media. Once the conversation picked up, she felt more in her element. She had another glass of wine. They gossiped about famous authors—who was rude to assistants, who had a drinking problem.

When a bunch of them went outside to smoke, she and Ezra stayed behind at the table. By that point, she was eager for a few minutes alone with him.

"So how long are you in the city?" he said.

"I'll probably go back tomorrow."

He nodded. "Where are you staying?"

"Shelby's letting me crash at her place."

Ezra nodded. "I heard a rumor that Shelby handed in a great book, then changed her mind and is refusing to publish it. Is that true?"

"Um, yeah. Basically."

"What happened?"

She shrugged. "Artists are temperamental, right?" She didn't want to gossip about Shelby. What she wanted was to kiss him, to ask him to come back to her hotel. But she didn't know how that would be received. She wasn't used to feeling uncertain when it came to men.

She put her hand on his leg underneath the table. "You don't have to ditch your friends right now or anything, but do you want to meet up later?"

"It's tempting," he said, leaning over and touching his forehead to hers. "But I don't sleep with friends. It gets too complicated."

She was confused. "We've already slept together."

"Right. But then you said you just wanted to be friends."

"No, I said I don't want a *relationship*. Sex—just sex—is fine."

"Not for me it's not," he said. "I mean, don't get me wrong: in college, sure. But I've kind of moved on. Don't you find that gets…boring?"

"No." She shifted uncomfortably in her chair.

"Well, if you ever change your mind, let me know."

Was he serious? His eyes, focused on her, left little doubt that he meant what he said. She felt put on the spot. But then his friends returned from their smoke break.

She didn't know what to do. Her black-and-white stance on relationships had never been a problem. Most men were fine with uncomplicated hookups—no questions asked. She should probably just write off Ezra as incompatible with her. But something stopped her.

For some reason, she found herself thinking about her conversation with Shelby the day of the baby shower. It had been the first time she'd articulated exactly what Shelby had done to upset her. It wasn't just the novel, but also the fact that she coldly and selfishly dumped Justin because he got in the way of her career plans. Wasn't that what Hunter was doing with Ezra? Not that he was getting in the way of her work; on the contrary, he fit perfectly into that part of her life. But she liked him, and that scared her. That would get in the way of her freedom.

Maybe it was time for her to reconsider what she really wanted.

Sixty

Shelby sat next to Duke in his living room while Justin set up a laptop for their video call with the Millers. The house was less cluttered than she'd ever seen it now that Seaport Press was half-boxed-up.

"How's the new novel coming along?" Duke asked her.

That was the last thing she wanted to talk about. "Well, my agent and I are parting ways. So things are in limbo."

"Sorry to hear that. Anything I can do?"

She shook her head and thanked him. Justin adjusted the brightness of the screen just as the Millers logged on. The hospital room came into view, with Colleen sitting in bed and her parents sitting side by side in chairs pulled up close.

As agreed, Duke presented their idea for using the town trust to buy the store for Colleen to run and operate. On the other end of the call, Pam and Annie were unreadable, while Colleen nodded and smiled vigorously to everything he said.

"Of course, this only works if you haven't signed anything yet with the Hendriks," Duke said.

Pam and Annie shared a glance, then Annie said, "No, we

haven't gone to contract yet." Even through the screen, the skepticism in her face was clear. "But we can't put them off indefinitely. How long would it take for the trust to decide?"

Justin leaned into the frame. "We have to present a case: why this is crucial for the town and why it's sustainable. Colleen, that's where you come in. A big part of our argument will be continuity—that you'll be running it. And it's actually a requirement that a local manages any trust-owned businesses. So we need to be sure this is what you want."

Pam passed the screen to Colleen, and Shelby noticed how tired she looked.

"Of course it's what I want," she said. "It's what I've *always* wanted."

"Great," Duke said. "That's all we needed to hear."

Shelby and Justin walked out together. She noticed the sun was setting earlier, a stark reminder that the summer was coming to an end. She felt a twinge. As much as she prided herself on being comfortable with change, it suddenly felt painful again, like when she'd been a child. She didn't know why. Maybe it was the realization that she might never truly belong anywhere. In New York City, she'd become the author she always dreamed of being. But the last week she'd spent there, she'd felt like a tourist in her own life. And sure, Provincetown was a lovely place to visit. But when would she ever feel at home?

They walked to the end of Duke's street towards Commercial, where they'd turn in opposite directions. A cyclist rode by, alerting them with the ring of a bell. The dusk light gave everything a soft glow.

"So that went well," he said.

"It did. But it was the easy part, right? I mean, I knew Colleen was in. And I had faith in Pam and Annie. But the town trust...what are the odds?"

Justin stopped to move a big branch that had fallen into the middle of the street. When he finished, he dusted off his hands and said, "I'll do my best."

She nodded. "I know you will."

They shared a smile and she felt a tension, a pull towards him. It shouldn't be surprising; of course they had a bond. Maybe they always would.

They walked to the corner of Franklin and Bradford, waiting to cross the street. At the first lull in traffic, they darted to the other side. A fox ran across their path and under a parked car. The light was fading quickly.

"You know, I understand you better now," he said as they made their way to Commercial.

"You do?"

"Well, I understand why you decided it wouldn't work out in the long run," he said.

A pedicab drove by, ringing a bell to alert them. She moved closer to the curb and he walked alongside her. It was a natural spot for them to part. But she wasn't leaving on that note.

"What do you mean?" Close to the water, the breeze was stronger. She pulled up her sweatshirt hood.

He looked at her with directness, an intimacy that made her stomach flip. "Do you have time to walk a little?"

"Sure," she said.

They turned right, towards the bend of Commercial's far west end. Beautiful clapboard homes lined the waterfront, and above them in the sky a half-moon shone bright. They made their way to the small beach where she and Colleen had gone a few weeks earlier. Someone had abandoned a beach towel on the bench.

"I realize, if you feel strongly enough about something, no matter how much you want a relationship to work, if it's in conflict with that, it's a deal-breaker. I'm in that situation now with Kate."

"I see," she said slowly. "In what way?"

"I can't be with her now that her father bought the wharf

building. Not just that, but the fact that she didn't tell me. And actually, it's not even that. We could get past that, I guess. It's that she doesn't care about this place, not in the big picture. Not in the ways that matter."

"I see how that's...complicated. But I don't see the connection to what happened between us."

His expression turned rueful. "It wouldn't have worked long-distance. I would be trying to get you to move here, and you'd resent me for not even considering New York City. With Kate, I made the mistake of trying to convert her into a Ptowner. And look what happened."

A lightning bug glowed over his shoulder. Jazz music played from someone's backyard. She heard laughter coming from an open window, a nearby dinner party. She could feel the warmth of the room they were in, imagine the table of food and the wine and the comradery. She wondered who owned the house. She wondered if they were a couple.

"Justin," she said. "When we said goodbye that summer, you said to me, 'I hope you find what you're looking for.' And I did. But there was a cost."

His eyes softened. "It's okay, Shelby."

"I thought it was. But I'm not so sure. Things are different now."

"You still live in New York," he said gently.

He was right. That hadn't changed.

"But I'm here *now*. I'm here tonight," she said. His expression shifted—a small smile, just enough to bring out the dimple in his cheek. His tensed jawline softened. God, she missed him.

"Are you saying you...don't have to rush back to Hunter's?" he said.

She nodded. Then he reached for her hand.

Three summers ago, Justin's bedroom had felt like her own. She knew the handblown glass lamp on the dresser was a gift after one of his parents' trips to Italy. The framed vintage map of Cape Cod on his wall had once belonged to the man who built Barros Boatyard. There was a watermark on the ceiling that he purposefully didn't repair because he thought it uncannily resembled the Cape.

It was dark, but moonlight streamed in through the ill-fitting window shade that somehow never bothered him. Across the room, a table fan whirred, and seemed particularly loud. Shelby felt hyperaware of everything: the way her cheek felt against his bare chest, the beating of his heart, the distant howl of a coyote.

She turned her face towards his, and he cupped her jaw with his hand. He kissed her.

He reached for his phone, checking the time. She remembered that it was a weeknight and he probably had to get to work in the morning. She sat up, looking around for her clothes. They were still on the floor.

"You don't have to run off," he said, touching her arm lightly.

Shelby stopped reaching for her clothes. This was it: she could speak now, or forever hold the proverbial peace. "Justin, maybe we're wrong about the long-distance thing. Maybe it can work."

He shook his head. "It can't. Not for people like us."

She turned away from him so he wouldn't see the hurt on her face. She couldn't argue with him because he wasn't wrong. In doing the job he loved, Justin was bound to that unique peninsula. And in doing what she loved, she had to be unbound.

"No," she said. "Not for people like us."

She stepped out of bed, her bare feet touching the plank wood floors. It gave her a chill she felt through her entire body.

Sixty-One

Hunter spent her first morning back in town helping Duke finish packing up the office.

"Can you put all the copies of the Cape Cod murder mystery series in one box? I'm going to send them to the author. That other box—of the poetry? That's for donation to the library."

He sat at his desk, feeding documents into a shredder.

Ironically, now that he was shutting down shop, she respected Duke more than ever. He created his own business; he was his own boss. He discovered fiction that he loved and was getting it out into the world. And when he felt he couldn't do that in a way that served the art, he stepped back. That was why she wanted his advice.

"I was offered a job at a literary agency," she said. She told him about Paragon, and the authors Raj Mason worked with, and that she knew she'd learn a lot but still hesitated.

"What's stopping you?" he said, pausing to give them a merciful break from the shrill grinding of the shredder. He switched to instead filling a cardboard box with books.

"I'm nervous about waiting years to represent my own authors. I know I have things to learn, but I know I'm going to be impatient. It's going to be frustrating."

"I think once you get started you'll be too busy to be frustrated. You'll see him pitch editors, you'll learn how to negotiate contracts, and with his roster, you'll read the highest quality fiction. And—no offense—it's not like you need to worry about your salary."

"It's not the money," she said. It wasn't even about the entry-level work. It was fear. Always fear. "I don't want to fail."

Duke put down the books in his arms. "Fail? You won't fail. In fact, I bet you can get a running start by bringing a new author to the agency."

"It doesn't work that way. They don't want me representing anyone yet. That's what I'm trying to explain to you."

"That's a shame," Duke said. "Because I know of a bestselling author looking for new representation." He went back to shredding.

She shook her head and resumed loading the book boxes. Then she stopped.

Was he suggesting what she thought he was suggesting?

"Duke, that's impossible."

His doorbell rang.

"Heavens!" he said. "I completely forgot: I'm hosting the Community Trust meeting. Hunter, I know you're practically a literary agent already, but can you do me a tiny favor and run out to fetch some cupcakes?"

Duke's back porch was big enough to host the group that included Bert Lombardo, town selectman, Gene Hobart, the owner of one of the art galleries, and a few people she didn't recognize. They spread out on cushioned patio furniture, facing the lawn where Shelby hosted Anders's book event. It seemed like that happened during an entirely different summer.

When everyone was settled, Duke served iced tea with mint

from his garden. Shelby and Justin stood facing them, their backs to the lawn. They'd decided he'd make the introduction, then she'd speak briefly on behalf of Land's End, and then Duke would conduct the vote. Pam and Annie had helped them pull together a package about the store's financials. The numbers seemed to make sense, but the deciding factor was whether or not Land's End was essential to the people of Provincetown. Justin said it might take a day or two for the committee to decide.

"Thanks, everyone, for showing up on short notice," Justin said. "This is a time-sensitive issue so we appreciate it. As you know, we're here to decide whether or not to take the funds raised for the wharf building and reallocate them to buy Land's End Books. Land's End has been a part of Provincetown—and the Miller family—for eighty years, and if this plan is approved, it will continue with Colleen running the shop. Shelby Archer, who took time away from her book tour this summer to run the store in Colleen's absence, wants to say a few words."

He turned to Shelby, and she had to avoid his eyes to keep her focus. She didn't regret sleeping with him again, but it complicated everything. Still, she was grateful they could end the summer on such a positive note: doing something together for the good of the town. It felt like a little gift from the universe, a way to move on to the next chapter of her life with peace of mind.

"Thanks for coming, everyone." She glanced at the notes on her phone, then at Duke. He offered an encouraging smile. "A wise friend once told me that this is a special place. And that if we want to hold on to it, we need to give more than we take. I hope that you'll keep that in mind when making your decision about the bookstore today."

The back door leading to the porch opened, and Mia walked out, looking around and finding a seat near her father. It distracted Shelby, just long enough to remind her that even if Mia still felt betrayed, she was getting the help she needed. And then she thought, *I was her age when I met Hunter. A year older when I started working at Land's End.*

"I started working at Land's End when I was a teenager," Shelby said. "The bookstore gave me a job for four summers—five if you include this one. When I wasn't even looking for a job." Someone gave a little laugh. Probably Duke. "Three years ago, Colleen and I stood in that store, surrounded by books, talking about our futures. All Colleen wanted was to continue the bookstore that her great-grandparents had started. I had no doubt that she would succeed, that Land's End would always be here. I'm sure everyone here believed that."

Shelby put her phone down by her side. She didn't need it anymore. "But things are changing. A lot's changing. Some of it is out of our control, or up to conservationists and scientists to preserve. But Land's End is something that can be saved by the people sitting right here, today. I hope you'll agree that it's worth whatever work and sacrifice it takes to make that happen."

Duke clapped first, and loudest. Shelby felt a flash of embarrassment, though she knew she shouldn't. She'd said what she wanted to say. What she'd needed to say.

Still, she didn't want to hear the group debate the pros and cons of buying the bookshop.

She made a discreet exit back into the house, where she headed straight for the kitchen. Shelby set her phone down on the counter near a few boxes from Scott Cakes, then opened the refrigerator for something cold to drink.

"Hey."

She turned around. Mia stood in the doorway. She wore a floral print dress and white Birkenstocks. Her ubiquitous headphones were gone.

"Hey," Shelby said, closing the fridge. "Good to see you."

"It's good to see you, too." She started to say something else, then stopped.

Shelby walked closer. "Mia, I've wanted to talk to you. I

only told your brother about your problems with reading because I truly believed it would make you happier in the long
run. The one thing I'm sorry about is that I had to betray your
confidence to do it."

Mia nodded. She looked down at the floor, then up at her.
"I'm glad you're trying to save the bookstore."

"Me, too."

"If it reopens, are you gonna stick around?" Mia said.

"I can't. But Colleen will find someone to manage the store
until she's back on her feet. And I'm sure she'll need a lot of help
if you know anyone who's interested in working part-time."

Mia smiled.

"Can we be friends again?" Shelby said. Mia nodded.

Her phone buzzed, a particularly loud vibration against the
countertop. She wondered if the vote was done that quickly.
Duke had warned her it could take a lot of discussion.

"These meetings are rarely efficient," he'd said.

The text wasn't from Duke. It was from Doug: Colleen in
emergency C-section. She's okay.

Shelby gasped, and pressed the phone to her chest.

"Mia… I have to go. But we'll talk more, okay?"

Heart pounding, she rushed back to the porch. Hunter was
standing up; from the look on her face, she'd gotten the same
message.

I'll drive, Hunter mouthed.

Shelby nodded. *Let's go.*

Sixty-Two

Hunter wasn't ready for motherhood. Not even Colleen's motherhood.

She clenched the wheel of the Land Rover so hard her fingers ached. Traffic was heavy on MA-3 North, and the two-hour drive to Boston was going to take somewhere closer to three. She impatiently switched the Sirius station, pressing up up up until she reached the New Wave channel and the song "Small-town Boy" by Bronski Beat.

"This traffic is a nightmare," Shelby said, propping her elbow on the passenger-side window and pressing her forehead into her palm. "Can we talk or something?" Shelby said. "I need to get my mind off what's happening at the hospital."

Hunter turned down the music. "Sure." There *was* something she wanted to discuss, although maybe it wasn't appropriate to talk about work at a time like this. But Shelby did say she wanted to get her mind off Colleen…

"I got the job offer from Paragon." She wasn't surprised when the call came. But was still ambivalent about it.

"Amazing!" Shelby said. "So happy for you. You'll be great."

Hunter shifted lanes, picking up speed after a lull and feeling a rush of adrenaline along with it. "Thanks. And on the subject of agents...when are you going to look for someone new? You're officially done with Claudia, right?"

A text alert appeared on the car's navigation screen. From Doug.

"Oh, my God!" they said in unison. Shelby grabbed her phone and read the text aloud: "Our twins are here! 5 lbs, 17. Mom is doing great."

Shelby looked at Hunter, and they burst into tears.

Hunter peered at the babies through the glass window of the NICU. Madeline and Mathew MacDougal were in clear little bins. They looked fragile and the room was filled with whirring machines and apparatuses. But the twins were healthy.

Beside her, Doug stood with his eyes locked on his brand-new son and daughter.

"They're just beautiful," Shelby said.

Doug nodded. "I feel torn every second because I don't want to leave them, but I also want to be with Colleen."

Hunter understood how he felt, but she was impatient to see Mama. "I'll go see Colleen now. Don't rush, Doug. We'll let you know if she needs anything."

Shelby held up her index finger to signal she'd join her in one minute.

Hunter set off down the hall nervously. She felt the weight of the moment. Colleen was no longer just her friend. She wasn't just Doug's girlfriend. She was someone's *mother*. Two people's mother!

Colleen sat propped up on pillows in bed, hooked up to an IV. She was surrounded by bunches of helium balloons with colorful ribbons hanging nearly to the floor. Hunter bent over to give her a hug, but Colleen stopped her.

"I'm a little sore," Colleen said.

"Oh! Of course. Sorry," Hunter said, taking a step back.

She looked exhausted, her hair lank, the back of her hand bruised from the IV. But Colleen's eyes were lit from within, and she was all smiles.

"Did you see them?" Colleen asked.

"I did. They're incredible," Hunter said, thinking of their little sparrow legs with a smile.

"You know, all summer I was so upset. Things were out of my control, and I was so certain that I knew how they were *supposed* to be. I was too much in my head instead of in my heart, you know? And it was all such a waste of time because now I can't imagine my life without them."

Hunter had a strange feeling in her chest. A tightness. She knew, as soon as she heard the words, that she was making the same mistake.

"I'll be right back," she said, leaning over to kiss Colleen on the cheek.

She slipped out of the room, following the narrow vestibule that led to a vending machine and a bench. She bought a pack of peanut M&Ms, sat down, and pulled out her phone. She tapped a message to Ezra.

I'm taking the job at Paragon. And u said to let u know if I changed my mind about relationships. I changed my mind.

Shelby followed Pam and Annie down the hall to Colleen's room. Just outside the door, Pam turned to her and said, "Remind me to talk to you about one thing before you leave. Don't forget."

"Okay," Shelby said, eager to see Colleen.

She sat propped up in bed, and Shelby leaned over the metal railing, and bent down to kiss the top of her head. She couldn't believe she was a mother.

"Did you see them?" Colleen said, smiling with tired eyes.

Shelby nodded. "I did. They're beautiful."

"I can't wait to hold them," Colleen said.

"Oh, you'll have plenty of that," Annie said, pouring Colleen a fresh cup of water. "In a few months, you'll be begging other people to take them off your hands."

"I can't imagine," she said.

Shelby's phone vibrated in her bag. She peeked at the screen to read a text from Justin: The vote is YES for Land's End.

Shelby looked up. Pam was adjusting Collen's hospital gown.

"More news," Shelby said, getting their attention. "Because today hasn't been exciting enough: Justin just texted that the trust wants to buy Land's End!"

"They do? Still?" Colleen said, turning to look at Pam. "Didn't you tell her?"

Pam and Annie glanced at each other, then uneasily at Shelby.

"Tell me what?" Shelby said, confused.

Pam stood up from the wooden chair she was sitting in against one wall. A balloon drifted in front of her, and she moved it aside. "I mentioned that I wanted to talk to you before you left. There's a wrinkle in the plan."

"Oh?"

Shelby had worried about this: the financial reality would hit them. They were taking a loss with the Community Trust offer. There had to be some way to get more for them. Maybe she could raise additional funds, pitch in, some of her own. Maybe the Dillworths would invest, though Hunter didn't like asking them for anything.

"Shelby," Colleen said, looking up with steady blue eyes. "I won't be able to run the store. Not now."

"Not right this *minute*, obviously," Shelby said. "You can hire someone to manage temporarily—until you're ready to get back to work. And Mia still wants to—"

"Shelby, I'm sorry. Everything's different now." Colleen's tone was hard-edged: this was not open for discussion. "I know it's hard to understand and I really appreciate what you did to save the store. The timing just isn't right." Shelby felt punched in the gut. She looked around for a chair and sank into one.

"I...don't get it. So what's going to happen?" she said.

"We're going to accept the Hendriks' offer," Annie said.

Shelby looked at Colleen, trying to figure out if this was Pam and Annie's idea. But the untroubled expression on Colleen's face told her that it wasn't. So she nodded with understanding, hiding her disappointment. She wasn't even sure why she felt so crushed. It was Colleen's store, so if she was prepared to let it go, why wasn't Shelby?

"We were going to tell you this week, but then everything happened with Colleen and the babies. I'm sorry." Pam looked uncomfortable.

"Did you talk to the Hendriks already?" Shelby asked. Pam shook her head. Okay. So there was still a chance. "Can I ask you a huge favor? Can you hold off on taking the Hendrik's deal? Just for a few more days?"

Pam and Annie glanced at Colleen, who shifted her body to face Shelby more directly.

"It's okay, Shelby. I'm fine with it. Thanks for everything you—"

"Just give me one more day," Shelby said, standing.

"For what?" Colleen said.

Shelby wasn't quite sure. She just wasn't ready to give up yet.

Sixty-Three

Commercial Street was painted yellow from end to end. Town Hall glowed in green lights as the Emerald City. Carnival "Somewhere over the Rainbow" had begun, and Shelby was on her way to see the closest thing she had to a wizard: Duke.

Hunter dropped her off in front of his house. They'd spent the entire morning drive back from Boston talking about the future of Land's End. They both felt that losing the store meant more than losing a store. Land's End was part of their personal history, the nexus of their three-way friendship. But it was also a piece of Provincetown history, and that gave them confidence that Duke would help them with the idea they came up with for a plan B.

Shelby walked up Duke's driveway and saw he'd posted a painted This Way to Oz sign in his yard. He'd also set out a vintage bicycle with a front basket holding a stuffed dog, and a bunch of haystacks made out of what appeared to be shredded cardboard.

Duke answered the door wearing powder blue pajama shorts

with navy piping and a matching top. Surprised, she checked the time on her phone.

"Did I wake you?"

"Unfortunately, yes," he said. "But it's obscenely late so I'm glad you did." He closed the door. "Tell me everything: How's Colleen? Did you see the twins?"

She followed him into the house.

"Colleen is great, the twins are tiny but healthy. Doug said it will be a while before they can bring them home."

The living room was cluttered with used dessert plates and mostly empty champagne flutes. "Apologies for the mess," he said.

"Looks like I missed a good party," she said.

"When I realized no one from the meeting yesterday was in a hurry to leave, Max ran out to get more food and drinks and it turned into a spontaneous pre-Carnival bash. Are you coming to the pier tonight? We're doing a dramatic reading of *The Wizard of Oz*. I'm the Tin Man."

"I don't know what I'm doing," she said. "I hadn't even planned on being here this week." She felt disoriented. Like she'd forgotten what character she played in her own life.

Duke pushed the plates and glasses to one side of the coffee table and made room for her next to him on the couch.

"This is my favorite line," he said. "'I shall take the heart. For brains do not make one happy, and happiness is the best thing in the world.' So true, right?"

She smiled. "Yes. Although, I imagine you more as the Wizard."

Duke looked reflective for a minute. "I take that as a compliment. So what brings you here not so early in the morning?"

Shelby leaned forward, hands on her thighs. "Colleen changed her mind. She doesn't want to take over Land's End after all—it's too much for her."

Duke's eyes widened. "Oh, dear," he said. "That's a bit of a curve ball."

"Pam and Annie think it's the right decision, and they want to move forward with the sale. But since the trust won't buy the business without a local on board to run it, they're back to entertaining the Hendriks' offer."

"Well, that's it, then," he said. "Personally, I think Colleen will wake up one day and regret it, but that's life, I suppose. We all have our regrets. And we learn from them." He stood and began gathering plates to bring to the kitchen. Shelby picked up a few, sticky with melted ice cream, and followed him. They loaded the sink and Duke ran hot water over the pile.

"It's not necessarily over," she said. "We just need someone who lives here to take on the bookshop."

He scratched his cheek. "Finding the right person could take a while. How long do you think the Millers are willing to wait?"

"Not long," she said, leaning on the counter and facing him. "That's why I was thinking...since Seaport Press is shut down, maybe you could take this on as your next venture?"

It seemed so obviously right to her. And from the look on his face, he agreed.

"I *love* the idea," he said, reaching out to touch her arm. "And I love you for thinking of me. But alas, I can't do it."

"You...don't even want to think about it?" She truly hadn't considered the idea that he'd say no. If anything, she suspected he might prefer to buy it himself. He'd taken joy in funding his press, he liked running the show, and he'd get to own a piece of Ptown cultural history.

"Shelby, in other circumstances, I would jump at the chance."

"So what's changed?"

"Max," he said. "I'm moving in with him. In Boston."

"You're leaving Provincetown?" It was unthinkable.

"We'll be back every summer. And holidays. But he's got his job, so I'm the one who has to be flexible."

She couldn't believe it. "That's more than flexible," she said. "That's giving up your whole life."

He shook his head. "No," he said. "It's me taking a leap to *have* a life. But I understand it doesn't help your cause much. I'm sorry."

Duke was leaving Provincetown to have the life he wanted. How could she blame him? She'd done the same. And she got some of those things—important ones, like her work. But what about the things she'd lost?

Shelby stood and walked to the sliding door leading to the deck, watching a dragonfly on the other side of the glass and fighting an idea she was afraid to let surface. Outside, a neighbor played Judy Garland's "Somewhere over the Rainbow." Duke began singing along, *"'There's a land that I heard of once in a lullaby...'"*

What if she didn't go back to New York? What if she turned down the Woodstock job, let go of her apartment, and just... stayed? The idea was so simple, so obvious, she realized the answer had been there all along.

"Duke," she said, turning around. "You *are* a wizard."

Sixty-Four

September rolled around and Shelby was still living at Hunter's. With the ongoing housing crunch, it could be months until she found a place of her own. The apartment above the shop was out; the Community Trust was keeping it as designated office space. As a group, they knew that saving Land's End was just the beginning of their work. If they wanted Provincetown to still be Provincetown in five years, there'd be more battles to come.

"You were always ashamed of this giant house," Shelby told Hunter. "But I wouldn't be able to get the store ready without somewhere to stay. So, I hope you see things a little differently now," Shelby said on one of their daily calls. Hunter was busy with her new job and her new boyfriend, Ezra, but they still checked in with each other constantly, leaving Shelby to wonder how she'd managed her own time in the city without their closeness.

"I see a lot of things differently," Hunter told her.

Shelby walked up Commercial towards Land's End. She still had another week to go before it was ready to reopen. The storm damage repair was finished, but they were now upgrading some of the shelving fixtures. The bookstore would now make it to its eighty-first summer, and rumor had it that the Hendrik's was closing next week, after Labor Day. It would not be reopening.

Apparently, Kate's enthusiasm for a Cape Cod outpost ended alongside her relationship with Justin. Shelby wasn't surprised: bookselling was a passion business. If your heart wasn't in it, what was the point?

Shelby peeked at Hendrik's from the opposite side of the street, keeping in stride with some tourists. The front door opened, and a familiar herringbone blazer caught her eye. It was Anders. His sandy brown hair was cut shorter than when she'd last seen him. She ducked behind a pilaster on the porch of a T-shirt shop, then peeked out again. He held the door, and out walked Kate. They turned in the opposite direction and he put his arm around her.

Shelby covered her mouth with her hand. She hadn't seen that one coming! The only thing she felt was mild amusement, as if she were watching two characters on a show. It was hard to believe that just weeks ago he had actually been a part of her life.

A block away from the bookstore, she stopped into a coffee shop.

Justin was walking out.

"Oh!" She hadn't seen him since the afternoon of the Community Trust vote. Doug had been scheduled to go on a research trip for CCS, but since he was on paternity leave Justin went in his place. The research trip must have been days on the water because he was tanner than she'd ever seen him. His forearms were brown against the white of his CCS T-shirt. The color on his face made his cheekbones more defined, and his irises looked like brown velvet. His dark hair poked out from under a blue baseball cap. "You're back."

"I am," he said. "And rumor has it, so are you. You're going to be sticking around for a while?"

She nodded. "Yep. I'm officially the proud new manager of Land's End."

"Congratulations," he said. They looked at each other for a second. To break the awkward silence, she said, "I'm a little apprehensive about my first winter on the Cape. I hope I can roll with the climate. You've told me it can be a test of endurance."

"I think you'll do just fine. You've proven yourself to be impressively resilient."

She smiled. "I'll take that as compliment."

"As it's intended. And speaking of climate, they're about ready to send our Kemp's ridley down south."

The turtle she'd found on the beach that night with Anders. "He's recovered?"

"She," Justin said. "We named her Ladyslipper. And yes, she's ready to go. I'm on my way now to see her off. Why don't you come along?"

Shelby climbed into the passenger seat of Justin's Jeep.

The worn passenger seat felt familiar. There was a tiny pebble crack in the windshield just below her eyeline, and the floor mats were faded by saltwater. The local radio station played an old Bruce Springsteen song. Justin cranked it up, looking at her with a smile, singing along. They cruised past the town limits, along marshes and green fields. She watched a slow-moving heron, astonishing with its long legs and curved neck.

"So. You're staying," he said, tapping the wheel. "I'm really surprised."

"I'm have to admit—so am I."

He laughed. "I don't think I fully believed it until right now. With you sitting here."

When he glanced over, their eyes met and she felt herself holding her breath. They didn't talk for the rest of the ride, letting the breeze and the music fill the silence.

The Marine Animal Rehabilitation Center was a large warehouse building in Wellfleet, complete with an adjacent landing field for emergency animal transport. Inside, it smelled like the aquarium room at the Central Park Zoo. They walked past cinder block walls to the inner sanctuary filled with turtle tanks. The expansive room was filled with round, waist-high, aboveground pools. She counted a dozen or so turtles.

"In the fall, we rescue so many turtles they can't house the long-term cases. That's when the volunteer flights taking them to warmer beaches really save lives."

"Yeah, your gal beat the rush," said the volunteer who greeted them. She wore khakis and a green MARC T-shirt and blue surgical gloves. She led them to the pool to see the Kemp's ridley. Shelby covered her mouth in awe.

It was hard to reconcile the robust animal gliding through the water with the stunned, still creature she'd found in the sand. Wildlife was resilient. And now, she realized, so was she.

The turtle swam close to where she stood, surfaced, and appeared to look at her. A number was written both on her shell and on a bright orange tag fastened around one of her front flippers. Her eyes opened and closed slowly.

"You're lucky to have a second chance," Shelby said softly.

"She looks good, right?" Justin said.

She nodded. They watched Ladyslipper swim as the loud ambient hum of the lights and the tanks filled the void between them. Neither of them spoke, and she didn't want to be the one to break the quiet.

A curly-haired technician walked over and scooped up the turtle. She waved her front flippers in protest.

"You're going home," Justin said.

Jan placed the turtle in the same simple cardboard banana box that they used to rescue her from the beach. She carried the turtle outside to a tarmac and the waiting Cessna, and they followed.

Justin greeted the volunteer pilot, someone he knew from the various organizations he was in constant contact with to coordinate rescues. He took the turtle box from the MARC biologist, and walked it over to Shelby so she could see her one more time before he helped load it onto the plane headed for Texas.

Shelby covered her ears against the roar of the plane propellers as it took off. With Justin beside her, she watched until it disappeared.

"Look at that," Shelby said. "Literally flying off into the sunset."

He looked at her. "Do you mean that thing you say—that you write fiction because it's the happy ending you can't have in real life?"

"Yeah. Maybe it's not *why* I write, but maybe it's the reason behind *what* I write. Am I wrong?"

"About happy endings in real life? It's tough to say," he said, his brow furrowed. "As a scientist, I like to have all the facts."

"Of course," she said with exaggerated solemnity.

"But I would theorize that happy endings are possible," he said.

She nodded as if considering this. "Tough to prove."

"It is. But I'd like to test the hypothesis. Know anyone who could help me with that?"

He looked into her eyes and smiled. She leaned against him, nodding, and he pulled her close. She tilted her head up, and he kissed her.

Sixty-Five

Two years later

Shelby stood on the beach behind Land's End, doing a quick head count. It was standing room only and she wondered if she'd ordered enough books. Concerned, she pulled Mia off to the side.

"I'm never doing this again." Planning her own book launch at her own bookstore was more stressful than planning a wedding.

"Sure you will," Mia said.

Shelby spotted Colleen rounding the building towards them. Madeline, holding her mother's hand, was dressed in a pink sequined T-shirt and a little denim skirt. Her fine blond hair was in two pigtails. Doug and Mathew followed close behind. Hunter called them over. Madeline scurried over to Shelby, and she bent down to hug her. She radiated heat and smelled like strawberries.

"Watch out—her hands are sticky," Colleen said.

"Everything is always sticky now," Doug said.

Shelby didn't care. It was hard to believe how she'd agonized over what to wear to her first book event years ago. Today, she'd barely been able to think about it long enough to make sure she had clean jeans to wear with her red Land's End Books T-shirt. Mathew was wearing the kiddie version of the same shirt.

"I tried to get Maddy to wear hers, but she insisted on glamour tonight," Doug said.

"Who can argue with sequins?" Shelby said.

"I'd say everyone is a little underdressed," Hunter said, walking up to them in an elegant, bone-colored Theory pantsuit. Gone were the concert tees and Doc Martens.

"We're at the *beach*," Colleen said. "Doug, can you watch them for a second?" She turned to Shelby and Hunter. "I'm not going to be able to stay for the party. I can't leave Doug to wrestle them into baths on his own. And I know you'll be mobbed after the reading. But I wanted to say I'm really proud of you."

Shelby hugged her. "Do you want to take a quick walk to the water? I could use a minute away from all this."

"Only if Hunter comes, too."

Hunter raised her eyebrows. "Do you see what I'm wearing?"

"So? What happened to our punk rock friend?" Colleen said.

"Yeah," said Shelby. "Now you're not just wearing a suit, you *are* a suit."

"And proud of it," Hunter said.

Walking to the water was a lovely idea, but there really wasn't time. Mia was already at the podium, asking guests to take their seats. After two years working at Land's End, she was leaving at the end of the summer for Boston University. Shelby was already wondering what she'd do without her. The only consolation was that in a few months, while Mia would no longer be her part-timer, she would officially be Shelby's sister-in-law.

Shelby hurried over to her spot in front of the crowd. She faced the audience and spotted all the familiar faces in the front rows: Duke and Max, the Lombardos, Colleen and her brood, Hunter, and Ezra Randall. He and Hunter were becoming quite the literary "it couple," and Shelby suspected some aspiring writers in the audience were more interested in seeing them than in meeting her.

The sun dropped lower on the horizon, casting everything in a pinkish-gold light. Shelby caught Justin's eye and he gave her a wink. She knew they were probably thinking the same thing: at the end of the summer, on Labor Day weekend, they'd be standing on that very spot together. She wondered how nervous she would feel taking her vows. It certainly put her pub day jitters into perspective.

"Thank you, everyone, for being here with me to celebrate the publication of *Beach Friends*, my second novel. And everyone, please—a big hand for my colleague Mia Lombardo. Mia, if I hadn't been able to leave this store in your capable hands so I could write a few hours every day, this book would not exist." People applauded, and Carmen reached over and squeezed Mia's arm.

"A special thanks to my agent, Hunter Dillworth. Knowing that you were waiting on the other end of this writing process gave me the confidence I needed to dust myself off and start over." Hunter stood up and turned to wave at the audience like she was the Queen. And she was. She'd read the first draft of Shelby's manuscript, took it to her boss, and said if they didn't let her represent it she'd leave and go out with it on her own. They promoted her.

Shelby still thought about Claudia Linden sometimes. She'd wondered if she'd hear from her when her new book deal was announced. Something along the line of "no hard feelings?" But maybe that was the type of neat resolution she really would have to save for her novels. In real life, some plot lines dangled messily until the very end. But she didn't need for real life to be perfect. Thanks to Colleen, and Hunter, and Justin, it turned out to be good enough.

"Most of all, I want to thank my friend Colleen Miller for bringing me back to where I belong. None of us would be here on this beach tonight without you."

The changing light cast warm gold on the white chairs. She could smell the salty bay breeze, and from somewhere down the beach, an '80s song played. It was all so familiar, but new at the same time. It felt as if she were standing at the intersection of her past and her future. But really, wasn't that always the case? Life kept moving forward. The difference was, she finally understood that didn't necessarily mean leaving things she loved behind. She'd have to learn to get comfortable with the idea.

Now that she was home, she would.

★ ★ ★ ★ ★

Acknowledgments

This book is in your hands because of my editor, Erika Imranyi. Erika, you're one of a kind. Thank you for your patience and for sharing your talent with me. Thank you to editorial assistant Nicole Luongo and copy editor Greg Stephenson. This is my first novel with Park Row, and as of this writing I don't yet know the names of everyone who will be part of my team heading into publication, but I thank you ahead of time. Thank you to my agent, Adam Chromy; thank you for always believing. You make me better.

I'd have to write an additional book if I tried to name every bookseller who has meant the world to me. But I would like to thank a special few who've been a part of my life the past few years. To Jeff Peters of East End Books in Provincetown: thank you for your friendship, for the celebrations, and for always giving my novels a home on your shelves. To Sparta Books in Sparta, New Jersey: Jennifer Carlson, Linda Schurmann, and Susan Perricone. Your passion for books and readers is unparalleled. I'm grateful to be able to call you my friends. To Zandra Senft of Bethany Beach Books: thank you for always having a place for me at your table. Finally, to Doylestown Bookshop and bookseller Krisy Elisii: I couldn't ask for a better hometown bookstore.

Writing is a solitary job but I'm never alone thanks to authors Fiona Davis, Lynda Loigman, Susie Schnall, Amy Poeppel, Nicole Harrison, and book maven Suzanne Leopold. It's an incredible luxury to have talented and kind friends just one text away, 24/7. I adore you.

To my husband, Adam: maybe someday we'll actually get that quiet week. Thank you for being my calm in the storm. I love you.